Rani Choudhury MUST DIE

Adiba Jaigirdar

HODDER

HODDER CHILDREN'S BOOKS

First published in Great Britain in 2024 by Hodder & Stoughton
First published in the United States by Feiwel and Friends,
an imprint of Macmillan Publishing Group, LLC

1 3 5 7 9 10 8 6 4 2

A CIP catalogue record for this book
is available from the British Library.

ISBN 978 1 444 96775 3

Printed and bound in Great Britain by
Clays Ltd, Elcograf S.p.A.

The paper and board used in this book
are made from wood from responsible sources.

MIX
Paper | Supporting responsible forestry
FSC® C104740

Hodder Children's Books
An imprint of
Hachette Children's Group
Part of Hodder & Stoughton Limited
Carmelite House
50 Victoria Embankment
London EC4Y 0DZ

The authorised representative in the EEA is Hachette Ireland, 8 Castlecourt Centre, Castleknock Road, Castleknock, Dublin 15, D15 YF6A, Ireland

An Hachette UK Company
www.hachette.co.uk

www.hachettechildrens.co.uk

To my Bangladeshi writer community:

Tammi Jahan and Priyanka Taslim,

I'm glad the three of us found one another

and made our khichuri wars squad.

1

MEGHNA

Sneaking out of a house full of Bengalis is not an easy task by any means. The incessant sound of Abbu's voice on the telephone floats all the way upstairs and through my closed bedroom door, mixed together with the dramatic music and Hindi dialogue from the natok Ammu is currently watching in the sitting room.

I glance down at the time on my phone: 8:45 p.m. There's only fifteen minutes until I have to meet Zak, and unless Ammu and Abbu are occupied for the entire time I'm there and the time it takes me to get back, they'll definitely notice my absence.

I look out my window and almost consider the few stories drop all the way to the ground. But I'm pretty sure seeing my boyfriend just to give him this once-in-a-lifetime (for me) news is not worth breaking my legs, or possibly dying.

So I slip my bedroom door open and clamber down the stairs, getting ready to lie my ass off to my parents. Something I'm surprisingly good at.

In the sitting room, Ammu's eyes are glued to the TV screen in front of her. I stay in the doorway, half-in and half-out of the room.

"Ammu . . . I'm going to the library, okay?"

Ammu's eyes snap to me immediately. She looks me up and down, at my black jeans and purple runners, and the pink blouse with the puffy sleeves. She has such a good poker face that I have no idea what judgment she makes of me from that once-over.

"Is the library open this late?" she asks finally.

"Yes!" I lie, with all the confidence I can muster. "But it closes at nine thirty, so I have to hurry!" I don't give Ammu a chance to ask any more questions. Questions are where lies go to die, and I don't have time for anyone to poke holes into mine today.

"Khodahafez!" I cry, stumbling out the door while nearly tripping on my untied shoelaces. Ammu calls out something indecipherable behind me, and I'm hoping and praying to God that it's *goodbye* as I leg it down the driveway and out of sight of our house. It's only then that I pause to catch my breath and tie my laces.

My phone buzzes in my pocket, and I dig it out. It's just a text from Zak, and not Ammu insisting that I get back home immediately.

Zak: where are you???

I glance at the time on the top of my phone screen, and it's already 8:55. Zak is early—for once.

Almost there, I quickly type back before giving my laces one final tug and starting to make my way to the park that's our meeting spot and has been for the past few months. It's only a twenty-minute walk, or five-minute bus ride. But I half run and half walk there today (I could definitely win gold for fast walking at the Olympics) and get there in ten minutes. Under the shroud of darkness, Blackthorn Garden almost looks creepy. It's completely deserted, and the looming trees sway in the wind as I slip through the gates. I can hear the creaking of the swing set before I see Zak. He's sitting on one of the swings, his face illuminated by the glow of his phone. My heart hammers in my chest at the sight of his lips puckered in concentration, and the arch of his eyebrows. It's strange—even three months into our relationship, seeing Zak sets fresh goose bumps running across my skin. Of course, he can never know about that.

"Hey!" I say, slipping onto the swing beside him and trying not to grin too wide.

"Took you long enough," Zak says, putting his phone away and looking up at me with a lazy grin of his own.

"Sorry. It's not always easy to get away from my house, you know."

"It's just fifteen minutes to the park."

"Twenty, actually," I say, and he rolls his eyes.

"Tell me your news," he says.

"Seriously? I don't get to build up to it? To set the scene and do a big reveal?"

Zak groans. "You know it's a twenty-minute bus ride for me to get home. And it's the middle of the week. I have a curfew."

I frown, even though I know I don't really have a right to be annoyed. He did come all the way out here to see me at the last minute, just because I told him I had big, exciting news I wanted to share. Still, I can't help the little pulse of disappointment that he doesn't seem as enthused about hearing my good news as I am about sharing it. But it must be because he had to get the bus all the way here, and probably had other things planned that he had to drop at the last minute for my sake.

So I shake the disappointment off and sit up with my shoulders straight. "I got an email today."

"Right . . ."

"And I got into the Young Scientist Exhibition!" I almost yell the last words, throwing my hands in the air with excitement. Zak's lips are pressed into a thin line, and he's looking down at the ground. "We're going to be there together this year. Like a science power couple!" I add. "Can you imagine if our projects are side by side, and we can—"

"I thought your project was about something to do with floods," Zak interrupts.

"Investigating rising water levels in Bangladesh and the various flood prevention mechanisms which can slow the process of creating eco-refugees." I rattle off the title that I've already committed to memory.

"Right. That's more . . . geography, isn't it?" His voice rises too high on the last few words, like he's trying really hard to emphasize the fact that he's just asking a harmless question and not questioning the reason why I got into the exhibition.

I try to bite down the annoyance gathering in my stomach. Annoyance that will definitely turn into fiery rage if I don't nip it in the bud.

"I thought you'd be happy. You were the first person I wanted to tell."

He finally meets my gaze, and I'm not sure what to read in his blank expression. "I just . . . I'm making sure that you're not being set up."

"Set up?"

"Like, for failure. Only a handful of people get awarded at the Young Scientist Exhibition, and I feel like your project will get lost in all the tech and actual science."

"Flood prevention *is* science," I say through gritted teeth, because otherwise I may shoot flames from my mouth.

"Meg, I'm just concerned about you." He reaches his hand forward like he's going to link our fingers together. But for once, I'm not getting goose bumps on my skin or butterflies in my stomach at touching him. I leap off of my swing instead, inching away from him and shooting him a steady glare.

"Are you worried about losing to me or something? Because I thought you were different than that," I say. And I really thought he was. For the past three months, Zak has been nothing but the perfect boyfriend. It's not like any other boy would be sympathetic with all the sneaking around and secret relationship stuff. But he's from Bangladesh, too. He understands that there are some things our parents just don't need to know about. His parents are the same as mine. I thought that—combined with his good looks, his charm, his kindness—made him the one. I'd never accounted for his strange reaction to this.

Zak sighs, letting his hand drop to his side. He doesn't make an effort to reach out to me again, but he does meet my gaze once more. "That's not what I'm worried about."

"I can't think of any other reason why you wouldn't be happy that I finally got in," I say. "I've been trying for years and—"

"I don't want this to be another thing you lose to Rani." Zak's words are like a gut punch. And they make me angrier than anything else he's said tonight—all of which made me pretty angry.

"Seriously?"

"Rani gets in every year," Zak says. "I know how you are about her."

I shake my head, but I know he's right. There are worse things than not getting into the Young Scientist Exhibition, and losing to Rani Choudhury is definitely worse.

"Imagine you're next to her," Zak says. "Imagine the two of you have to be side by side and you have to watch the judges marvel at her brilliance and—"

"Okay, okay. I get it. You've painted a pretty picture." I sigh.

Zak does stand up this time. He shuffles forward, closing the distance between the two of us. He reaches out and takes my hands in his, warming my fingers against the cool September air. "I'm just thinking about you," he says softly.

"I know," I say, thinking that I should have known it all along. There's no way Zak—*my Zak*—would be threatened by me being in the same competition as him. "And you could have done so without bastardizing my name! You know I hate that. *Meg*? That's some white girl with—"

I don't get to finish my sentence, though, because he leans closer and presses his lips against mine, cutting me off. I forget the rest of my words as I wrap my arm around him, run my fingers through his hair. And I almost—almost—forget about Rani Choudhury. But somewhere in the back of my mind, I'm already thinking about how I'm going to go into the Young Scientist Exhibition, and how I'm going to destroy her.

2

RANI

"Rani!" The sharp sound of Ammu's voice pulls me out of my concentration. I blink for a moment at the bright lights of the computer screen in front of me, the half-finished code, and my hovering cursor.

"Rani!" The call comes louder before I've even had the chance to slip out of my chair.

"Com—"

"RANI!"

I sigh and fling the door open, hurrying downstairs as fast as I can before Ammu's screaming bursts my eardrums.

"Yes?" I say in my most polite voice, though really, I want to scream *WHAT?!* Very loudly. I just know I can't do that without receiving a lengthy lecture that I don't have time for.

Ammu frowns at me like she's unhappy I'm here after all her god-awful screaming.

"You're not dressed," she says.

"There's still time until . . ." I cut myself off when I spot the time on the clock above the TV. It's 6:00 p.m. already. "Sorry," I mumble instead. "I guess I lost track."

Ammu shakes her head like she's not sure what she's going to do with me, but she points to the brown paper shopping bags on the couch. "I bought you a few things. There's a new dress that I thought you could wear today."

"Oh." Ammu and I don't have the same fashion sense, but she still loves to buy me the kind of clothes she insists suits me the best. It's not like I can say anything when she's already bought them. It's not like I even have the right to complain.

In front of me, Ammu pulls out a white knee-length dress with a printed floral design across it. She holds it up to me and frowns. "You've gained a few kilos, but it should still fit. And the white will look really good with your skin."

What she means is that it'll give me the illusion of having a lighter skin color than I do. Having spent the last seventeen years of my life hearing all kinds of comments from my mother, I've become pretty adept at cracking her codes. Not that they're particularly difficult to crack, anyway. Anyone who is paying close attention can figure them out.

"I was going to wear that black dress Aarti brought me back from Bangladesh last time she was there?" I ask. It's midnight black with sparkles across it so it looks like a night sky.

But Ammu just shakes her head again. "You want them to think you're dark?"

"I'm pretty sure they already know what my skin color is, Ammu. I've known them pretty much my whole life," I say.

"You want to look presentable, Rani." She hands me the white dress like the conversation is over before digging into the bag once more to pull out some eyeliner, powder, and lipstick, and shoving those into my hands, too. "Not too much, but a little makeup will make you look nice." She smiles for the first time this entire conversation. So I smile, too, because I know she's just doing all this because she always wants me to make a good impression. She always wants our whole family to make a good impression.

"Okay, I'll go get ready," I say, turning around and making my way up the stairs. I lay the dress down on the bed and pile the makeup on top of it. Pink lipstick, dark black eyeliner, and a powder that's a whole shade lighter than my skin.

For a moment, I envision walking over to my wardrobe and putting on the black dress instead. But then I remember the way Ammu's eyebrows furrowed together the first time I wore it out to a dawat. There's no way she'd let me get away with wearing it to have a meal with the Sardars. So I tuck away my thoughts of the black dress and do as Ammu wants me to.

THE SARDARS ARE ALREADY AT THE RESTAURANT BY THE TIME WE arrive. Thanks to Parisa and Neelam arguing about what dresses they wanted to wear, we were delayed. Ammu and Abbu groaned and complained the entire drive over, but as we step into the restaurant, instant smiles appear on their faces like magic.

Ammu embraces Sardar Aunty like they haven't seen each other for an eternity while Abbu and Sardar Uncle exchange salams and handshakes. It's not long, though, before both my parents turn to Zak, who is sitting at the far end of the table and scrolling through his phone like he hasn't even noticed our presence.

"Zakkariyah!" Abbu says. "Huge, huge congratulations on the rugby win!"

Zak finally looks up, and a smile flits across his face. "Thanks, Uncle," he says. "It's not that big a deal." But from the way he says it, it's clear that he thinks it's a pretty big deal.

Ammu nudges me with her elbows and nods at Zak, so I clear my throat to speak. Everyone's eyes snap to me, and I try to ignore the heat that rushes up my face.

"Congrats, Zak," I say, my voice sounding more like a squeak than anything else.

"Thanks, Rani. You sitting down?" He pats the seat right beside him, and both our parents beam like this is the best interaction they've ever witnessed in their whole entire lives. I try very hard not to roll my eyes as I shuffle over and take a seat beside Zak.

Thankfully, our parents and my sisters take their own seats, too, drawing attention away from me and Zak. Attention is the last thing we need.

"Are you wearing makeup?" Zak asks, looking at me a little too closely with his piercing brown eyes. I pull at my hair so it falls in a curtain between me and Zak.

"Yeah, a little."

"Since when do you wear makeup? And pink lipstick? Really?"

"Ammu got it for me," I say.

"Ah." He leans back in his seat, like that explains it all. Like he's got me pinned down just because our families have known each other for the past few years and decided that the two of us are destined to be. The thing is, it makes sense on paper. It's not like Dublin is crawling with eligible Bangladeshi, Muslim bachelors. Technically, I've hit the jackpot with Zak. The problem is, I'm not sure I actually like him like that, or like the fact that the two of us are in a kind-of sort-of relationship. As a friend, he's fine. As more than that? I'm not so sure.

"I want a doner kebab," Parisa says before anybody else has even had a chance to glance at the menu.

"I want chips!" Neelam chimes in quickly, like if she doesn't, she might lose her shot at them.

"I think we should order whatever Zakkariyah wants. It's his day, after all," Abbu says. Pari lets out half a groan, but as soon as I poke her in the stomach with my elbow, she shuts up. She should know by now that Zak is the favorite child of our family . . . and he's not even in our family.

"Uncle, you can call me Zak," Zak insists.

"Zakkariyah is a much better name than Zak," Ammu says. Uncle and Aunty nod in agreement.

"I don't know why he tries to change it to that awful Zak. Zakkariyah is strong, Muslim," Aunty says.

"There are so many amazing people with your name," Uncle adds. "Zakariyya al-Ansari was an Islamic scholar in medieval Egypt."

"There's also that Indian cricketer, right? Zakkariya . . . Zakkariya . . ." Abbu drifts off, trying to find his exact name.

Zak turns to me with a look of utter frustration, and for the first time tonight it feels like we actually have something in common.

"Zak is a better name, right?" he asks me quietly, like he values my opinion on it more than anyone else's.

"Not the way you say it."

"How do I say it?" he asks.

"*Zack*, like it's a Western name. Zakkariyah and Zack, they're not the same." I shrug.

"You're really going to mansplain to me about my own name?" he asks.

I scoff. "I'm just answering your question."

Strangely, Zak smiles instead of retorting with something smart. Like he's letting me win this one.

"The makeup looks nice, by the way," he says after a moment.

If I were a normal girl, the compliment would probably make me feel something. Like a thrumming in my chest, or heat rising up my cheeks.

But I guess I'm not a normal girl.

3

MEGHNA

CAR RIDES WITH MY PARENTS ARE HELLISH, BUT WHAT'S EVEN worse is what waits for me at the other end of the ride.

"I don't understand why we're going to this dawat," I complain.

"Because we were invited," Ammu says matter-of-factly. Ever since Abbu's business went bankrupt a few years ago, the Bengali people we used to hang out with rarely—if ever—invite us over. Still, when they do, Ammu and Abbu jump at the opportunity.

"But we hate them," I point out, crossing my arms and glaring out the window at the passing cars. I know I can't do this once I get into the dawat, so I might as well get it all out of my system now.

"We don't *hate* them," Abbu says at the same time that Ammu exclaims, "We don't hate anyone!" They exchange a quick glance, like they're embarrassed to have gotten their signals mixed up this one time.

"They're part of our community," Ammu adds after a second. "So, it's important to be a willing participant of that community, even if things are sometimes a little complicated."

"They didn't care about community when things were hard for us," I say.

"Things aren't always so black-and-white," Abbu says in a firm tone that tells me the conversation is over. So I groan and slump back in my seat, even if it messes up my hair a little bit, waiting for the car to pull up to the driveway.

The Bhuiyans' house is nothing like ours. That's probably why it's on the complete other side of the city and secluded with a gate and red-brick fence. The gate opens automatically once Abbu presses the buzzer on the wall, and we drive in. There are already a dozen cars in front of the house, and Abbu parks just to the side of the gravel pathway.

"I think we might be late," Ammu mumbles as she grabs hold of the bouquet of flowers she bought for the Bhuiyans.

"I bet none of the other families had to drive from the other side of Dublin," I point out. But instead of agreeing with my very valid point, Ammu fixes me with one of her signature glares.

"Meghna, I know you don't like the Bhuiyans—"

"Or anybody else here," I say.

"—but you have to be on your best behavior."

"I'll try." I shrug. It's the best she's going to get out of me. Ammu sighs before ushering me and Abbu toward the oak double doors and ringing the bell. Even though she's been trying to justify our coming to this dawat this whole time, a flicker of nervousness crosses her face as the doors swing open. Bhuiyan Uncle stands in the doorway, and his smile feels plastic.

"Ah, Rahman Bhai, Bhabi!" he says. "Long time no see! Come in, come in!"

He waves us in and looks at me with surprise as I pass by. "Meghna, you're all grown up."

"I have been for a few years now," I say with a sickly sweet grin. He doesn't seem to get that it's a jibe against them for basically shunning us for the past few years.

"Your new house is . . . amazing," Abbu says, staring in awe at the white-tiled floors of the grand entrance and the spiral staircase leading upstairs. I'm pretty sure our entire house could fit in just this space, but I can already see it leads into a lounge area filled with aunties and uncles who don't pay any mind to our presence.

"It took a while for it to come together," Uncle says, as if he built the place with his own two hands or something. "I could give you all a tour?"

Ammu and Abbu nod enthusiastically, but the last thing I want to do is trail behind them as Bhuiyan Uncle boasts about all the expensive things he has no doubt filled this house with.

"Where's the bathroom?" I ask.

"There's one just up the stairs. First door on the right," Uncle says.

"Thanks." I slip off my shoes and make my way up the stairs; I can still hear the sound of Bhuiyan Uncle telling Ammu and Abbu about the tiles they had to have specially imported from Italy for their kitchen.

I don't actually have to use the bathroom, so I pause at the top of the stairs, unsure of where exactly to go. If I go downstairs, I'll have to deal with the aunties and uncles asking questions that'll no doubt lead to the rumor mill talking about my family. I definitely don't want to give them any more ammunition, or to even really be in their presence.

"Are you lost?" Rani's familiar voice snaps me out of my thoughts. She's looking at me with her wide-eyed deer-in-the-headlights expression. And of course, she looks stunning. It's not like Rani has ever not looked stunning, when her parents give her absolutely everything that money can buy. She's wearing a cream-colored anarkali dress with indigo flowers printed all over it. Her deep-blue urna hangs effortlessly off one shoulder and glitters when it catches the light. Compared to my simple, pink-patterned salwar kameez, Rani is basically dressed like royalty.

"It's a house. How could I get lost?"

"It's a pretty big house," she says. "The bathroom is just over there." She points to the door right in front of me, as if I'm incapable of finding the bathroom by myself.

"I'm not looking for the bathroom."

"Well, all the kids are over in the bedroom watching *Boss Baby*," Rani says. "They're mostly pretty young."

"I think *Boss Baby* is really incisive commentary on how we need to prioritize love and family over the evil that is capitalism, so it's good that kids are watching it," I say, even though I hated *Boss Baby* and would definitely never watch it ever again.

Rani smiles like I've said something funny, and it makes anger pulse through my veins. "I heard that you got into the Young Scientist Exhibition. With observations like that, I'm not surprised. Congrats."

I can read between the lines of what she's saying. She's surprised I got in even though I've watched movies like *Boss Baby*. She doesn't know what's coming, though—how my project is absolutely going to destroy hers.

"Isn't it, like, your millionth time at the exhibition? Hardly something to congratulate me about when it's something you can do in your sleep, apparently."

Rani blinks her long, black lashes a little too slowly. "Well, I think it's a really big achievement, regardless. We should celebrate all our accomplishments, right? I can't wait to see your project."

I know she's fishing for information, but there's no way I'll give away anything about my project.

"Can't wait to see yours, either," I say, though I definitely don't mean it. "I assume it's something genius to do with tech." Last year, she designed an app that helped students work on group projects together. It was really just a fancier version of Google Docs, but my parents talked about how smart Rani was for creating it for so long that I seriously wished I had the ability to turn my ears off at will. If only Rani had designed the technology for *that*.

"It's to do with languages," Rani says with a small nod. I make a mental note of it, but it makes me feel a little bit more at ease about beating her. If the judges at the exhibition weren't moved by her app that was supposed to help students, there's no way they'll give her a prize for an app about languages. There are a million language apps already out there.

She doesn't elaborate any more. Instead, she just looks at me, like she's waiting for me to douse her in compliments for her brilliant app idea. No doubt that's what everybody else in her life does 24/7.

"Well, I hope it can beat out all the other language apps on the market!" I say cheerily.

Rani's smile flickers for a moment, but before she has the chance to say anything else, Bhuiyan Aunty's voice floats up from downstairs.

"Dinner is served! Come to eat!" she says in a singsong voice that grates on my nerves.

"Bhuiyan Aunty makes the best biryani," Rani says.

"I hate biryani," I lie with a smile before turning around and marching down the stairs. By the time Rani follows me down, I'm already at the kitchen, piling my plate with food and looking for a secluded corner to eat in by myself. I'd rather spend the whole dawat alone than spend another minute with Rani, or really anyone else here. Thankfully, nobody bats an eyelash when I slink off into a corner of the sitting room with all the uncles. Abbu even gives me a smile, like he's glad I'm here. Probably because none of the uncles seem particularly interested in speaking to him, either.

I stuff a handful of biryani in my mouth, savoring the taste of the rice and meat and spices all mixed together. Rani was right—the biryani is good. But that doesn't mean I can't hate Bhuiyan Aunty and Uncle, or all the other people at this dawat who were all too happy ignoring my family for the last few years. And it doesn't mean that I can't hate Rani and every awful thing about her.

My parents may think Rani is the best thing to come out of Bangladesh since Muhammad Yunus won the Nobel Prize, but I know the real her.

And I have to beat her.

4

RANI

For some reason, I think about Meghna for a long time—during the dawat when she avoids me like the plague, after on the car ride home, and even throughout the rest of the week as I try to figure out my presentation for the Young Scientist Exhibition.

"You're not thinking about your science project, are you?" Aarti asks at lunchtime on Wednesday, when the silence between us has stretched out for a little too long.

"You know I hate it when you call it a science project. It sounds so . . . childish," I say. Aarti just rolls her eyes and takes a bite of the spinach frittata that the cafeteria is serving today. I know she has more she wants to say, and she's just drawing out the conversation. Ever since befriending her four years ago when I first started in Sacred Hearts International School, I've quickly realized that this is Aarti's method of ensuring that people are *really* paying attention when she has something important to say.

Now I watch as she takes an agonizingly long time chewing her food. Finally, she swallows and says, "I'm just tired of every single conversation revolving around it for the past couple of weeks. I know it's important to you, but you can't live, breathe, and eat it for months and not expect me to complain at least a little."

"Well, good thing it'll be over by this time next week." My mind drifts to Meghna again—because she'll be there at the exhibition.

After not seeing her for months, maybe even a whole year, I get to see her twice in the space of two weeks. If I was someone who believed in superstitions, I would think maybe it was some kind of a sign. "You know, Meghna is going to be there," I blurt out, against my better judgment.

Aarti's eyebrows scrunch up for a moment. "Meghna?"

I can't tell if she's pretending she doesn't know Meghna or if she's really forgotten about her. It's not like there are a million Meghnas running around Dublin.

"You know, Meghna Rahman. You definitely saw her in some dawats back in the day."

Recognition flickers in Aarti's eyes, and she sits back in her chair, slowly chewing another bite of her frittata. "The Rahmans. They were the ones who went bankrupt because the uncle did some shady deals and went into major debt, and then they had to move, and nobody wanted to associate with them anymore. Right?"

I sigh. Leave it to Aarti to remember Meghna and her family for their scandals and nothing else.

"I'm pretty sure that's not what happened. That was just a rumor."

Aarti raises an eyebrow. "I didn't know you were friends with . . . Meghna." She says her name like it's something distasteful. I knew I shouldn't have brought her up.

"I'm not. It's just last weekend at that dawat at the Bhuiyans' house, she was there, and I heard she was going to be at the Young Scientist Exhibition. I don't know, it was kind of nice to see her again after so long." I pause, not sure how much information is appropriate to divulge here. After all, whatever friendship I had with Meghna is from the past. From before starting at Sacred Hearts. From before befriending

Aarti. And I'm not sure I really want to dredge it all up and have Aarti put it under a microscope. Especially when even I don't know what really happened. "I guess I just think it's cool that there will be multiple Bangladeshis presenting. Bangladeshi representation, right?"

Aarti squints her eyes at me like I've suddenly grown two heads, so I quickly stuff the most humongous bite of my own lunch into my mouth so she can't ask me any more questions. That doesn't stop Aarti, though—almost nothing does.

"Who is the other one?" she asks. When I look at her questioningly because I'm too busy chewing to speak, Aarti just presses even more. "You said there were multiple Bangladeshi people presenting. So, it's you, Meghna, and . . ."

"Zak." My voice comes out in a squeak. Aarti's expression hardens at his name.

"Seriously? He has time from his busy schedule of rugby and being a smug asshole to present at a science fair?"

"A science exhibition," I correct her. "And he's not that bad. He's smart, clearly, otherwise he wouldn't be the only student from his entire school picked to present. And his project sounds amazing. He's working on an app that's supposed to help athletes keep track of everything in one place. Their diet, their exercise, and the app is supposed to calculate statistics about your body, how it's changing, and even give you advice on what you can do differently depending on what changes you want to see."

"So, an app for sports bros." Aarti sounds so unimpressed it's actually a little funny.

"Athletes are not 'sports bros,'" I say, but Aarti just rolls her eyes. Zak may be the most charming guy I—or my parents—have ever met, but something about his charm just never works on Aarti. And he's definitely tried his best—from cracking jokes in the middle of dawats, all the way to going over her head to impress her parents. But none of it made any difference to Aarti, even if she knows that being my best friend means she'll have to put up with Zak one way or another.

"I hope you beat him," she says. "God knows he's had enough wins in his lifetime. He doesn't need anything, or anyone, else to stroke his ego."

I bite down a laugh because it's not the first time I've heard this sentiment from Aarti. I hear it with every match of Zak's that I drag her to, every single Young Scientist Exhibition where we're both up for the same award, and every time his parents call mine to tell them the good news about his results.

"His results are not even as good as yours!" Aarti had cried in an exasperated voice last summer. Our report cards arrived in the mail and my parents fawned over Zak's like they always do while dismissing mine as though they had never expected anything else.

"I guess you'll have to come to the exhibition to cheer me on, then," I say with a smile.

Aarti just sighs and says, "Like I've got nothing better to do with my life?" But I know it's her way of saying that I couldn't keep her away even if I tried.

5

MEGHNA

I've been to the Young Scientist Exhibition almost every year since I started secondary school.

But this is my first year as a participant. As a scientist. And, as soon as I arrive in the massive hall at the RDS, I can't help but be enthralled by everything. My eyes widen to the size of saucers as I take it all in: the other students setting up their tables with posters explaining exactly what their projects are about, the signs hanging up on the wall telling people what they can expect in each section of the venue. That's how big the hall is—there are sections!

"You know you're supposed to be setting up, right?" Yemi's voice is muffled behind a box of materials they're carrying in front of them. When I turn around, they're being guided by Janella, who has one hand firmly pressed against Yemi's wrist and is pulling them along gently.

"How do you know I'm not setting up?" I ask.

"Because I know you," Yemi huffs. Janella drops their wrist and pulls the box from Yemi's hand, only to place it with a plop on top of the desk I've been assigned, already scattered with the stuff I brought in earlier. "And I was right." Yemi says this with all the theatrics that only someone who has been part of their local drama group their entire life can. So, basically, with some jazz hands and an over-the-top singsong voice.

"The exhibition starts in, like, an hour," Janella half whispers, checking the time on her phone.

"I'll be ready in time. I can get it set up in a few minutes, no problem!" I say, even though when I glance down at the box and everything I have to do to prepare, it doesn't seem like it's a *no problem* situation.

Janella and Yemi exchange a glance between them like they know this. And I know they know. I'm not exactly the most organized person in our friend group.

"We could stay?" Janella asks, though she's looking at Yemi instead of me.

"We've got double biology first anyway, so it's kind of like we're in science class already." Yemi shrugs.

"You're not staying!" I exclaim. "I've got this. Go to school, study science, and I'll see you when Ms. Ennis brings the whole year down." I all but shove the two of them through the double doors by my table. They protest halfheartedly before finally succumbing. They've never been able to hold their own against me in an argument, anyway.

Once the double doors shut behind them, I feel anxiety pool in my belly as I look around at everyone else, total strangers who've probably been presenting here every year since they started secondary school. I don't really believe in impostor syndrome—I know the only reason I ever feel it is because I'm a woman of color in a country where I'm a minority. And an immigrant and from a working-class family, on top of all that. But I can't help but feel like I don't belong here at all.

I shuffle back to my table, because I have work to do. But before I begin, I type a quick text to Zak: *can you tell me everything's going to be all right? I'm feeling way more nervous than I should be.*

For a moment, I just stare at my phone. I will Zak to start typing, for the three dots to appear. But nothing happens.

I know he's here somewhere in this massive events hall, and he's probably setting up his own project, like I'm supposed to be doing. I can't wait for him to come to rescue me—to make me feel like I belong here. I don't have time for that.

So instead, I take a deep breath and put my phone away as I start emptying the box of everything I need to set up my table. I've worked hard for this, and I know that I can win.

At least, that's what I repeat to myself for the next hour.

I DON'T KNOW WHY I EXPECT PEOPLE TO COME POURING IN AS soon as the exhibition officially begins. That obviously doesn't happen, because this is a science expo and not a Beyoncé concert that people have been queuing up for for hours on end.

Instead, once the doors open, a trickle of people come in slowly throughout the day. I stand by my table, hands clasped in front of me like I'm a polite person who knows how to behave in decent human society. I even smile—big—at all the white people strolling around the hall, their eyes on the different projects on display. It's not lost on me that I'm one of a handful of people of color in this room.

"What do we have here?" a white woman with dark red hair asks, pausing in front of my table and waving over a group of students. Their navy-blue uniforms are only a shade darker than my own, but the school crests emblazoned on their sweaters is completely different.

"Hi, welcome!" I say, my voice sounding a little too cheerful and fake. None of the students look particularly impressed as they take in the posters plastered around my desk. But I know I have more to offer.

I move over to the other side of my station, giving them room to take everything in.

"My project is all about flood prevention, which is especially important in this day and age when rising sea levels are cause for huge concern. Did you guys know that it's predicted that seventeen percent of the country of Bangladesh will be underwater by the year 2050? Which means more than twenty million people will be displaced!"

The redhead nods as if this is the most fascinating tirade she's ever heard in her life, but her students blink at me like they haven't processed a single word I've said.

I take a deep breath and continue, "You see, Bangladesh deals with floods every year because so much of the country is under sea level, which means that every year the rain and the rising water levels give way to them."

I press a button on the tablet set up against the posters, and the graphic I worked so hard to create starts raining onto the map of Bangladesh until much of the green on it disappears into blue water.

This time, the students shift on their heels, their eyes glued to the tablet. A few people from the surrounding area even shuffle over.

"Wars and famines have already led to a rise in refugees in recent years, but if this problem persists—not just in Bangladesh, but across the globe"—at this, I tap on the tablet again and the image zooms out to show all the countries that are in a similar amount of danger from rising sea levels—"we're going to see millions of people displaced without a home and with nowhere to go. The rise of climate refugees is imminent if we don't find a solution to the problem now.

Bangladesh is not the only country affected, but it is one that's in immediate danger."

I continue my presentation with images of parts of Bangladesh that were ravaged by floods. The pictures show people's homes swept away, and crops destroyed. It shows people knee-deep in water, and even cars and rickshaws half-submerged. None of it is pretty.

I watch as the students' eyes widen more and more with every picture. I imagine some of them have never seen—or heard of—floods like this before. Even I hadn't before my parents told me about the ones from when they were younger and lived in Bangladesh. It's not like floods are a common occurrence here—and definitely not like the ones we get there.

"How can we stop Bangladesh from going underwater?" one of the students asks. I grin. It's the question I'd been hoping for.

"Well, there is something called the Delta project. It was successfully implemented in the Netherlands. The project in Bangladesh will be a long-term one that prioritizes the drainage of water and the embankment systems on Bangladesh's river deltas. It'll be a complicated and expensive process, but it can save a lot of people from homelessness and poverty," I say. I press a button so graphics showing potential delta swamps around Bangladesh appear on-screen. "But ultimately, sea levels are rising because of climate change. And our governments need to commit to doing better for the climate."

Once my presentation is over, the teacher and students give me a small round of applause, and I can't help but feel a swell of pride.

"I went to the climate protest a few years ago," one of the students chimes in. "But my parents say climate change isn't real."

"From looking at these photos, do you really believe that?" I ask.

The student shakes her head slowly.

"This was an excellent presentation. Remember this one, girls," the teacher says sternly to her students. "We will definitely discuss it further in class tomorrow."

The girls groan as their teacher sweeps them away to another table, but I have to stop myself from squealing with happiness. I thought that once it came time to do my presentation, I would somehow screw it up. Start nervously stuttering or something. But it was like once I began, everything just flowed out of me.

I pick up my phone once more and shoot off another text to Zak.

Me: things are going so well!! come here whenever you get the chance, okay? I want to show you my project.

I barely have the time to put the phone down when it buzzes. It's a text from Zak. Two, actually.

Zak: can't
Zak: busy

I frown, about to start typing when my phone buzzes two more times.

Zak: sorry
Zak: tell me about it later

All my excitement deflates. Tell him about it later? Does that mean he's not going to come see my project at all? Surely he has five minutes to spare to see his girlfriend present in her first ever Young Scientist Exhibition.

I'm considering setting my tablet to auto-play my presentation and leaving my table to scour for Zak, when my parents finally decide to make their appearance, with my older brother Mahin on their heels.

"Meghna, why are you in this corner, so far away from everything?" is the first thing Ammu asks, shaking her head solemnly.

"I'm by a door." I point to the door that's to the right of my setup. It's not the main entrance, but from the way Ammu is speaking, you'd think they'd shoved me into a dank, dark corner filled with cobwebs and no light or something.

"You should see where Rani is, right in the middle. And so many people around her project," Abbu says.

I have to stop myself from letting out a frustrated sigh, but Bhaiya catches my eye with a knowing look. We're both used to our parents singing Rani's praises every chance they get. She's probably their favorite child, and she's not even their child.

"How have you already seen Rani when you just got here?" I ask, trying very hard not to let any of my frustration seep into my voice.

"Because her project is amazing!" Ammu says. "She's teaching people Bangla, Meghna. Bangla! Why couldn't you do a project about Bangla?"

Of course Rani is doing a language-learning app that centers Bangla. Like she couldn't be any more of the perfect Bangladeshi daughter my parents have always wanted.

"Ammu, Abbu, come on . . . Meghna's project is about Bangladesh, too. Look," Bhaiya says, coming to my rescue as he often does. He points to the photos I have on my posters that show the areas in the Sundarbans that are already underwater.

My parents take in the posters for a moment, even though they've heard me talking about this project for months, and I've even barraged them with research questions.

"Yes, it's very important," Ammu finally admits.

"Thank—"

"But," Ammu interrupts. Of course that couldn't have been the end of it. "Flooding is not Bangladesh. It shows the bad side of our country. But Bangla, teaching people Bangla—what could be better than that?"

"We're *Bangla*desh," Abbu agrees.

"Who here would even want to learn Bangla?" I ask, crossing my arms in a huff. In reality, I would love to use whatever app Rani is working on to learn Bangla. It's not like you can find our language on Duolingo, even though it's the seventh most spoken language in the world. Nobody knows anything about it, just like few people know anything about our country at all.

I can speak conversational Bangla well enough, but reading and writing it? That's not one of my abilities. Rani probably has a master's degree in it from Dhaka University somehow, even though she's the exact same age as me.

"It's not just Bangla," Bhaiya says, avoiding my eyes. "Her prototype is for Irish, too. And she's developing it further to teach yet another language." He finally looks me in the eye with a sheepish smile. "I hate to say it, but it's a pretty good app."

"Why do you hate to say it?" Ammu berates Bhaiya before I even have a chance to digest his words. Bhaiya just started a medical research position with a start-up company that helps implement tech into medicine, so that's how I know Rani's project must be even better than good. It must be amazing. And now, just because she's decided to teach people how to speak Bangla, even my parents are obsessed with it.

"I'm screwed, aren't I?" I ask.

Bhaiya doesn't say yes, but from the look in his eyes, I already know I don't have a shot next to Rani Choudhury.

I was delusional to think I ever did.

6

RANI

I DON'T KNOW IF IT'S FATE OR MY BAD LUCK, BUT SOMEHOW ZAK and I are right next to each other at the Young Scientist Exhibition. Which means that while I'm trying to give people a chance at testing out my language app, I have to deal with all of Zak's rugby friends obsessing over *his* app.

"You know, we're kind of the dream team," Zak says halfway through the day, when there's a lull in our area.

"I didn't even realize we were a team," I say while trying to rearrange my table to look a little more enticing and presentable. The judges haven't been by yet, so my nerves are running high. Even though I've always done well in *this* exhibition, I have never placed high enough to go on to the European exhibition. I'm not going to let Zak's constant barrage of conversation keep me from that.

"I just mean, you know, because one day we're going to be," Zak keeps going, like he doesn't even realize I'm only half listening to what he's saying. I don't think Zak has ever quite understood the concept of not being the center of the universe. My parents and their fawning over him probably don't help. "And we're side by side, taking this competition by storm."

When I finally turn toward him, he actually looks like he genuinely believes we're some kind of team. Even though we've done completely different projects, and they just happen to both be apps and they also just happen to both be placed next to each other. I hope the judges don't put too much stock in that. I don't want to come in second to Zak. My parents would never stop praising him.

"Since we're such a great team, maybe you should keep an eye on my project while I walk around for a few minutes?" I ask. "I've been really wanting to check out Meghna's project."

"Meghna?" Zak asks, his voice taking on the same tone that Aarti's had last week. Like he doesn't know Meghna.

"Seriously, how many Meghnas do people know? I only know the one. Meghna Rahman, she's here. Or she's supposed to be. We used to be friends. You don't . . . remember?" I ask.

Zak blinks like he's having a difficult time processing my words. "Why do you want to look at her project?" he asks finally.

"Because I'm curious, I guess," I say. "She wouldn't tell me anything about it, so—"

"Wait." Zak steps forward, suddenly a little too close to me. He doesn't have that signature smirk on his face, and for once he doesn't look amused. He actually seems serious, with his eyebrows furrowed together and his lips set into a thin line. "When did you and Meghna talk?"

"There was a dawat, and I was there. She was there, too, but I didn't know she would be. I was just asking her about her—"

"What did you guys talk about?" Zak's voice gets more and more somber with every word he speaks.

"Just . . . the exhibition." I shrug. "Why? Do you not like her or something?"

Zak's face finally softens. "I just heard her family was bad news. I don't know if it's a good idea for you to talk to her, that's all."

"We used to be friends with her family," I point out.

"That was a long time ago," Zak says. He steps away from me once more and makes his way over to his project. He almost seems back to his normal self, but there's a strange tension in his body as he moves around. "Anyway, I can't watch your project. The judges will probably be here soon."

"Zak, I'll be, like, five minutes. Nobody will even know I'm—"

"Rani, you need to be taking this seriously," Zak says. "When I said we're a team, I meant it. You really think you're going to win this thing by hanging out with Meghna?" He says her name like it's something distasteful. He says it all like I'm doing something distasteful. I don't know why, but it sends a weird thread of shame through me. Maybe he's right—maybe I shouldn't take off to visit Meghna. She probably wouldn't want me there, anyway.

My phone buzzes with a text, and I pick it up to see a message from Aarti.

Aarti: how's the science fair?
Aarti: sorry—exhibition!

I thought it had been going well—great, even. I was nervous, as I always am during the Young Scientist Exhibition, but I'd also been feeling excited to be here once more. But now, I'm not so sure.

I can't really explain that in a text, though, especially since I don't even know why I'm suddenly feeling so deflated.

Me: you're getting here soon, right?

It's the only thing I can think to text back. Aarti just sends me a thumbs up, which I know can mean she's five minutes away or five hours. Instead of dwelling on it, or giving too much thought to the sudden weight on my chest, I simply tuck my phone away.

My family arrives within the next hour. But rather than spending any time at my table, my parents spend most of their time oohing and aahing at Zak's app. Abbu even tells him that this was the app he needed when he was a kid in Bangladesh playing cricket with his cousins. I want to point out how at that age he couldn't even fathom the idea of an app, considering he was still using a rotary phone. But of course, I don't.

Instead, I chew on my lips and watch Ammu and Abbu fawn over Zak. And when Parisa and Neelam get bored and decide the best use of their time is to go up to every single person at the exhibit and ask them to sum up their project in one sentence so they can pretend they are the judges, I just sit in my seat and hope that the actual judges arrive soon.

Finally, I spot them coming around the corner. Zak tries to catch my eye, but I stand up with my shoulders straight, putting on my best smile. This year has to be the year. It just *has* to be.

"Good luck!" Ammu and Abbu whisper as they pull Pari and Neelam away and duck out of the way. I turn to say thanks, but then I realize they're wishing luck to Zak. Not to me.

"Rani Chow-do-ree." The judges completely butcher my name as they approach my project. I keep my smile plastered on.

There are four judges this year, each of them from one of the fields of science represented here: social and behavioral science; technological and mechanical sciences; biological and ecological sciences; and, finally, chemical, physical, and mathematical sciences.

After the past few years, I'm pretty sure I've cracked that the best way to place well in this exhibition and get an invite to the European one is to do something that's a crossover: a project that combines two or more of the scientific fields. That's why I chose to do an app on languages, which should ideally appeal to both social and technological sciences.

"Yes, Rani Choudhury!" I say, my voice sounding a little high-pitched and enthusiastic. I clear my throat and start my presentation. "I created a language-learning app for my project and designed the prototype, which already features two languages: Bangla or Bengali, which is my mother language. And Irish. Two languages that couldn't be more different from each other; one is one of the most spoken languages in the world, the other sadly considered a dying language. But that's why I wanted to start off by focusing on them."

I pull up my app on my phone, plug in a pair of headphones, and hand it all over to the judges.

"My language-learning app is immersive. It's not just about learning vocabulary and grammar; it's about giving people access to conversational language. It's a digital experience that tells a story. It's creating living language. With more development, not only will I be able to add more languages to the app, but I'll also be able to make each language more and more enhanced. So it's not just a linguistic experience, it's a cultural one, too," I finish off, blinking at the judges with wide eyes. They play around with the app for a few minutes, each of them taking a turn listening to the voice-overs I carefully recorded to try and create my immersive experience. It's not exactly as polished as I would like it to be, but it has to show them the potential that this app—and I—have.

"This is really good, Rani," one of the judges says. She has honey-blond hair and passes me a small smile as the other judges nod along.

"We've seen a lot of language apps, both here and in the wider world. But yours definitely stands out," one of the other judges, a man with a tuft of red hair and a goatee, adds.

Inwardly, I let out a sigh of relief. Outwardly, I say, "Thank you," trying not to beam at the compliments.

But when the judges move on to Zak, my face falls. Their excitement for his sports app is unparalleled. Almost all of the judges say that they've never seen an app like this before, and that it's one they could have used back in their sporting days—just like Abbu.

Only the blond-haired judge—the one woman among all of them—frowns as she taps away at the app.

"This interface looks familiar," she says.

"I mean, nothing is exactly original when there are new apps being designed every day," Zak says with a bashful smile and a shrug. "But I did take inspiration from a few different apps in designing this. There are some good medical apps out there that definitely motivated me to put this together."

"Right." The judge doesn't look even half as impressed as the others, but she says nothing else.

By the time they move on to the next table, there's an uncomfortable feeling in my stomach. It's not often that the judges choose two people from the same field of science to invite to Europe.

As I look at the huge grin on his face, I realize that for all his talk of teams, Zak might have always been too aware of this truth: If he wins, I lose.

And the worst thing is that my parents wouldn't mind.

7

MEGHNA

By the time Ms. Ennis arrives with the entire science class in tow, my parents and Mahin have disappeared. I shouldn't be glad for it, but with the amount of praise they had for Rani compared to me, I'm a little glad. Even more so when I spot Yemi and Janella's familiar faces in the crowd of students Ms. Ennis brought with her.

"Meghna!" Ms. Ennis says, the smile on her face so bright that it could probably put the sun to shame. If there's one person who knows how hard I've been trying to get into the Young Scientist Exhibition, it's her. She's the person I brainstorm ideas with every year, and she's the person who suggested that I look into climate change and Bangladesh this year.

"Climate change is big!" Ms. Ennis said. "It's important, it's timely, and now more than ever, people want to understand it."

"But will anyone even care about climate change in Bangladesh?" I asked. Last year, I tried to do a project on arsenic contamination in groundwater, and specifically how this had become a problem in water in Bangladesh. Clearly, it wasn't something the judges thought was a necessary investigation, despite all my hard work and research. The year before, I attempted a social and psychological investigation into the Rohingya genocide and the integration of Rohingya refugees into Bangladesh. But I quickly realized that nobody here cared about the Rohingya genocide, and they certainly didn't care about the refugees. I realized it even more when I dragged Yemi and Janella to the Rohingya solidarity protest in Dublin that year, and the numbers there were abysmal. There wasn't even any media coverage. A far cry from when Yemi, Janella, and I go to the March for Choice every year. Or when Yemi and Janella bring me as their token straight friend to the Pride march every single June.

Despite all that, Ms. Ennis had been right this year: Climate change and rising sea levels apparently are more universal than all the other things I had tried to research. At least, according to the judging committee of the Young Scientist Exhibition.

"Do you want me to do the whole song and dance for you?" I ask Ms. Ennis now, my smile almost matching hers but not quite.

"Maybe later," she says. After all, she's the person who has gone over my presentation with me again and again on her lunch breaks, and even after school, when she really didn't have to. "I'm going to take the girls"—at that, Yemi clears their throat a little too loudly—"the students," Ms. Ennis corrects herself, "and show them the rest of the projects. They even have an entire worksheet to fill out." Nobody quite looks happy at that.

"Can Yemi and Janella . . ." She nods before I can finish. So we watch as Ms. Ennis and the rest of the class drift around the hall, peeking at the different projects.

"Well, you got it done." Yemi stands with their hands on their hips, looking at my table with some admiration. "Has it been everything you've ever dreamed of?"

I want to say yes, but instead, I shake my head. "Rani's going to win. Again."

Janella frowns and exchanges a glance with Yemi. I'm not sure exactly what it means, but Yemi and Janella have been friends far longer than me. Sometimes, they communicate in a language that doesn't need any words. One that I have no hope of ever understanding.

"They're not announcing the winners until the end of the day, Meghna," Janella says, soothingly. It's the voice she uses on me when I get angry and go off on one of my rants—so one she uses often.

"I know, but my brother was here, and even he said Rani's project was amazing. I mean, it sounds amazing," I say.

"They choose one person from each of the four different categories usually, right?" Yemi asks. "Well, you and Rani are in completely different categories. Hers has nothing to do with the climate. You're not really even competing."

I sigh. "There are times they choose two people from the same category. If their projects are really impressive, and Rani's is. And tech is always the one that the judges love the most. Tech is the future, as they believe."

"Don't give up hope." Janella smiles. She's always the voice of reason. "And look, even if you don't get to go to the European exhibition, you got all the way here. There will still be a chance next year, right?"

"Right." But I can't help the dejection in my chest at that thought. I worked so hard for so many years just to get here. If I fail at this point, I only have one more year of school left. I'm not so sure it will be enough. And I'm not sure I have what it takes to get to Europe. Most people don't even consider the work I do to be "proper" science. When I first told Ammu and Abbu that I was going to submit to the Young Scientist Exhibition, they could not have been more excited. They thought that somehow, against all odds, one of their kids would pull themselves together and become a doctor. Then they learned that

I was interested in social science and climate science: two things that should have a lot of importance, especially to Bangladeshi people. But they saw it as lesser even than what my brother did. Because he may not be a doctor they can brag about to Bangladeshi uncles and aunties, but at least he's working adjacent to the right field.

"Something else is wrong," Yemi says after a few too many moments of silence have passed between us. "I'm assuming it's the boyfriend. Did he not show or something?"

I let out a frustrated puff of air. I have been trying to put Zak out of my mind for the past few hours, even though all I want to do is find him and figure out what the hell is going on. Ever since I told him about getting into the exhibition, he has been weird. I thought it was the Rani thing, but not even wanting to come see my project? That can't have anything to do with Rani.

"He's here," I say. "But he's busy. With his own project. He said he can't come see mine."

"That's it? That's the whole problem?" Yemi asks, like it's barely a problem at all.

"You should go see his project instead," Janella says.

"But I can't just leave. What if somebody comes around and they want to see my presentation?"

"We'll handle it." Yemi shrugs. "You're not the only smart science person around."

"*You* are going to do my presentation for people?" I ask.

"Don't look so shocked at the idea!" Yemi holds their hand over their chest, like they're very offended. "Janella and I can hold our own if need be. You go, sort things out with your boyfriend, and get that sad-puppy-dog look off of your face."

I stick my tongue out at the both of them, but still shuffle away, into the growing crowd. The longer the exhibition has been on, the more people have trickled in. Now I just need to find Zak. I glance down at my phone, at the last text exchange between us.

Zak: sorry. tell me about it later.

My fingers hover above the on-screen keyboard for a moment before I close out and take a deep breath. Zak and I have never been great at communicating via text. He is different in person—more vibrant, emotive. I need to not read so much into those few words on my screen.

I make my way through the exhibition more slowly than I would like. There are so many amazing projects that it's sometimes difficult to look away. A girl from our neighboring school built a water purifier as her project. It takes all my willpower not to rush over and check it out. I slip past her table and toward the tech section. This has even more people than the biological and ecological sections. I weave around, trying to spot Zak's familiar face. It shouldn't be hard. There aren't exactly a lot of brown people here.

Finally, after what feels like forever, I spot him at the edge of the room. In deep conversation with none other than Rani Choudhury. For a moment, I stop in my tracks, blinking at the two of them side by side. Zak says something to her with a grin on his face—one that seems too easy. Too bright. Rani doesn't return his smile. Instead, she glances down at her table, picking up her phone and scrolling through it with her long fingers.

I look at the crowds of people who seem to be completely unaware that there is something strange going on here. That it feels like I've stepped into some kind of an alternate reality. Zak ignoring me all day, telling me he's busy and couldn't come see me for even a minute. Zak laughing and talking with Rani like she's not my archnemesis.

And then, somehow, it gets even worse. Zak reaches in the space between the two of them. I watch as his hand brushes hers. She glances down, but she doesn't pull away. Almost like it's not unexpected. Not out of the ordinary.

My heart is thundering in my chest, my blood pumping so fast I can hear it in my ears. Like I'm running a marathon, not standing in the middle of a crowded room, watching my boyfriend . . . what? Flirt with another girl? Flirt with my archnemesis? Or something more? Something deeper.

If this were Janella watching her girlfriend, Saya, holding hands with another girl, I would tell her to stomp over there. Demand answers. That's what I want to do. But my throat is dry. My feet feel like lead glued to the linoleum floor of this hall. All I can do is stare, trying to understand, and wishing for some other explanation for what I'm seeing.

It's my phone buzzing in my pocket that takes me out of my trance. I dig it out with shaking fingers, turning away from Zak and Rani, who are evidently still too wrapped up in each other to notice that I'm only several paces in front of them. They'd only have to look up to see me, but they don't.

I have a string of notifications from both Janella and Yemi. The last of which reads:

Yemi: THE JUDGES ARE HERE. GET HERE NOW!!!!!!!!

I take one last, fleeting look at Zak and Rani before turning around and rushing back to my project. There is no way I'm letting the two of them sabotage me when I've come so far.

8

RANI

By the time the judges start the awards ceremony in the auditorium next-door, I've heard Zak's *we're a team* speech about a million times in a million different ways. Aarti—who finally showed up minutes before we began wrapping up the exhibition—drags me away from Zak as soon as the opportunity presents itself, claiming that we need an emergency bathroom break and will meet him there.

"Can we just ditch him?" Aarti asks as soon as we're out of his earshot.

"I don't think so," I say, "but hopefully by the time we catch up with him all the seats near him will be gone."

"Unless he saves us a seat," Aarti grumbles while pushing open the door to the bathroom. "What the hell is going on with him today, anyway?"

"I think he believes he's going to get a trophy," I say slowly. I don't have to use the bathroom, and apparently neither does Aarti. I take a moment to look at my reflection instead. The long day has definitely taken a toll on me. There are dark circles under my eyes, and my hair is a total mess.

"So . . ." Aarti urges when I haven't spoken for a moment too long.

"He's trying to act like him winning is somehow in my best interest," I say. It took until the third time he started talking about us being the ultimate team to figure out what he was doing. I don't really understand it. I wouldn't be angry at Zak if he won. But I also know that Zak hates it when people don't like him. It's why Aarti's dislike of him grates on his nerves so much. So, he's probably just making sure that I'll be on his good side, no matter what happens. He should realize it's not like I really have a choice, anyway. Not if I want to make my parents happy. Not if I want things to be good for my family. We're both in the same boat: stuck with each other. Zak just seems a little happier about it than me.

"He's such an ass," Aarti says. It's her signature line about Zak.

I sigh, trying to fix my hair in the mirror, but with only my fingers, it's not quite working. "He's really not that bad. And, you know, his app idea is good. I wouldn't be surprised if he does win over me. His appeal is to . . . a certain demographic, not you or me, really, but—"

"His demographic is meathead jocks like him," Aarti says. She digs up a hairbrush from her bag and hands it to me, along with a tube of concealer and a stick of eyeliner.

I take the hairbrush but refuse the rest. Though I'm sure Ammu wouldn't be happy about that, if she were here. "His demographic is athletes," I say while tying up my hair out of my eyes. "And I'm sure a lot of people could do great things with it. Athletes are important. The . . . Olympics."

Aarti just purses her lips tightly and stuffs the hairbrush back in her bag once I'm done with it. "Shall we?"

I take a deep breath. "Let's."

The seats are almost completely full by the time Aarti and I get there. She doesn't even let me search for Zak, and, honestly, I don't really try to fight her on it. Spending the entire day with him was more than enough.

We've barely sat down in the back row, right by the door, when the stage lights up with a spotlight. The four judges walk onto the stage, their footsteps echoing loudly across the entire auditorium.

"Welcome, everyone!" The blond-haired female judge speaks into the mic. "I'm Rachel McGill, and I work as a physicist in an aerospace laboratory. Some of you may recognize me as one of the judges of your wonderful exhibition today, alongside my three colleagues." At this, Rachel pauses to glance at the other three. She introduces them one by one and tells us their jobs: a specialist orthopedic surgeon, a professor of psychology, and a senior software developer.

The four of them give speeches about how over one hundred of us presented at this year's exhibition, and even list the statistics in each category. Beside me, Aarti's legs impatiently jiggle up and down, but I appreciate that for once she doesn't complain about how my science project is taking up all her time. She could be doing something much more interesting, but instead she's here supporting me.

"Now, as always, choosing the four best projects from all the presentations was an incredibly difficult decision. But there *were* four that stood out above the rest," Rachel says. "These four students will not only win a prize of one thousand euros, which will be donated to the science fund in their schools, but they'll also take home a trophy and a coveted invitation to submit to the European Young Scientist Exhibition. This year, the exhibition will take place in Amsterdam." Rachel pauses, and the room fills with breathless anticipation.

Even though I'm sure that I have no chance next to Zak, I can't help that my heart speeds up. That my breath hitches in my throat. Aarti passes me a supportive smile, but I barely even register it.

"First, we have Troy Abbott, whose investigation into lying as a social skill was seriously impressive!" Rachel announces. The room bursts into applause as Troy heads to the stage and collects his award.

"That was social and behavioral science," I whisper.

"I figured," Aarti replies, though she sounds far less snarky about it than she would otherwise.

"Next, we have Bryan Newman, whose interactive rocket launch was masterfully done," Rachel announces.

"Physics," I whisper, more to myself than to Aarti, as I watch Bryan walk up to the stage, collect his trophy, and shake hands with all the judges.

"Is it just me, or are these awards very white and male?" Aarti whispers back.

"That's always the way it is," I say. "I think they got Rachel specifically as a judge this year because they were criticized for the lack of women in both the judging panel and in the winners lineup last year."

"Up next, this mobile app . . ." Rachel begins. My breath becomes shallow as my eyes focus on her. Willing her to say me. My name. Rani Choudhury.

". . . by Zakkariyah Sardar, pulls off a brilliant combination of technology and biomedical sciences, showing true innovation."

I feel the pinprick of tears behind my eyes as a beaming Zak bounds up the steps. Even though I know I shouldn't. Even though I had already expected failure.

"There's always next year," Aarti says with a sympathetic glance toward me. "It's not the end of the world, Rani."

"I know, I'll be okay. I just—"

"And last, but certainly not least, we have Rani Choudhury!"

Rachel's booming voice cuts me off. "Whose immersive language app shows some serious coding and development skills."

For a moment, I can only just stare at the stage. But then Aarti shoves me to a stand and, somehow, I find my wobbly legs carrying me forward. Toward the stage, the spotlight. Toward Rachel, and the rest of the judges.

"I—thank you." That's all I can say as I collect my trophy. My mind is racing, and adrenaline pulses through me with every movement. This all feels surreal. I reach forward to shake the hands of the judges, barely managing to whisper a *thank-you* to each of them. My mouth is dry; my heart is thudding so loud I'm surprised everybody in the auditorium can't hear it.

The moment is over too soon. I turn around, taking a deep breath to calm myself. A smile stretches over my face. I try to catch Aarti in the crowd, but there are so many people that I can't find her. I can't believe I've won. One of four winners.

And then I catch sight of her: Meghna. She's sitting in the front row, her black hair like a curtain around her. And her eyes bore into mine. If looks could kill, Meghna's glare would decimate me on the spot. The smile vanishes from my face. But when I blink, Meghna isn't looking at me anymore. Instead, she's staring straight ahead at the stage. At Rachel giving closing remarks.

If Meghna's glare hadn't had the intensity of a thousand suns, I would have wondered if I had imagined the whole thing. But I know I didn't. Her rage was real.

And it was for me.

9

MEGHNA

I DON'T SLEEP THAT NIGHT. INSTEAD, I TOSS AND TURN FOR HOURS, feeling anger seep into me little by little, every passing second. I can't get any of it out of my head; it's like a movie that keeps playing the same few clips on repeat. Rani and Zak. Zak and Rani. Together. Zak walking up to the stage with that grin on his face. Searching for someone in the audience—but not me. Rani onstage with that fake, wide-eyed shock. Finding me in the audience.

By the time dawn breaks on the horizon and I hear Ammu rustling around in her bedroom to pray Fajr, I haven't slept a wink. I crawl out of bed and splash water on my face, hoping to make myself feel better. To let go of some of my anger. But it doesn't help, at all.

I open up my phone. There are dozens of text messages from Yemi and Janella. I didn't explain anything to them. Not after I came back to the table and gave a less-than-enthusiastic presentation to the judges. Not after they pestered me on the way to the auditorium. Not even after Rani and Zak won, and I was left with nothing.

Janella: you still have next year! you'll get them then!
Yemi: screw the judges! if they can't see what a visionary you are, that's their loss
Janella: let's watch a movie this weekend?

Yemi: you guys can come over to mine, we can order your favourite pizza Meghna

Janella: or we could get chinese food!

Yemi: and bubble tea, your favourite!!

Janella: we can print out photos of Rani and draw devil horns on her

Yemi: we can stalk her social media and laugh at all her snooty friends!

Janella: it'll be okay Meghna

Yemi: you'll be okay Meghna

They think I'm just upset because Rani won and I didn't. They don't know how wrong they are. That Rani didn't just take my win—she took Zak, too. And Zak was the only one in the world who really got me, through and through.

I didn't let myself cry before, but with Janella and Yemi's "it'll be okays" in front of me, a wave of sadness washes over me. And with my bedroom door closed and the dancing colors of dawn filtering in through the window, I let some of that sadness overwhelm the anger. I let myself cry.

It feels ridiculous to cry over losing. To cry over Zak and Rani, and everything they've both taken from me. But freeing in a way, too.

My phone buzzes once more and I look at the screen through a film of tears.

Bhaiya: heard about Rani . . . sorry Meghna

For a moment, I think he means he heard about what happened with Zak. But of course, that's ridiculous. Bhaiya doesn't even know about Zak. Nobody knows about him except Yemi and Janella. So unless I want to spill my guts to them about what I saw, I just have to sit here and wallow on my own. That may be the worst of it.

And it's that idea of sitting in my bed at the crack of dawn feeling sorry for myself that lights the fire in me once more. I wipe away my tears, changing out of my pajamas and into the first blouse and jeans in my wardrobe. I even manage to quickly put on a hint of concealer, blush, and eyeliner. Enough makeup to ensure that I don't look like I haven't slept all night and then just spent the past ten minutes crying. There is no way I can explain any of that to Ammu and Abbu, and no way I want anyone to even know that I had a breakdown.

With that done, I shuffle down the stairs to where Ammu is frying porotas and aloo bhaji. It's a Saturday morning tradition in my house.

Ammu almost recoils when she sees me. "You're up early."

"I just woke up and couldn't fall back asleep." I shrug. "Can I . . ." Before even finishing my question or letting Ammu reply, I grab one of the already-made porotas and pile a heap of aloo bhaji onto my plate.

"Wait for your abbu and Mahin," Ammu cries, though she makes no attempt to stop me.

"Bhaiya is coming today?" I make myself comfortable at our little dining table before tearing off a piece of the porota and stuffing it into my mouth with some aloo bhaji. The potatoes mixed with cheese, peas, and eggs nearly melts in my mouth. Nobody makes aloo bhaji like Ammu.

"He said he missed having homemade food." Ammu almost has a wistful look in her eyes as she says it, like all she's ever dreamed of doing is cooking for her children to their hearts' content.

"If he wanted homemade food so much, he could make it himself. In his own home," I say, through another mouthful of food. "Anyway, I have a busy day today, so I can't stay and hang out with him."

"Busy day?" Ammu asks. She sits down opposite me and settles me with one of her stern gazes. "Where do you have to go? What do you have to do?"

"I promised Yemi and Janella that I would hang out with them today. And we're going to study," I say.

"Hm." Ammu doesn't quite look like she believes me, but she doesn't say anything else. I guess she, too, must be feeling pretty sorry about the fact that I didn't win yesterday. Even if she should have seen it coming, considering how much praise she had for Rani and her project. "You should get some Bengali friends."

"You like Yemi and Janella," I groan, like I always do when this conversation happens. It's always the same thing: I talk about my friends, and Ammu grumbles about the fact that they're not Bengali, even though she loves to feed them Bengali food and be showered with their compliments about how good her cooking is.

"Yes, but they're not Bengali. Having Bengali friends is important, you know. Bengali people understand each other," Ammu says.

I want to argue back with her, but in some ways she's right. I love Yemi and Janella. They're my best friends in the world. But there are still some things they don't completely get. Like when I find a hilarious skit online about Bengali people, but they don't even understand it. I'm sure they feel the same way about me since I'm not Nigerian or Filipino. Yemi is close to their Nigerian cousins from London. They always talk about their shared WhatsApp group chat and how they spend their holidays in the UK trying out different African restaurants (to conclude that Nigerian jollof rice is the best), and going to various Afrobeats concerts. Janella has a small group of Filipino friends (and frenemies) from her mom's church, and their favorite pastime is going to the Filipino café near there for ube cake and siopao. I had Zak—that's why it felt so important to have him in my life. And now . . .

I shake my head and push my half-empty plate away. "You want the rest?"

Now Ammu really looks concerned. I'm not usually one to turn down food. She reaches her hand across the table toward my forehead. "Are you feeling okay? Are you feverish?"

"Ammu!" I duck out of her reach before coming to a stand. "It's early and I'm just . . . not that hungry. And I'm late!"

"Why are you always in a rush these days?" Ammu asks, watching as I slip on my runners. "The other day you had to rush to the library before closing. Now you're rushing to meet Janella and Yemi. Sometimes it's good to slow down, really see the world around you. Appreciate life and all the beautiful things that Allah has created in this world. Because before you know it—"

"Ammu, I'm going to be late." I interrupt her when I'm right by the front door, my hand on the doorknob. She would find a way to go on for another hour, otherwise.

"Home before Maghrib," Ammu says with a sigh. "Khodahafez."

"Khodahafez!" I call back as I open the door and slip outside. When I get to the bus stop, I open up Google Maps on my phone, putting in the address that I still remember from all those years back. It'll take me two buses and an hour to get there if I'm lucky, and neither of the buses is late. Otherwise, I'm looking at an hour and a half. Maybe even two.

When the bus pulls up, I board and find a window seat. And as it rushes forward, dread slowly builds inside me.

Rani's house is in a secluded corner of the road, with a gate and a stone fence cutting it off from everything. A plaque on the right side of the gate reads CHOUDHURY in shiny golden letters. I stand outside it for a moment, staring up at the looming house in front of me. It's been years since I was last here, but everything about it still feels familiar. Back when we used to be friends with the Choudhurys, we would be at their place every other weekend. And they'd be at ours the weekends we weren't at theirs. By the time they cast us out because we weren't good enough anymore, everything about their home was imprinted into my memory. I know every nook and cranny like it's my own.

The door swinging open takes me out of my reverie. For a moment, I expect Rani to step onto the porch and tell me to go away. But it's just her little sisters, Parisa and Neelam. They swing the door shut behind them and run into the front garden, their laughter high-pitched. They don't even notice me standing by the gate until they've pressed the button to open it.

"Hey Parisa, Neelam!" I say, trying not to feel like too much of a creep.

"Who are you?" Neelam asks. I try not to be offended. She was too young to remember how often I used to come over.

"Meghna? You don't remember me?" I ask. "I used to be friends with your sister."

Parisa at least seems to remember who I am, but she doesn't seem happy to see me. "Does Apu know you're here?"

"I'm just—"

"She's busy studying, you know." Parisa crosses her arms over her chest, and I try to ignore how weird it feels that someone who used to be like my own little sister just a few years back is treating me like I'm a complete stranger.

"I'm here to study with her," I lie.

Parisa doesn't look convinced, but she doesn't say anything when I slip in through the open gate. Instead, she takes Neelam's hand and begins to lead her out, no doubt to visit one of their rich friends.

"She's in her bedroom," Parisa calls back after a moment. "You remember where that is, right?" She doesn't even wait for me to answer before turning out of sight, with a confused Neelam in tow.

I walk through the front garden, up the stone steps to the porch, and try the door handle. Locked. I hover here for a moment. I could still turn back. Parisa and Neelam may have seen me, but I don't have to talk to Rani or risk running into Aunty and Uncle.

But then I take a deep breath, remember what Rani did to me, and press the doorbell. I can hear its hollow ring throughout the house. For a moment, there's only silence. Then, the creak of a door. The gentle sound of footsteps down the wooden staircase. Getting closer and closer.

I take another deep breath, preparing myself.

The door swings open, and suddenly there she is, looking down at me with her wide, confused eyes: Rani Choudhury.

10

RANI

"What are you doing here?" They're the first words out of my mouth when I spot Meghna standing in the doorway. I regret them almost instantly, because I realize it comes out less as what are you doing *here,* and more as what are *you* doing here. And clearly, that's how Meghna takes it, because her lips curl in disdain and she takes a step back as if she's ready to flee at a moment's notice.

"I'm sorry." I shake my head, looking away from Meghna and pushing the door open wider. "I just . . . wasn't expecting . . . come in."

Meghna looks me up and down but pushes past me a moment later. The movement feels so familiar it's strange. I can't help but think back to just a few years ago when Meghna would be here all the time. Sometimes even when her parents weren't over. Just to hang out. Just to talk.

I watch as she slips off her shoes and slides them into the little alcove under the stairs. She doesn't even wait for me before hopping onto the first step, then glancing back. Like she's the one who has lived here her whole life and I'm the guest.

"Upstairs? We need to talk." Meghna's voice is grim. She's not exactly enthusiastic when she talks to me these days (and we don't talk these days), but I've never heard her voice so . . . flat. If there's one thing everyone knows about Meghna, it's that whatever she does, whatever she says, there's exuberance to it. She's the most passionate person anyone will ever meet.

"Sure, yeah. Upstairs." I nod slowly. Meghna doesn't wait for me to lead her. She turns around and hurries up the steps, and I follow behind while she leads me to my own bedroom door. She hesitates for a moment before pushing it open and stepping inside. I follow, feeling like I've stepped into some kind of an alternate universe. Or maybe like I've stepped into the past.

Meghna takes in the mess in my bedroom with pursed lips before plopping herself down on the chair in front of my computer—the only chair that isn't piled with clothes or books.

"If I had known you were coming, I would have cleaned up or something," I mumble while trying to clear out some of the clothes on my bed. Since the win last night, I have been trying to think up how I can better my app for the European exhibition. I haven't really given much time to cleaning up.

"I don't care about whether your room is clean or not," Meghna says, some of the familiar fire finally back in her voice again. "I'm here because . . . because . . ." She pauses, and when I turn to her, she's looking down at the ground, her eyebrows scrunched together like she's trying to find the words. Meghna is never a person who has difficulty finding the right words. Mostly because she just says the first thing that comes to her mind.

"You stole my boyfriend!" Meghna finally blurts out. Whatever I was expecting to come out of Meghna's lips, it certainly wasn't *that*. I can only stare at her for a minute, trying to process what she's just accused me of. But it's a mistake, because Meghna seems to take my silence as some kind of admitting of fault.

"I know that things haven't been great with us or whatever. And I know your parents hate my parents. And I know that you love being better than me at everything, but this was the one thing, the *one* thing I had. You have everything, *everything*!" Meghna's voice rises with every word she says, her chest heaving. She's still not looking at me, but I can see the anger behind her eyes. The anger in her words, in her clenched fists.

"Meghna, I—" I step forward, but I don't know if she actually hears me.

"I don't even understand. I didn't know the two of you were friends. We don't even talk, but somehow you found a way to take him from me, when he was the only person who really understood me. You have everything, Rani, and all I had was, was—"

"Meghna!" My voice is not exactly a shout, but it's stern enough that Meghna stops talking. She finally glances up at me, holding my gaze. She's not glaring at me—not anymore. She doesn't even really look angry, even if she sounds it. She looks sad. Heartbroken. "I have no idea what you're talking about. Did . . . something happen?"

"You can't be serious." Meghna laughs, but there's no joy in it. She curls her hands up into fists and then uncurls them again, shaking her head. "You know what you did."

"If this is about the Young Scientist Exhibition . . . look, I know that you worked really hard and—"

"Don't be condescending," Meghna snaps at me. "I'm not a child who can't handle losing. I can *handle* losing." She says it like she definitely can't handle losing, but then she says, "It's about Zak."

I blink at her slowly. Her words from earlier have been running circles around my head, and with Zak's name uttered, it's like everything suddenly clicks into place. *You stole my boyfriend*, Meghna said. Zak was her boyfriend. But how was that even possible?

"What about Zak?" It's the only thing I can think to ask because surely it can't be what she's suggesting. Zak has been a part of my family for a long time now. We've been friends for forever, before we were ever anything more. Zak wouldn't do that to us. He wouldn't do it to my parents, who adore him like he is their own. He wouldn't . . . right?

Meghna takes an exasperated breath. "I don't know if you're just pretending, or you really don't know, but Zak and I, we're seeing each other. Or, well. I guess we *were*, because now I've seen the two of you . . . canoodling."

"Canoodling?" I ask.

"At the science exhibition, you were, like, holding hands or whatever. It was . . ." Meghna shudders like it was the most horrific thing she's ever had to watch.

"He wasn't . . . I wasn't . . ." But I'm not sure what to say. Whatever Meghna saw was right, but what she's saying can't be. "Zak and I have been together for a while now. It's not new. And he's . . . he wouldn't ever do that. Lie to us."

"Us?" Meghna asks.

"My family. He's like part of the family."

"Are you guys, like, betrothed or something?" Meghna's lips curl like she can't even believe she's asking that question.

"Something like that." I cross my arms over my chest, suddenly feeling a little defensive.

"What century is this?"

"It's not like that. It's . . . our parents just thought we'd make a good match, so we've been seeing how it's going," I say. "And there's no way he'd go against his parents like that." And no way he'd lie to my parents.

Meghna scrutinizes me, like she's trying to figure out if I'm telling the truth or not. She must see something in my expression, because her face softens. She drops her glare and turns away from my gaze.

"Zak and I have been together for three months," she says finally. "And it's been mostly a secret because, well, my parents would probably freak out if they knew. And he said his would, too. But apparently, it was less about his parents and more about you." She pauses at that, and her gaze flickers up. "You really didn't know?"

"No, because it can't be true," I say the words, but I know they're wrong. They feel wrong on my tongue. Meghna wouldn't lie about this. What reason would she have to lie? What reason would she have to come all the way here and scream in my face about me stealing her boyfriend? But it also can't be the truth. I can't accept that.

"I'm sorry," Meghna says slowly. She doesn't exactly sound sorry, though. "I thought you must have known because . . ." She pauses for a moment. "It doesn't matter why, but I was sure—"

"I had stolen your boyfriend on purpose?" I ask. "Well, I didn't, because it's not true."

"Just because you keep saying it doesn't make it true," Meghna says matter-of-factly.

"Well, just because *you* say it doesn't make it true, either," I counter.

For a moment, we just take each other in, face-to-face, potentially tied together by a boy who's duping us both. Or connected by a lie that Meghna's told.

“I can prove it,” Meghna says finally. She takes out her phone and types out a text so quickly that it shouldn’t be humanly possible. Her phone buzzes only a moment later. She turns to me, grim faced. “Zak is going to meet me at our usual spot in one hour.”

“Okay . . .” I say. “That doesn’t prove—”

“Get your coat, and let’s go.” Meghna doesn’t wait for me to finish. She doesn’t even wait for me to agree to go with her. She just turns around, opens the door, and thunders down the stairs. For a moment, I can only blink after her, wondering if this was all real or some kind of an ethereal dream. It’s not like I haven’t dreamed about Meghna in the years since our friendship ended.

But then Meghna’s voice floats up from the downstairs hallway. “Either you come, and I prove to you that I’m telling the truth, or you keep being duped by some asshole!”

I take a deep breath and, against my better judgment, call back, “Coming!”

11

MEGHNA

Rani is silent on our bus ride, though I see her sending off the occasional text. If I hadn't been raised right, I would lean over and peek at who she's texting and what she's texting them. But I don't. Instead, I open up my own phone to my conversation with Yemi and Janella. To the dozens of texts they've sent since I lost last night and left the RDS hall almost in tears. My hands hover over the keyboard, but I still don't know what exactly to tell them.

"Do your friends know?" I ask, turning to Rani while stuffing my phone back into my pocket. Rani looks up, blinking her too-long lashes and her wide doe eyes.

"Do they know what?"

"About you and Zak."

"Everyone knows," Rani says, like it's an obvious fact.

"Your sisters?"

Rani nods slowly. It sends a surge of anger through me, but I know I shouldn't be angry at Rani. Not about this. Not when she didn't know, purportedly.

"I just don't understand," I say after a moment of silence has passed. "How did he even . . . I mean, how could he . . . and how did . . ."

"Maybe it's all a big misunderstanding," Rani says.

"How do you accidentally get two girlfriends?" I ask, cocking my head slightly. "I've never heard of anyone doing that before."

"Well, I'm not technically his girlfriend. We don't use that word. It's more complicated."

"Well, how do you accidentally get one girlfriend," I say, pointing at myself in case it isn't clear who the girlfriend is, "and one . . . complication?"

Rani furrows her eyebrows, like she doesn't like how I used the word *complication*. But it's the word she used, so it's not like there's much to say.

"Do you really not believe I'm telling the truth?" I ask finally.

"Well, you believed I was capable of stealing your boyfriend," Rani points out. And I guess she's not wrong—but that's a little different.

Thankfully, I don't have to go into all the ways in which, throughout the years, Rani has beaten me out for everything and made me feel like the less accomplished version of her, because the bus pulls up to our stop. I lead Rani out just as my phone buzzes with a new text message.

Zak: here

That's all he wrote. Usually, Zak's texts make butterflies flutter around my stomach. Today, it sends a rush of nausea through me. I wave the text in front of Rani, but she just looks at the message blankly like it doesn't prove anything.

"Where are you taking me exactly?" Rani asks with a sigh.

"The park. Zak and I usually meet here, though mostly later in the day," I say, leading her toward the gate. "He can't see us together. Well, he shouldn't see you at all."

"So, you want me to hide in the bushes like some stalker?" Rani asks, looking with distaste at the tall grass on the other side of the park fence. Given her oversize sweater and worn jeans, I don't think a few grass stains would really mess up her fashion. But I guess I wouldn't want to be rolling around in the bushes, either. Not for Zak. Not now.

"Go around to the other side; there's another set of gates. Head toward the swings, that's where we usually meet. There's a big tree that you can hide behind," I say.

"Okay." Rani nods and turns around. But she doesn't take a single step forward before she turns back again. This time, worry tugs at her expression, making her look even more doe-eyed than usual. "Meghna, will you be okay?"

It's not the question I expect her to ask. I half expected her to exclaim that I was being ridiculous and that nothing I did would prove to her that I was telling the truth.

"I'll be just fine," I lie.

12

RANI

I ALWAYS KNEW HE WAS A TOTAL ASS. DIDN'T I?

I shake my head at Aarti's text as I make my way to the other side of the park. I don't know why, but my hands are clammy, and my heart is beating a little too fast. With every step I take, it all feels a little too serious. Like, if it *is* true that Zak has been seeing Meghna this whole time—for three months—what does that mean for me?

I text Aarti back quickly.

Me: nothing's been proven yet

Her reply comes lightning fast.

Aarti: but you believe her.

She doesn't ask it like a question, though she doesn't even know Meghna. But she's right: I believe Meghna. I don't think I would have come here if—somewhere in the back of my mind—I didn't already know that she was telling the truth. But it could still be some kind of misunderstanding. I'm not sure how, but it's all that I'm holding on to as I step through the gates of the park.

It's not a big park. In fact, it might be about the size of our back garden. There are some bright blooming flowerbeds scattered to one side. On the other, I spot the swing set that Meghna mentioned. There's a figure standing by it with a head of black hair bent over his phone: Zak. I traipse forward slowly, making as little noise as I can, and duck behind the tree like Meghna suggested. Not that my sneaking around really makes a difference, because Zak doesn't look up until Meghna stops right in front of him. Like he was so immersed in whatever he was doing that he wasn't paying attention to anything else. But he pays attention to her now.

"Hey." Meghna's voice somehow sounds normal. Not like the hurt anger that it had back in my room. Not even a hint of sadness is betraying her.

"Hey," Zak says with a grin. He steps forward and links their fingers together. Easily, too, as if he's been doing it his whole life. All the while, my heart feels like it's about to burst out of my chest. "I'm sorry about yesterday, that I didn't get to see your project, but you know how it is. It's busy, and there are judges, and my parents were there." A total lie—his parents had work the entire day, which is why they made *my* parents take a million pictures of him. And why my parents spent more time obsessing over Zak than paying any attention to me.

"Well, I wish you could have seen my project. I put a lot of work into it, and you didn't even . . ." Meghna says. Her voice wavers a little. Not like she's about to break down into tears, but more like she's trying hard to keep her anger at bay. If Zak thinks this is weird, he doesn't say anything. Instead, he leans closer to Meghna, using his free hand to brush her dark hair away from her face. I have to give props to Meghna for somehow managing to look at him without revulsion. Maybe if science doesn't work out for her, she could try Hollywood.

"I know, and I know you're angry because of Rani."

At my name on Zak's lips, my heart skips a beat, and my skin prickles. Does he know, somehow, that I'm here?

"Yeah." Meghna sighs. She unravels her hands from Zak and steps back from him. For a moment, dread washes over me as I wonder if this is some kind of elaborate prank. Then Meghna adds, "I should have known she would win. She always does better than me at everything."

"Her project was terrible," Zak retorts, a little too fast. My stomach twists, and I almost wish I could walk away from this conversation. But I can't—I'm rooted to the spot. And I have to hear it, don't I? I came here to know the truth. And now I'm hearing it, from Zak's lips.

He keeps going. "I don't know what the judges saw in it, honestly. Languages? How many language apps are there already? You should have won." He steps forward again, reaching his arms out to Meghna, but she steps back, shaking her head.

"I just wish you could have been there yesterday. Did you see her? Her project, I mean?" I lean forward, pressing myself against the tree until I can feel the grooves of wood on my skin.

"No." Zak lies so easily, like he's been doing it forever. I guess he has. "We were probably on completely different sides of the hall."

"Right." Meghna's eyes flicker toward me for a moment. Our eyes meet, and I don't know what she sees there. She must see that I believe her. That I've heard it all, and there's no point in pretending it was some kind of a misunderstanding anymore. Zak isn't just a cheat, he's a liar. One who has no problem acting like he hates me to his . . . girlfriend. And who knows who else?

Meghna takes another step away from him, and this time he *does* seem to notice that something is off. "Meg, what—"

"I told you not to call me that!" Meghna snaps.

Zak sighs, like he has any right to be upset about anything. "Look,

I get that you're angry that you didn't win, but I told you it would happen, didn't I? You shouldn't have gotten your hopes up. It was your first year there, but she's been there every single year since she started secondary school. And I should be angry too, right? You didn't even say congratulations." He pauses, like he's waiting for her to say it now. When she doesn't, he sighs once more. "But it doesn't matter, I have to get going. My parents are taking me out for a celebration dinner tonight."

Celebration dinner. I check the time on my phone. It's already 3:00 p.m. I'm not sure how long it'll take me to get back home on the bus. Not that it matters, anyway. Am I really going to let my parents join his family for a meal celebrating him?

I glance up when I hear footsteps approaching, but it's only Meghna. Zak is out of sight already.

"Well?" Meghna presses.

"You were right," I say, my voice deflated. "Why didn't you break up with him? You had the chance."

Meghna rolls her eyes, crossing her arms over her chest and leaning on the tree. She's suddenly a little too close for comfort. "When I break up with Zak, it's not going to happen in this stupid park. I don't want to contaminate this place for myself. Plus, I'm not going to let him have it easy. And anyway . . ." At this, she pauses to glance at me. "I don't think it would have really been fair to you. You've been with him longer; you should get to have the grand breakup."

"Right." Except, I'm not sure how to tell Meghna that I don't know if I can have a grand breakup. Or if I can have a breakup at all. It's not like we were really together, and how do I tell my parents that the boy they've been treating like their precious son for the past few years has betrayed their trust?

"You *are* going to break up with him, right?" Meghna narrows her eyes at me, like she somehow knows what's going on in my head. It's a little creepy because this is the most we've spoken or spent time with each other in more than five years. The most since we were twelve and joined at the hip, both excited to start secondary school in Sacred Hearts and convinced that nothing in the world could tear us apart. But then Meghna's dad's company went under, and suddenly our parents were only arguing over the phone, and I wasn't allowed to see Meghna anymore. And Meghna wasn't interested in seeing me anymore. Before all that, we could read each other's minds. Maybe that part of us never went away.

"I don't know," I admit. "I mean, I have to talk to my parents and my sisters and tell them about this. And I don't know if they'll believe me or how they'll take it or what will happen. And maybe it's just better if . . . I don't . . . ruffle any feathers."

"Let me get this straight." Meghna stands up once more but leans toward me. She's a little shorter than me, but, somehow, her being this close while glaring at me like she wants to take a knife to my throat is pretty intimidating. "You would rather keep seeing Zak, who has been lying to you and cheating on you, because you don't want to tell your parents about this?"

"No." I take a step back from her, trying very hard not to inhale her sharp peppermint scent that seems to have invaded every part of me all of a sudden and is making it a little difficult to think straight. "I just mean that, maybe it's easier if—"

"You just get married to him after you graduate university because he's the only eligible bachelor around and your parents like him?" Meghna asks. "Seriously, Rani. Even you deserve better than that."

Somehow the "even you" hurts more than Zak's betrayal. But Meghna doesn't see my face fall because she's already turned around and marching toward the front gates of the park.

"Where are you going?" I call after her.

"Home," Meghna says. "To think about how I'm going to give Zak exactly what he deserves." She glances at me out of the corner of her eye for only a moment, passing me a mocking wave goodbye.

I can only watch her leave, feeling dread wash over me.

Aarti doesn't look surprised when I show up at her house. In fact, she opens the door and steps aside almost like she's been expecting me.

"It was true, right?" is the first thing she says when she closes her bedroom door behind us. Thankfully, she doesn't say it with the smug tone that all her texts had.

"Yes," I mumble. I don't know why, but I feel ashamed somehow. Like Zak lying to me and cheating on me is my fault in some way. And maybe it is—maybe if I was the kind of girl who flirted with him and gave him the attention that he clearly craves, he would have been happy with our arrangement, and I wouldn't be wondering how to break the news to my parents.

"So? What are you going to do now?" Aarti asks, plopping herself down on her bed while I take my usual seat on the nook by her window. It overlooks the rest of her neighborhood, showing rows of almost-identical, picture-perfect houses, and the lush greenery surrounding it all.

"I guess I should talk to my parents," I say. "I'm supposed to have a celebratory dinner with Zak and his parents in a few hours."

"You're not going to go to that, are you?" Aarti asks.

"I don't know how I'm supposed to get out of it." I sigh, looking out the window and wishing that none of this had happened in the first place. Still, there's a strange part of me that feels this sense of relief. I finally have a reason to end things with Zak. And maybe when I tell my parents, they'll be devastated, but they'll have to see that it wasn't really my fault. It was his.

"What's Meghna going to do?" Aarti presses. When I glance back at her, she's almost at the edge of her bed, face resting on her palms like this whole situation is the most interesting thing to her.

"She's apparently going to give him what he deserves, whatever that means." I shake my head, because I can imagine what it means. Meghna never does things halfheartedly, and she's not the kind of person you want to get on the wrong side of. "I'm sure she'll find a way to break his heart, even if he got there first."

"Now that's my kind of girl," Aarti says, sitting up straight. "And honestly, you should take a page from her book."

"Get revenge?" I chuckle.

"Why not?"

"Because that's ridiculous. People don't get revenge in real life, only in music videos, fantasies, and movies."

"Have you never heard about crimes of passion?" Aarti asks.

"That's not what a crime of passion is," I point out.

"My point is, Meghna has the right idea. You were with him for a year, Rani. You two had plans to get married after you graduate university. You *parents* had plans for that. He doesn't just get to lie to you, and cheat on you, and get away with it all without any consequences."

"But we weren't really—"

"If someone did that to me, what would you say?" Aarti asks.

I try to think about it for a moment. It's not like Aarti has ever been in a serious relationship. She's had a few boyfriends here and there, but she never gets too attached to anyone. I'm surprised she ever got attached to me. But if someone was with Aarti, and they were serious, and then they cheated on her . . . well, she wouldn't deserve that. No matter what. Just like Meghna didn't deserve it.

"Maybe you're right," I say. But really, I'm not thinking about the revenge; I'm thinking about Meghna and the way her voice had wavered when she was speaking to Zak. She had done it to prove to me that she wasn't the only one being cheated on, even if I was adamant to stay ignorant about it. She didn't owe that to me. Really, she didn't owe me anything at all. "Maybe I need to team up with Meghna."

13

MEGHNA

For some reason, Bhaiya is the first person I see when I get home. He swings the door open, all the while looking at me like I'm a kicked puppy.

"You okay?" he asks, instead of saying *hello* like a normal person.

"Why are you still here?"

"I wanted to see you," he says, stepping aside as I slip in and take off my shoes. "You never answered my text."

"What did you want me to say? Yeah, it sucks and I hate Rani, but whatever, I'm already over it." I barely look at him as I push past him and up the stairs. I know that if I look at him and start talking, I'm going to somehow start spilling my guts. And he doesn't know about Zak, so he wouldn't get it at all. Or he would try to get it, but that would just make the whole thing a million times worse.

"I'm here if you want to talk!" Bhaiya calls from the bottom of the stairs. I know he means well, but it's not like the two of us are the kind of siblings who sit around having heart-to-hearts. Before, we mostly just argued about everything, or texted each other Bengali memes. But ever since he moved out, it's like he suddenly thinks he has to take care of me, or something. He's always asking me too many questions, giving advice about my Leaving Cert, and even keeps offering to let me spend the weekends at his house.

"Go home, Bhaiya!" I call back before shutting my door and locking it.

Usually, coming into my bedroom feels like entering my sanctuary. But today, the first thing I see is the poster board of my project, thrown haphazardly into the space between my desk and wall. It sends a jolt of pain through me, and I'm not even sure if it's because I'd gotten my hopes up about winning, or because I've lost more than I thought was possible. All I know is that all the bravado I showed Rani, telling her about giving Zak what he deserved, is gone. All I feel is deflated, like a balloon with all the air let out of it. So I crawl into bed and close my eyes, ignoring the rest of the world, for once.

IF AMMU AND ABBU NOTICE THAT SOMETHING IS OFF WITH ME throughout the weekend, they don't mention it, even though Ammu does offer me food a few more times than usual. Bhaiya doesn't come around again on Sunday, but he does send me half a dozen TikTok videos. The ones who notice my mood are Yemi and Janella, who text me almost nonstop.

And on Monday morning, they all but accost me at my locker.

"You can't let losing this science competition take everything from you!" Yemi exclaims as soon as they see me. They grab me by the shoulders and give me a dramatic shake, like they're trying to get the feeling of loss out of me.

"I'm not," I say firmly, brushing Yemi's hands off my shoulders and trying to flash both of my friends a smile. One that says *yes, I've been ignoring you all weekend, but I am completely and totally fine and haven't been crying in my bedroom for the past two days.* "It's just . . ." I trail off. I've been practicing in my head how to tell Yemi and Janella about what happened, but, for some reason, it's hard now. I thought I could march up to them with righteous anger blazing in my belly, but instead what I feel is this niggling thread of embarrassment. "I . . . saw something. At the exhibition."

"Saw something?" Yemi asks, exchanging a glance with Janella. "Like, you were looking at all the projects around you and you realized that because of human greed we really are ruining the world around us?"

"No," I say, rolling my eyes at Yemi's theatrics. "I didn't realize something, I *saw* something."

"You saw the logical fallacy of having a science exhibition which has a dedicated section on climate change but also a dedicated section on tech that includes projects that glorify NFTs, and the whole thing is sponsored by a multibillion-dollar company that is for sure contributing to the destruction of this earth?" Janella asks.

I sigh. "Is this all you two talked about while at the exhibition?"

Janella nods. "And after."

"Well, and you!" Yemi adds. "What did you see?"

I take a deep breath and study the speckled gray tiles of the floor. "I saw Zak. And he was with Rani."

"Okay . . . ?" Yemi and Janella say simultaneously.

"Isn't that kind of like how I have to be nice to Sofia whenever I see her, even though she thinks she's better than me because she has a perfect Christian boyfriend and I'm a lesbian and will never have a boyfriend, because she and her mom go to my mom's church and we're both Filipino in our tiny Filipino community?" Janella asks.

"No, it wasn't like that. It was . . . they were . . ." I glance up to see my friends studying me with concern written all over their faces. Concern for me. And as much as they're making jokes about the science exhibition, I know they've probably spent all their time since Friday worrying about me while I've been ignoring them.

So, I take a deep breath and tell them everything. From what I saw at the science exhibition—what I pieced together—all the way to Saturday; how I went to Rani's house, everything Rani said, and everything that happened at the park. Janella and Yemi listen with rapt attention, not a word out of either of their lips. And when Yemi doesn't speak for longer than five minutes, you know they're taking something seriously.

"That—"

"—asshole!" Yemi finishes off for Janella.

"How could he do that to you?" Janella asks.

"How could he be lying for your entire relationship?" Yemi asks.

"I thought he was a nice guy," Janella says.

"I always thought something was off about him," Yemi adds.

"Well, I thought he was perfect," I sigh. And I did, even though there must have been signs. Like when he tried to convince me not to do the Young Scientist Exhibition, not because he was worried about me losing to Rani, but because he was obviously worried I'd run into Rani. And his worst fears came true.

"I'm sorry, Meghna," Yemi says. They lean forward and pull me into an embrace. A moment later, Janella is in as well. And it feels nice, actually, to be hugged by people who I know actually love and care for me. People I know won't lie to me or betray my trust. The only thing that pulls us apart is when the bell rings a minute later.

I sheepishly wipe my eyes of the moisture that formed during our way-too-long hug and avoid looking at either of my friends. I may be the overemotional one in our group—*overemotional* meaning irate and angry—but that usually doesn't mean breaking down into tears in the middle of the school hallway.

"See you guys at lunch?" I ask.

Janella and Yemi nod simultaneously, and we wave goodbye. As I walk to my first class of the day, I actually feel at least a little bit lighter.

ALL THROUGHOUT THE DAY, I WISH JANELLA, YEMI, AND I SHARED A few more classes together. But Monday morning means double chemistry for me, followed by higher math, while Janella and Yemi are in double geography, followed by ordinary math. And during the twenty-minute first break, I have to multitask by stuffing a cereal bar into my mouth while taking notes at our green school's committee meeting. All of this followed by double French for me, and Spanish for Janella and Yemi.

Finally, at 12:30 P.M., we meet up in our little corner of the lockers with our lunch boxes, and I feel like I can take a breath. The good thing—at least—is that the busy morning has kept my mind from thinking about Zak.

"So, have you broken up with that son of a bitch yet?" Yemi asks before we've even had a chance to sit down.

"Yemi." Janella's voice is soft, but stern.

"Not yet," I say. I'm not even sure how you're supposed to break up with someone. I've never broken up with anyone before; Zak is my first real boyfriend. Well, as real as a boyfriend who you have to hide from most people can get. Or as real as a boyfriend who has been lying to you for your whole relationship can get.

"What about Rani?" Janella asks.

I eye her warily while biting into the cold chicken sandwich Ammu packed me for lunch. "What about her?"

"Isn't she . . . I mean, maybe you two should, I don't know. Coordinate or something," Janella says.

"Coordinate breakups?" I raise an eyebrow in her direction.

"Well, not exactly. But you could support each other. You both got screwed over by the same guy," Janella says.

I stop mid-chew and look at Janella like she's lost her mind. Because she must have, if she thinks I'm going to support Rani. Or worse, that I'd ask her for any kind of support.

"You know we're talking about Rani, right?" I ask. "My sworn enemy?"

"Also known as your ex–best friend," Yemi adds.

"Yes . . . but, Rani has never purposefully done anything bad to you, has she? I know there were things with her parents and your parents, but maybe it would help to talk to her about this. And not just . . . accuse her of stealing your boyfriend." Janella is using that soft, reassuring voice she usually has when she's trying to reason with us. In our friendship group, she is definitely the voice of reason, considering Yemi is the dramatic one, and I am the impulsive one. It helps to have someone rational to balance us out. But never have I ever heard something so unreasonable come out of Janella's mouth.

"I'm not supporting Rani through this. Maybe she didn't steal my boyfriend, but that doesn't change anything else. She's still the absolute worst, and I still hate her." With that, I stuff the rest of my chicken sandwich into my mouth, because it means I can't speak until I finish chewing.

Janella gives me a look, but she doesn't try to push the Rani thing again.

While I'm finishing off my lunch, and Janella and Yemi enter a conversation about how Yemi had a dream last night where they were flying over the school on a bed made of lollipops, my phone buzzes with a text. Technically, we're not supposed to be using our phones during school hours, but nobody pays that rule any mind.

I slip my phone out of my bag, only to see a message from an unknown number.

hey Meghna. It's Rani. I hope this is still your number . . . look, I've been thinking about what happened and what you said, and I think we should talk. about Zak. and maybe how we can deal with what happened. what do you think?

I stare at the message for a long while, trying to process all of it. I don't even understand why Rani has my phone number. I deleted hers a long time ago. But she wants to talk? About Zak? Yesterday, it seemed like she wouldn't even consider breaking up with him. I can't help but wonder what's changed.

At any other time, I would have ignored her message completely. But then I think about Janella. Maybe her idea of speaking to Rani is ridiculous, but maybe it's not. Rani is the only other person dealing with the same situation I am. Well, similar, at least.

I type out a reply to Rani before I can change my mind.

Me: meet me after school. 4pm. our old spot.

14

RANI

I HAVEN'T BEEN BACK TO MINE AND MEGHNA'S OLD SPOT IN YEARS. After Meghna and I fell out, even thinking about this place was like picking at an old scab. It's not like we discovered it, but considering it's hidden underground, it often feels like we did.

When I spot the set of stairs leading down to Café Nightingale, my stomach lurches. I'm not sure if I'm anxious or excited. When I texted Meghna, I half expected her to ignore me, as she has for the past five years. I definitely didn't expect her to agree to meet up so soon, and I'm not sure what exactly I have to say to her. Or what she has to say to me.

Still, I tread down the spiral staircase and into the café. I'm immediately overwhelmed by the smell of coffee that always lingers in every inch of this place, and the sound of ethereal piano music floating around like it's coming from nowhere.

A woman in a black blouse which announces CAFÉ NIGHTINGALE beside a bird and coffee bean logo approaches me with a customer-service smile. "Hi, welcome to Café Nightingale. Can I help you?"

"I'm just meeting someone here," I say, even though I have no clue if I'm the first to arrive or if Meghna's already here. Both of those options make my heartbeat speed up just slightly. "I'll just . . ." I mumble, stepping forward and past the main lobby of the café. I walk past a narrow hallway filled with bookshelves and into a much wider room lined with colorful couches and armchairs. There are some people dotted around the room, but not enough that I don't spot Meghna in the corner, glaring at her phone screen. Taking a deep breath, I march up and slip into the seat next to her.

"Hey."

Meghna glances up, tucking her phone into her pocket. The glare remains. "Hi."

"I haven't been back here in years," I say.

"Yeah, me neither." Meghna's face softens, but only a little.

"It's still all the same," I say. Meghna's expression flickers with . . . something. But I can't quite read it. Maybe she's thinking about the fact that this café might not have changed, but we definitely have. Silence settles between us, and there's nothing comfortable about it, like there once might have been. I pick up the menu from the table in front of us, mostly to avoid the awkwardness of this non-conversation.

"Even the menu is the exact same." I chuckle, flicking from one page to the next. It has your garden variety of coffees; flat whites, Americanos, cappuccinos; a selection of cakes that are available to browse at the counter; and of course, their specialty: the bulbul baklava, or the nightingale's nest baklava. It's a type of Turkish dessert. When Meghna and I first stumbled in here many years ago, we were amused at the fact that they had a dessert named after a Bengali bird. Of course, later we discovered that Bengali isn't the only language in the world to call a nightingale a bulbul. But at the time, there was something magical about coming across a café in the middle of Dublin and finding something that felt so familiar to just the two of us. Like a little secret that bound us together.

"Remember when we used to get the most gigantic piece of cake to share?" Meghna surprises me by asking.

"That was our favorite thing about this place: gigantic portion sizes," I say.

Meghna's glare has definitely subsided now. Maybe some of our memories have thawed her a little.

"Why did you want to meet?" she asks after a moment. "Because I think we said whatever we had to, at the park the other day."

"I've just been thinking, I guess. About everything. About Zak, and us, and how you said he should get what he deserves. I think I agree with you. Neither of us deserved what he did to us."

Meghna narrows her eyes at me, like she's trying to figure out what my game is. "Okay. And?"

"And . . . I had an idea, I guess." I shrug. "I was thinking about the Young Scientist Exhibition. Zak is really determined to go to the European exhibition with his project and win. His family, and honestly even mine, think that he can do no wrong, so he's feeling pretty confident."

"So what, you're going to go and beat him and that's going to show him?" Meghna asks. She was always good at reading my mind.

"Not exactly. I was thinking *we* could. That would show him, right? These two girls who he's been lying to this whole time, playing with, but he can't even beat us. He would hate that."

Meghna doesn't look convinced as she crosses her arms and sets her lips into a thin line. "In case you forgot, I lost."

"Well, if the two of us create a new project, that won't matter. We can enter the European Young Scientist Exhibition as a team," I say. I looked up the rules before coming here, and since the European exhibition is completely separate from the Irish one, it means that new projects and new collaborations are definitely allowed. Even encouraged. There have been times when winners from different European countries decided to team up, and even develop their original ideas into collaborative projects.

Meghna, though, still looks unconvinced. "I don't know. I mean, is that really the best we can do? Beat him at a competition where there are going to be so many other people who could take home the prize as well?"

"Look, I know it may seem small, but you know Zak as well as I do," I say. Meghna sits up straight at this, like she hadn't expected me to take her seriously as someone Zak was seeing. "You know how much this means to him. You know how much winning means to him. And honestly, yesterday at the dinner with his parents, he was going on and on about the internships they offer to the winner. He was acting like it was a done deal, even though he knew that I was going to be competing against him, too. He won't see this coming, and it's majorly going to bruise his ego."

Meghna glances down, like she's considering it. "And you would really be okay partnering up with me for your European exhibition project?"

"Yes, of course." I chuckle. I half want to tell Meghna that more than getting back at Zak, I want to partner with her. Not just because I know she's going to help me in winning the European Exhibition, but because I hope that it will help me figure out why we ever drifted apart. And maybe it will help us drift back toward each other.

Meghna looks up to meet my gaze. There's something in her eyes that I can't quite read. But then she nods and says, "Okay, I'm in."

15

MEGHNA

I DUCK INTO THE BACK OF YEMI'S REHEARSAL JUST IN TIME TO catch them in the midst of a long monologue from *Hamlet*. Since *Hamlet* is the Shakespeare play we're studying for the Leaving Cert this year, this is probably giving Yemi a bit of a leg up. They kill the performance, and the rest of the group bursts into enthusiastic applause. Me, in the back, included.

Yemi finds me almost as soon as their rehearsal is over, slumping into a seat beside mine and tossing all their things—coat, bag, script, and water bottle—into another empty seat.

They let out an exhausted sigh and say, "Don't you have homework to do or something?" as a way of greeting. It's not like I often make my way to Yemi's drama class after school.

"Yes, I have homework. But I needed to talk to you. To see if I'm making a bad decision or not," I say.

"Isn't that Janella's department?" Yemi asks.

"Yemi." I groan.

"Okay, okay." Yemi waves their hand, as if for me to continue.

But I'm not sure how exactly to launch into it. When Rani had told me her suggestion to team up and beat Zak at the European Young Scientist Exhibition, it had seemed like an opportunity. The perfect one, on a silver platter.

"So, I just had coffee with Rani," I begin.

Beside me, Yemi's eyes widen to the size of saucers, and they turn their body completely toward mine, like they need to get a proper look at me to ensure I'm telling the truth. "Choudhury?" They get the pronunciation exactly right.

"How many Ranis do you know?" I scoff. "Look, it's not a big deal. You know, Janella told me that maybe we have more in common now because of the whole Zak cheating on us thing, and I was still feeling kind of shitty when Rani texted me about talking, so I went to meet up with her and . . ."

"And?" Yemi repeats with an encouraging nod.

"She told me that we should collaborate on a project for the European Young Scientist Exhibition, and beat Zak. Get back at him in that way for what he did to us. And I said yes."

"Wow, Meghna." Yemi gives me an appraising look. "You definitely should have had this conversation with Janella, because this is pretty mature of you."

"Getting revenge is mature?" I ask.

"It is, when you're teaming up with someone who you claim is your sworn enemy."

"Right, about that . . ." This is the part that I've been dreading saying to anyone. Even though I know there's really nothing else to be done about it. "The thing is, I've been studying the European Young Scientist Exhibition and everything that comes with it since before I lost. Obviously. And there are two prizes you can win: the team prize, and the individual prize. Normally, the individual prize goes to someone who is working on their own; no teams involved. But, there have been rare cases where the prize has been awarded to individuals from a team, instead of the entire team."

"Meghna." The grin on Yemi's lips is so wide I'm surprised it hasn't split their face open. "That's amazing. That means you'll have two shots at winning."

"Right, two shots. But it means that . . ." I mutter, not sure how to say the next part. Every single individual prize that's gone to a team member has led to the dissolution of the team. Usually, it means that the individual member of the team went above and beyond in terms of leadership skills and showed the judges that they are absolutely instrumental to the project. It means I'd have to throw Rani under the bus.

"It means?" Yemi urges, raising an eyebrow.

"It just means Rani might be pissed, you know. Because they only award to an individual and not the team. So, she'd lose out, and she's the one who's inviting me to this thing," I say.

Yemi rolls their eyes. "Honestly, considering how many wins Rani has had, does it really matter? As long as you two can rub it in that asshat, Zak's, face, Rani should be happy. And if she's pissed, who cares? She *is* your archnemesis."

I nod. And even though I know I should tell Yemi what winning the individual prize really means, I know that they're right, too. Rani has won everything that the two of us have ever competed in. If I came home with a report card of six As, Rani came home with seven. If I was third place in our primary school science fair, Rani was first. Even her accomplishments topped mine—at least in the eyes of my parents. I may be secretary of our school's green school committee, but Rani is secretary of her school's student council, and a shoo-in for head girl next year.

Ever since I met Rani, I've been compared to her by Ammu and

Abbu. Why can't I bring home all As like her? Why can't I be polite and well-mannered like her? Everything has been about *her*.

Well, if I win the individual prize at the EYSE, it won't just mean defeating Zak. It'll mean destroying Rani, too.

It'll mean my parents might finally stop comparing the two of us and realize that Rani is not all she's chalked up to be.

"You're right," I say. "Rani can take one loss, no big deal."

But in my head, I'm thinking: *Rani Choudhury must be destroyed*—and this is my one chance to do it.

16

RANI

I WAKE UP ON SATURDAY MORNING TO A TEXT FROM MEGHNA: still on for today?

I rub sleep out of my eyes before typing: yes!

But staring at the phone screen for a moment, I hit backspace and add a full stop. Now the text just says: yes.

Maybe a smiley face?

yes :)

Shaking my head, I erase the message altogether. I haven't even asked Ammu and Abbu if it is okay for Meghna to come over. Considering that her parents and mine haven't had anything to do with each other for the past five years, I definitely should seek permission first.

Putting my phone down, I stumble out of my room and down the stairs. Ammu is over the stove, frying some luchi for breakfast while Parisa and Neelam are helping set the table.

"Alur dom?" I ask, when Parisa passes me with a bowl of the spicy potato dish.

"Yup!" Parisa exclaims, grinning at me. Alur dom—or really anything with potatoes in it—is her favorite.

I grab the plate of fried luchi and carry it over to the breakfast table. All the while, Ammu observes me with a frown.

"Rani, you should really get out of your pajamas before coming downstairs," she says after a moment.

"It's just breakfast, Ammu. It's not like there's people over, or like I'm going somewhere," I say, trying not to point out the fact that Parisa is dressed in her panda onesie, and Neelam is wearing a set of heart–print pajamas. I'm just wearing an oversize T-shirt and gray pajama bottoms: much more presentable on a comparative scale.

"You're not a kid anymore, Rani. It's important how you present yourself. Yes, even at the breakfast table." Ammu tuts. "You know, your sisters look up to you as their older sister."

"I don't look up to her," Parisa says before sticking her tongue out at me.

Ammu keeps going, like she hasn't heard Parisa. "And as their older sister, and the eldest in this whole family, it's your responsibility to always set a good example. Waking up before your sisters, helping out around the house, being presentable. Me and your abbu aren't always going to be here, you know. If anything ever happens to us, it's going to be you taking care of your sisters." Ammu says this like she and Abbu are already on their deathbeds, instead of about to sit down to a very Bengali breakfast.

"I know, Ammu," I mumble, mostly because it's sometimes the only way to get Ammu to stop one of her overly long lectures.

Ammu gives me a look like she doesn't know what she's going to do with me if I don't even have the basic etiquette to not wear pajamas to the breakfast table, but then she marches over and flips the luchi she was frying onto my plate. Steam rises off the flatbread. The last one off the stove is usually the best. It's nice and warm, just the way luchi is supposed to be. So I guess that's Ammu's way of telling me that she loves me.

"Eat, come on," Ammu says, sitting at one end of the table while Parisa and Neelam climb into their respective chairs. Abbu struts in from the sitting room, saying khodahafez to whoever he was on the phone with, and greets us all with a smile.

The five of us are the picture of the perfect family as we pile alur dom onto our plates and begin to slowly chew our breakfast. I'm not sure how exactly to bring up Meghna, between Neelam's long monologue about how one of the girls on her junior swim team got an ear infection last week and Abbu's belligerent questions about Parisa's after-school piano lessons.

Finally, when there's a lull in the conversation, I jump in.

"Ammu, Abbu," I say, swallowing down the bite of alur dom and luchi in my mouth. I don't look at either of them, but at my plate instead. "Um, Meghna was going to come over to study later. Is that okay?"

When I glance up, I meet Parisa's confused glance.

"Meghna?" Ammu asks in the same tone Zak used at the Young Scientist Exhibition. I don't know why everyone acts like there are a million Meghnas in Dublin.

"Meghna Rahman," I press.

"You two don't go to the same school anymore," Abbu says matter-of-factly.

"Yeah, but we ran into each other at the Young Scientist Exhibition," I lie. "And we share a lot of the same classes. Obviously, we're both into science."

"I don't remember seeing her there," Ammu muses.

"Is it okay if she comes over?" I ask.

Ammu and Abbu share a glance between them. Neither of them looks happy, and I'm half-afraid they're really going to say no. They've never had a problem with my friends before. Even though Ammu has never been a big fan of Aarti ("that girl talks too much," is Ammu's reasoning), she's never told me to not befriend her.

"I don't see why not," Ammu says finally. I breathe an internal sigh of relief.

Later, after I finally text a reply to Meghna (*yes, we're still on* with no smiley faces or punctuation) and start cleaning out all the mess in my bedroom, Parisa knocks on my door.

"Door's open," I say, not even glancing up.

"Are you and Meghna, like, friends again?" Parisa asks.

I sigh, even while moving my books into their proper place on my bookshelf. "Not really."

"So why did she come over last week? And now she's coming over again?"

"We're working on our science project together."

"*Our* science project?"

I finally turn around, giving her an exasperated look. "Two heads are better than one, right? This is my first time at the European Science Exhibition. I thought having Meghna as my partner would be good."

"I don't think it's a good idea, Apu," Parisa says. "I mean, Ammu and Abbu aren't friends with the Rahmans anymore for a reason. And . . . Meghna kind of . . . broke your heart."

I can only stare at my little sister in surprise. "Meghna didn't break my heart," I scoff. I don't even know how she remembers the end of our friendship—she was only seven years old when it happened. I bet she barely even remembers Meghna, and she's just projecting whatever rumors she's heard about Meghna's family from Bengali dawats.

"You were pretty upset when the two of you stopped talking. Because you kept texting her and calling her, and she wouldn't even talk to you. Or explain what happened," Parisa says. "I just don't trust her."

"I'll be fine, Pari," I insist, even though the memories of those days, when Meghna decided to cut me off with no explanation, lodge a rock in my throat. I don't know how Parisa remembers it all so vividly, but I remember how hurt I was that after everything the two of us had been through, Meghna wouldn't even return a text. Not even to tell me that we couldn't speak anymore. "I'm sure everything that happened was because of her parents," I add. "And you know, the fact that they moved, and she started a whole new school. None of that could have been easy for her."

"Well, Ammu told me that the Rahmans were bad news," Parisa says.

I should have known most of this was coming from Ammu. Pari is usually not someone who listens to her, though. If anything, her favorite hobby is finding new and innovative ways of giving Ammu headaches. I don't know why she's decided to trust her about Meghna.

"Ammu doesn't always know best," I say.

Parisa just purses her lips tight, like she knows I'll be annoyed if she says what she's thinking out loud.

"If you get to know Meghna, you'll see she's really great," I say with a smile. "Anyway, leave the protective act to me, right? Since you're so into listening to Ammu all of a sudden, remember she said that

I'm the one setting examples here; you and Neel just watch and learn from me."

Parisa rolls her eyes. "Just be careful," she adds before turning back toward her own room.

Careful. That's a difficult thing to be when what Meghna and I are doing isn't exactly conventional. I wonder for a moment what Parisa would say if I told her the truth about Zak and Meghna, and that the only reason we've been brought together again is because of him.

17

MEGHNA

Being outside Rani's house again feels like some kind of fever dream. Still, I take a deep breath and march past the front gates and up to the porch. The bell sounds shrill and empty on the other side when I ring it. It takes a moment for the sound of footsteps to echo down the stairs and all the way to me.

When the door finally flings open, Rani stands in front of me, smiling with all her teeth. Last time I was here, Rani was wearing a baggy gray sweater and pajama bottoms. Today she's swapped those out for a fitted sweater with pink-and-blue stripes and a pair of black skinny jeans. Her long, black hair is brushed away from her eyes, pushed back with a floral hairband.

"Hey, you're early," Rani says.

"I'm right on time." I pull up my phone to show her the digital clock flashing 3:00 p.m. on the dot. I had hovered by the gate for about ten whole minutes to make sure that I wouldn't be early even by a minute.

Rani's smile doesn't falter as she waves me inside, where I spot Choudhury Aunty hovering in the kitchen.

"Assalamu alaikum," Choudhury Aunty says, waving me over before I can even slip off my shoes.

I cast a glance at Rani, and she nods, like it's okay to approach her mom. Like I was looking for permission, when really I was looking for a chance to escape.

"Walaikum salam, Aunty," I say, shuffling toward her. "How are things?"

"Good, great," Aunty says. "How are you? How's your new school?"

It feels strange to have it called my "new school" when it's the only one I've known for years. "It's pretty good, yeah. I'm part of the green schools committee."

"Green schools committee?" Aunty frowns.

"It's for . . ." Rani thinks for a second. "Environmenter bepare . . . shochetun howa?" she says in Bengali.

I roll my eyes. I could have done better than that. Still, Aunty nods like she gets the idea. Though she doesn't look particularly impressed.

But Rani doesn't stop there. "Meghna's entire project in the Science Exhibition was about Bangladesh, Ammu. Bangladeshe kibhabe bonna hoi, ar kibhabe amra prevent korte pari."

Aunty seems a little more impressed by that. "Kono solution ber korecho?"

I shake my head slowly. "Solution . . . ektu complicated . . ." I half want to launch into everything I learned about the Delta project, but I'm not even sure how to translate all that into Bengali, so I just leave it there.

Thankfully, that's also where Aunty's line of questioning ends, and she doesn't delve into asking about Ammu and Abbu, or even giving them salam (both a relief and, honestly, a huge insult). When Rani says that we're going to go work in her bedroom, Aunty just nods and smiles.

"So, Aunty and Uncle were just totally cool with you hanging out with me again?" I ask, once inside Rani's room. Unlike last time I was here, it's totally spotless. Not a thing is out of place.

Rani waves me over to a seat at her desk. "Why wouldn't they be cool with it?"

"Rani, come on." I raise an eyebrow at her.

She sighs and takes the seat beside mine while unlocking her computer. "They didn't ask any questions. They know working on this project together is important."

"Because you told them about Zak finally?"

Rani chuckles. "Did you tell your parents about him?"

"That's kind of a different case," I counter. "They didn't even know about him to begin with. Aunty and Uncle, though . . ."

"Look, let's just figure this out first, okay? It'll be easier to tell my parents about Zak once he throws a total tantrum about losing to us, I bet. Right now, they think the sun shines out of his behind."

I have to bite back a smile at her avoidance of the word *ass.*

"So, about our project." Rani turns to me, her voice suddenly alive with excitement. I've never seen someone look so happy at the idea of doing a science project. "I was thinking since it's my language app that got me in, we could further develop that. I already had a few ideas about how to expand it."

"So did I," I say. "I think you should make it even more interactive. Kind of like Duolingo, but better. Like maybe something with vocabulary games. Grammar games. You know, to help incentivize learning the language?"

"Hm." Some of the excitement dims in Rani's eyes even though she nods. "That sounds like a really interesting idea. But I don't know. There's already a lot of language apps that focus on games. Mine is more about the immersive, narrative quality, you know?"

"What's more immersive than games?" I ask.

"Well, a story? Setting, mood, all those things," Rani says. She opens up her coding software to the preview of her language app. It's the first time I'm seeing it, since I missed it completely at the exhibition thanks to Zak and his cheating ways. It's a pretty minimalistic app; there's just a black-and-white ombré background with the two language options indicated with flags: red and green for Bangladesh, and the tricolor Irish flag.

"Since you're so good at coding," I say slowly, "I think I can contribute with ideas. And you execute them."

Rani turns to me once more. Her smile is a little strained this time. "I mean, this language app was my idea to begin with. So, it's not like I don't have ideas."

"Sure, you do. But look at this design." I wave my hand at her screen.

"What's wrong with it?"

"It's so minimal and boring. Who would be tempted to download and use this?"

"People who like learning languages without any, you know, jhamela," Rani says.

"A better design would be jhamela?" I scoff. "Come on, it would be more eye-catching if there was some color. Better UI. User interface is one of the most important things in an app. It can set one apart from another, even if their functions are the same."

"If our app doesn't have basis in what it can actually do, the design is useless. A pretty app that doesn't function well is not an app at all," Rani counters.

"You're right. So, you bring the coding, and I bring the substance."

Rani is full-on glaring at me now. "Meghna. I appreciate your input, but I developed this app from scratch. I brought the substance *and* the coding. You can't relegate me to the role of a coding monkey."

"Okay, I never said that."

"You didn't have to!"

"Well, you don't have to keep talking about how this is your app!" I exclaim. "I get you created it, but now we're supposed to be teaming up, aren't we? So, shouldn't you welcome my input?"

Rani looks at me like the last thing she wants to do is hear any input whatsoever from me; truth be told, it's a little amusing to see Rani riled up. She's always the image of calm, polite, perfect. This is a side of her that I rarely saw even when we were best friends. I didn't know I could push her buttons like this.

"Fine, Meghna. I'd love to hear your input. As long as you realize that both you and I are bringing substance to this app development," Rani says.

"Okay, whatever."

"Okay." Rani stares at her computer with a stern expression for a moment before shaking her head like she's washing herself of her anger. "Maybe we should brainstorm our ideas separately, and then put them together?"

I shrug. "I guess that's as good a plan as any."

Rani opens up the drawer under her desk and pulls out a blank notepad and a few pens. She tears off two pages and hands them to me.

“Let’s put twenty minutes on the clock,” I say, laying the blank pages out on the desk in front of me.

Rani purses her lips but nods. “Twenty minutes.” She sets a timer on her phone before wandering over to her bed with her pen and notepad.

I write out *language app brainstorm* at the top of the page and underline it three times. Then I begin scribbling down my ideas. I have to come up with ideas that will make this app feel less like Rani’s and more like . . . well, mine, if I have any hope of beating her out for the individual prize at the European Young Scientist Exhibition.

18

RANI

By the time my phone beeps after the twenty-minute timer I set, I've barely written down a single thing. I stare forlornly at the page in front of me.

BRAINSTORMING LANGUAGE APP IDEAS:
-more immersive, for each type of learner
-auditory: add music and sound
-visual: add illustrations
-kinesthetic: ???
-reading and writing: ???

Before I even have the chance to get off of my bed, Meghna plops down beside me. The bed creaks loudly, but she doesn't seem to even hear.

"Okay, so. This is what I have." She flashes an entire page. She's even doodled things on the edges of the page that seem connected to her ideas. There are little cartoons of people with Bengali speech bubbles and a phone screen on the corner with a new UI design mock-up.

I gawk. "How did you come up with so much in twenty minutes?"

"How did you come up with . . . so little?" Meghna asks, staring at my bare page.

"Hey, quality over quantity," I say defensively.

Meghna shrugs, as if she's daring me to show her quality, and I flush. My ideas are hardly quality. Still, I continue, "I was thinking about, you know, the different learning styles and how we can develop the app so it caters to all of them. So auditory and visual are pretty easy. Not so sure about kinesthetic and reading and writing. You'd think reading and writing would be obvious, but—"

"What the hell is kinesthetic?" Meghna asks.

"Well, it's basically the type of learning where you have to carry out activities in order to take something in. Like—"

"Games?" Meghna's voice drips with smugness.

"I mean, I guess technically, yes. But it still has to be connected to the rest of the app, otherwise it's not going to work."

"Okay, whatever," Meghna huffs. Apparently, "okay, whatever," is her new catchphrase. It's a pretty annoying one, if I'm being perfectly honest.

"Well, what about your ideas?" I ask, though I'm dreading her answer. But before Meghna can say anything, her phone buzzes loudly from where she placed it on the bed between us. Zak's name flashes up on the screen, along with a photo of the two of them at the very same park Meghna took me to last weekend. For a moment, I can only stare at the photo of them snuggling by the swings. Meghna actually looks . . . happy. She's smiling like I haven't seen her smile maybe ever.

Meghna grabs her phone and places it face down, letting it ring.

"I'm guessing you haven't broken up with him yet," I say.

"I don't want to talk about it," Meghna says. And she doesn't sound angry. She sounds . . . sad, almost. Even if she doesn't look it.

"You want some tea?" I offer. Obviously, tea is the solution to everything. A smile tugs at Meghna's lips, and she nods.

"But after the tea, we're discussing my ideas," she insists.

WITH AMMU AND ABBU SAFELY IN THEIR BEDROOM, MEGHNA AND I sit in the dining room with mugs of warm tea and a plate full of Jammie Dodgers, Bourbons, chocolate Digestives, and Mikados.

"You know, your house hasn't changed, like, at all," Meghna comments as she cradles her tea, taking small sips.

I glance around the kitchen, at the fridge filled with magnets from different countries, the shelf full of trophies that Pari, Neel, and I have brought home over the years, and the wall that has our latest family portrait taken at the studio last summer. We're the image of the perfect family; all of us dressed to the nines and smiling with our teeth showing. But I remember what a struggle it was to get Neel into her salwar kameez and keep it clean; how Ammu had insisted that I had to wear makeup, and that Pari was too young to wear makeup. I didn't point out the irony of it all to Ammu, even though I wanted to. I just bit my tongue and put on the makeup. Pari, though, had put up a bit more of a fight. In the end, Ammu let her line her eyes and apply a dab of lip gloss, but nothing more than that.

Meghna follows my gaze to our family portrait, and something unreadable flickers in her expression. "I can't believe you guys still do that every year."

"Yeah, it's tradition, I guess." I shrug, then stuff a Jammie Dodger into my mouth.

"Hey, how did you know what my project was about earlier?" Meghna asks after a moment of silence. "I distinctly remember not seeing you the day of the exhibition."

"Yeah, I was curious. So, I looked it up. All the projects are on their website," I say. "Honestly, your project was really good. It should have won, but the judges loved that Zak's combined biomed with tech. They love things like that which combine two or more categories together."

"I guess Zak figured it out from all of his years being a participant." There's a bitter note to Meghna's voice, especially when she says Zak's name. Like she can barely get it out.

"Did you and Zak . . . I mean, you guys must have been . . ." I'm not sure how to ask the question. I just can't help but wonder. It's not that I don't think Zak is, on paper, an ideal candidate for a boyfriend. Even more than a boyfriend. It's just that in person, he definitely leaves much to be desired. Sure, he's good-looking and charming, but there seems to be so little to him outside of that.

Meghna, on the other hand, is nothing but substance. If I could choose one word to describe her, it would be *passionate*. She cares so deeply about so many things. I just can't imagine what they really have in common.

Meghna gives me a stern look, almost like she can see into my head. "I think we should just stick to talking about our project." With that, she slips out the paper she's been writing on.

"I was thinking we need a completely new design, something like this." She points to the sketch of the phone screen. "Maybe we can even do this kind of cartoon style to fit into your audio, visual . . . learning style thing. And obviously games for the kines-whatever.

I can help with design and illustration, you can do the coding, and we should be good."

She smiles at me like it's all a done deal.

"Meghna, I don't think a cartoon style is a good idea. It's too . . . immature."

That's clearly not the right word to use, because Meghna's smile falters immediately. "You think I'm immature?"

"Not you, the style of the—"

"You're not taking any of my ideas seriously," Meghna counters before I can even finish what I'm saying.

"Well, your ideas don't go with my vision for the app, which I—"

"Developed from scratch. Yeah, whatever." Meghna rolls her eyes, and I feel an itch of irritation crawling up my skin. "Look, you have to be open to new ideas if you want to work together."

"And you have to be open to my ideas. Not just see me as someone who can code, since you can't."

Meghna's expression shifts. A flicker of anger is recognizable behind her eyes. But for once, she doesn't launch into one of her tirades. Instead, she discards the piece of paper with her ideas and stands up. Her chair scraping against the wood of the dining room floor sounds a little too loud.

"I think . . . I should go. It's getting late."

"It's only five p.m.," I say softly. But she doesn't even look at me. I already know I've lost her. Still, I have to try to rectify whatever I've said to upset her. "Meghna, I'm sorry . . . I didn't mean anything by it. You can't take me too seriously about these things."

"It's fine," Meghna says in a voice that tells me it's decidedly *not* fine. She shuffles toward the front door, and I follow, not sure what I can say to make things better when I don't even know what I've said to make things bad.

"Maybe we can brainstorm and catch up next week?" I ask hopefully while Meghna slips on her shoes.

Meghna turns to me with a tight smile. "Sure. Next week. I'll see you later."

With that, she pulls open the front door. She doesn't even glance back as I call out a *goodbye.*

19

MEGHNA

If there's one thing that's solidified in my mind after leaving Rani's house, it's that the choice I made to win the individual prize is absolutely right. Because Rani only cares about herself, and her own project.

Further proved by Rani's text the next day as I'm at movie night with Yemi and Janella: the EYSE is at the end of november. can you ask your parents for their permission and get them to sign the permission slip? also, you need a permission slip from your science teacher. they'll need to do an approval of the project idea as well. I sent you the proposal.

permission_slip.pdf

language_app_proposal.pptx

I glare at the text. "I hate her."

"You have to give her a chance," Janella says. This is Janella's tune about everyone and everything. She's never met a person that she hates. Maybe some people she has a dislike of, but she'd rarely say a bad word about them, regardless.

"I *have* given her a chance. I even went over to her territory yesterday," I grumble.

"What is this? Gangland wars?" Yemi asks.

"Shut up. Look, I tried, okay? I went over there, and I tried to improve Rani's ridiculous language app. But her ideas are so mechanical! Where is the creativity behind any of it? You should see how blah her UI is. She hasn't even come up with a cool name for the app. She literally calls it her language app!" I throw my arms up in frustration so my friends can see just how ridiculous this girl is, even though they should already know. They may not have met Rani before, but I've regaled them with enough tales of her infuriating perfection for them to recognize just how horrid she really is.

"So you're just going to give up?" Janella asks.

"No, but I can't work with her," I say. "And honestly, her whole plan to beat Zak at the European Exhibition seems like a delay tactic. She doesn't want to break up with him or talk to her parents about him. Which is *her* problem, not mine."

At that, Janella and Yemi exchange a worried glance, which just makes me feel even more annoyed than I already do.

"What?" My voice definitely comes out a lot more abrasive than I mean it to.

"It's just . . . it's not like you've broken up with Zak, either," Janella says slowly, like she's speaking to someone who is on the verge of a breakdown.

"I'm waiting for the right time," I say. "I haven't seen him in person since . . . since the park."

As if Zak can hear me from wherever he is right now, my phone buzzes with a text. His name and message flash on my screen, and I feel heat rush to my face.

"And that's not him trying to get in touch with you?" Yemi asks.

"Shut up." I pick up my phone, but my heartbeat quickens at the thought of reading his text. Zak has been texting me on and off for the past few days. Trying to arrange a meetup, asking if I'm okay. And I haven't responded to a single one. Every time he sends me a text, all I can think is that it's all a lie. It was *all a lie*. And I haven't been able to face up to that yet—not really.

"I know it's hard, Meghna, but maybe it's hard for Rani, too, in the same way. You're being a little harsh on her," Janella says. "That's all we're trying to say."

But Yemi and Janella don't know Rani like I do. She's much more concerned about winning the EYSE than anything else—because that's the kind of person she is. Zak comes second. And me? I'm probably not even part of the equation for her.

Janella presses play on the movie we were watching, as if to declare an end to our conversation. As the movie begins, I can't help but glance at Zak's message: hey, my rugby game is after school on wednesday. my parents won't be there, so thought it might be nice if you were? I've missed you Meg.

I try to ignore the way my heart clenches at his words. But at the same time, a plan begins to form in my head. Maybe I don't need Rani at all to get my revenge on Zak.

"THIS IS THE WORST IDEA YOU HAVE EVER HAD!" YEMI EXCLAIMS with a grin when I tell them my plan on Wednesday afternoon. I wouldn't have involved Yemi at all, but I need a lookout.

"So, you'll help?" I ask.

"You know what Janella would say . . ." Yemi says. "I mean, is it the healthiest way to cope with being cheated on? No. Is it the most chaotic way?"

"I can think of more chaotic ways," I say. When Yemi gives me a sharp look, though, I quickly add, "But I'm not going to do any of those, obviously."

"You're going to do this with or without me, right?" Yemi asks.

"Yes, but with you, the chances of getting caught are a little lower."

"Well, I'm never one to pass up on some chaos. Especially when it involves getting back at that cheating bastard," Yemi says with a nod.

That's how Yemi and I find ourselves outside Zak's school twenty minutes and a trip to the pharmacy later.

St. Patrick's Academy is nestled inside a massive residential area, and it's double the size of our school. It doesn't just have a main building like ours, but private dwellings branching off the main one. It's big enough to even warrant a map by the front entrance.

Yemi is taking the whole place in with wide eyes while I try to navigate the position of the rugby field on the map.

"Excuse me." An unfamiliar voice disrupts me. It's the secretary, peeking out through the window partition that separates her from the entrance hall. "Can I help you?" She observes Yemi and me with a frown.

"We're here for the rugby match," I say.

"You're early," she huffs while checking her watch. "The match doesn't start for a little bit. The last class of the day doesn't end for ten more minutes."

"Oh, we can go wait at the field?" I offer, exchanging a glance with Yemi. I had faked a doctor's note to get out of school early, and Yemi had faked a stomachache. I'm glad that it wasn't for nothing.

The secretary doesn't look happy at the idea of letting us on the rugby field early, but she nods her head slowly. "If you go through these double doors here and straight through to the end of the hallway, you'll come across another set of doors which will take you to the rugby field."

"Thanks!" Yemi and I paste on grins before turning to the set of double doors she pointed out. The hallway we enter is lined with doors on either side, and we can hear the murmur of ongoing classes.

"We don't have a lot of time," I mumble as we push open the second set of doors. We stumble out into the daylight once more. The green rugby pitch is right in front of us, with benches to the side for spectators.

"So, we need to find the changing rooms." Yemi glances from one side to the other.

"There!" I exclaim, pointing to the prefabs on the other side of the field. "That has to be it." I take a deep breath and turn to Yemi. "Okay, I think you should stay here as my lookout. Text me if you see anyone coming around here."

"We should have a code word. SOS?" Yemi asks.

I nod. "That should work. You text me SOS and I'll bolt right out of there."

"Be careful," Yemi says.

"I always am."

My heart beats faster and faster the closer I get to the changing rooms. By the time I arrive and read the plaque on the door announcing RUGBY CHANGING ROOMS, my heart is about to beat right out of my chest.

I take a deep breath and step inside. Immediately, I'm hit with the distinct smell of perspiration. I guess even the fancy private school can't stop the smell of boys' sweat—especially ones who play rugby.

I pinch my nose to make the smell more tolerable and approach a group of lockers lining the side of the room.

Each of the lockers is decorated with a slew of stickers. I see one with an Arsenal sticker, another with an Ulster Rugby club logo. Most of the locker doors have a label with a name or nickname written in black marker. Finally, I spot one that says SCIENCE NERD and underneath, in Zak's wiry handwriting, *Zakkariyah*. I'm not sure why he's chosen to claim his full name on this locker when everywhere else he insists on being just Zak, but I don't give it much more thought.

I pull the door open. Zak's rugby jersey hangs on the back, emblazoned with his surname and his number. There's also a pack of energy bars and his water bottle. I grab the bottle and unscrew the top. From my backpack, I bring out the laxatives Yemi and I bought on our way here. I'm not sure how many of the pills I'll need for my plan to work.

I pull open my phone to ask Google when it buzzes with a text.

Yemi: SOS!!!!!

Shit. I nearly drop my phone in my anxiety but catch it at the last minute. I chance a glance at the door. It took me about two minutes to walk to the prefabs. I know I shouldn't risk it, but I have to. I came all the way here. I'm not going to let it be for nothing.

I grab a fistful of the pills and dump them into the water. I screw on the lid as fast as I can and give the bottle a good shake. I can hear the water sloshing around in there, but no sound of the pills. Good—that must mean they've successfully dissolved. I'm about to close the locker door when I hear the first sounds of people.

Shit shit shit.

My phone buzzes once more and, even though it's silent, it seems to echo around the whole locker room. I stuff it into the pocket of my shirt and slam the locker door shut. That sound *does* echo loudly, but the drone of the students entering seems to drown it out.

I duck out of sight, behind a bank of lockers.

"Two more games and the championship is ours," one of the boys says, throwing open his locker on one side of the room. Another locker slams closed a little too near me, and I wince at the sound.

"Don't get too confident, we still don't know how this match will even go," Zak's familiar voice rumbles. I feel a twinge of sadness. It's been so long since I've heard his voice, and it feels a little surreal to hear it here. In a place so unfamiliar to me.

"So, did your girlfriend say she's coming to this one?" one of Zak's friends asks, thumping him in the back. It's almost comforting to see, like he's been confiding in them about how we haven't really spoken recently.

Zak sighs. "No, she's busy today." I know Zak is a practiced liar because he sounds totally believable. Sympathetic. "I'm hoping the next one."

I try to ignore the pinpricks of tears behind my eyes. I have to get out of here. I glance around the locker room once more. The front door is too far away. There's no way I'll make it all the way there. But then I spot another door hidden away in the very back: the emergency door.

The boys are too busy pulling on rugby jerseys and hyping each other up for the match to be paying much attention.

I take one last glance around the room, making sure nobody's watching.

Then, I make a run for it.

20

MEGHNA

THE DOOR OPENS AS SOON AS I CLASP THE EMERGENCY HANDLE. I push it easily—only by a crack—and slip outside. My breath is coming in fast and heavy. Even though I only ran a few steps, it feels like I've run a marathon.

"Where have you been?" Yemi asks when I join them by the benches. "I've been texting you!"

"I got stuck in there," I say. "Almost didn't make it out. Had to sneak out through the emergency exit at the back."

"Nobody saw you, did they?" Yemi sounds worried.

I shake my head. "I don't think so. I can be sneaky when I want to be." I collapse onto one of the benches beside Yemi. "We should stay, watch the fruits of our labor."

"What if Zak sees you?" Yemi asks. "Are you ready to face him?"

From the way I teared up at just the sound of his voice and his steady stream of lies, I already know the answer is no.

"Let's just make sure he doesn't see me," I say.

It's not long until the bus pulls up with the players from the other team. Their jerseys are a stark maroon with white lettering on the back, compared to Zak's team, whose jerseys are navy blue with gold lettering.

Yemi and I watch as the prefab doors open and Zak's team streams out slowly. We back away from the field until we've blended into the crowd. It's a little difficult since I'm pretty sure Yemi and I are the only people of color in this crowd of white spectators. But unless Zak looks very hard, I don't think he'll be able to spot us.

"Do you know anything about rugby?" Yemi asks once the match begins.

"I mean, yes . . . Zak has told me about it," I say, even though most of the things Zak told me totally went over my head. I've never been to a match of his, either, because usually his parents make sure to take time off to watch him play. Now I'm realizing that it was probably less about his parents and more about Rani.

"So, explain." Yemi crosses their arms and glances between the field and me expectantly.

"You know, it's like football but with your hands, and an oval ball," I offer.

"You've been dating a rugby player and you don't even know the basic rules of the game?" Yemi asks.

"There's a lot more to Zak than rugby," I say defensively, even though now that I stop to think about it, Zak did spend a lot of time telling me about his games, his teammates, his opponents, the championship, but he never stopped to ask me if I knew or cared about rugby. He never even invited me to the rugby games that his parents got him tickets for. I assume those were saved for the girlfriend his parents approved of. Now I wonder if the girlfriend he told his friends about was me, or Rani.

We don't get a chance to finish our conversation, though, because the crowd's gasps draw us back to the game. In the middle of the field, Zak is doubled over, clutching his stomach as if he's in pain. The coaches and both teams are looking at him with concern etched all over their faces.

"How many did you put in?" Yemi asks in a whisper.

"Um, I wasn't, like, scientific about it," I say.

"Meghna!" Yemi exclaims.

"I didn't have time! I just grabbed a handful and . . ." I make a motion of dropping them in, and Yemi shakes their head slowly. We watch as the coach and one of Zak's teammates carry him over to the bench on the other side of the field. They speak in hushed voices for a moment while the rest of the field and spectators watch on. Zak waves his hands around aggressively, a pained look on his face, before he goes into the school building, presumably to a bathroom.

"Do you think we've gone too far?" I ask after a moment.

"Meghna, I know you cared about him . . ." Yemi says slowly. "But the bastard cheated on you. He still is. If he doesn't care about you, why do you bother caring about him?"

Yemi's right. I shouldn't care about him. It makes no logical sense to spend even a moment worrying about him. But the way you feel about someone doesn't just vanish in an instant. However I felt about Zak is nestled somewhere deep inside my heart, and it clenches tightly around me every time I see him. And that's why I have to bury it down as far as I can. Replace it with hate—that's the only way to deal with this.

That's the thought that I hold on to as the match continues without Zak. And when Zak finally returns to the sidelines, his face crumples, realizing they've lost.

21

RANI

I TEXT MEGHNA ON AND OFF FOR THE NEXT FEW DAYS, BUT TO NO avail. It's like after the first hiccup, Meghna has already given up. That's definitely not the Meghna I used to be friends with, the one who would fight tooth and nail for everything she believed in, whether that was as small as wanting to eat ice cream when she wasn't supposed to or as big as convincing her parents that when she grew up, art was a viable career she could have. So, either Meghna doesn't actually care about the EYSE, or she's changed. Neither of those things makes me feel better in the slightest.

"It's been a long time since Meghna and you were friends," Pari aptly points out when I complain to her about being ghosted. "And she did pull this before."

I want to tell her that everything was different before. Our families went from talking every day and visiting each other every other weekend to complete silence. Everything was so tense, and I felt like I was always walking on eggshells around my parents. I couldn't even really blame Meghna for choosing to stop talking to me, if that's what made things with her parents easier. Not talking about Meghna definitely made things easier with mine.

But things are different now. At least, I thought they were.

"Maybe she's just busy with school," I tell Pari defensively. Pari rolls her eyes, like she can't believe I've succumbed to Meghna once more.

But then, something happens that makes speaking to Meghna a necessity.

At the dinner table on Thursday night, Ammu and Abbu bring up Zak's latest rugby match.

"I can't believe their team is already out of the championships. They still had multiple matches to get through," Abbu says. For once, he actually sounds . . . disappointed in Zak. Disappointment is something I've never heard in my parents' tone when it comes to him. That seems to be almost exclusively reserved for me.

"He says he was sick. That someone put something in his drink to sabotage the match." Ammu clicks her tongue like she can't believe someone would make up such lies.

"He wouldn't make up a lie like that!" This comes from Pari, surprising us all.

"You don't know what he would and wouldn't lie about, Pari," I say with a frown directed her way.

"It seems like an excuse to save face," Abbu says in agreement. "Which is . . . disappointing."

"Why lie about someone putting something in his drink, though?" Pari asks. "That's a weird lie to make up to save face. Why not being sick? Didn't Uncle and Aunty say he had to be carried off the field in the middle of playing as well?"

"He did?" I hadn't really had a proper conversation with Zak since the science exhibition. Even during the celebratory dinner afterward, I had mostly avoided him, giving him one-word answers.

Pari nods, and Ammu and Abbu actually seem to reconsider their stance.

After dinner, I pick up my phone and scroll to the end of my thread of texts with Zak. We don't text often so it's not exactly a long thread, but the last few messages he sent me have been left unanswered in my inbox.

Me: hey, heard you got sick in the middle of your match yesterday. you okay?

The three dots indicating Zak is typing appear immediately.

Zak: fine now. pretty sure someone put something in my drink though. was doubled over with stomach pain and my water tasted a bit weird. probably someone from the other team.
Me: isn't that a bit conspiracy theorist?
Zak: call me a flat earther I guess
Me: Zak . . .
Zak: look, it's all grand anyway. in the end, it saves me the trouble
Me: the trouble of winning a championship game???
Zak: no, but the championship game was scheduled for the same week when we're supposed to travel abroad for the EYSE. my coach was pressuring me to drop out to concentrate on rugby, because he reckoned we couldn't win without me. well, he was right. we couldn't even win this match without me.

I have to stop myself from rolling my eyes at his cockiness.

Me: so . . . I guess I'll see you in amsterdam
Zak: what, you planning on avoiding me until then?
Me: I'll be busy with my project
Zak: you should be, you'll have competition ;)

I shake my head and close out of our chat. I'm pretty sure I have a good idea about who sabotaged Zak, and it definitely isn't someone from the opposing team.

I click into my even shorter text thread with Meghna.

Me: tell me you weren't the one to sabotage Zak's rugby game

This time, Meghna's response comes almost immediately.

Meghna: so what if I was?

I knew somewhere in the back of my mind that it had to be Meghna, but I didn't want to believe it. Meghna always had a taste for doing things like this. I remember when we were kids, one of the main victims of her pranks was Mahin Bhaiya.

My fingers hover over my keyboard for a moment as I wonder how to tell Meghna that she's only made things easier for Zak. But I don't know how to write it out, so I press the call button instead.

Meghna picks up after the first ring.

"You know it's weird to call people these days, right?" she asks, as a way of greeting.

"You know it's illegal to spike someone's drink, right?" I ask, trying to mimic the fervor in her voice.

"It's not spiking someone's drink," Meghna says defensively.

"It's literally the definition of spiking someone's drink, Meghna. How . . . why . . . would you do that? We already had a plan on how to deal with Zak and you just go and—"

"It was a ridiculous plan," Meghna interrupts. "It's not going to work. You know that, right?"

"You never even gave it a chance." I hate how small and resentful my voice sounds. And I hate that I can feel my throat clog up with tears. Maybe Pari was right: Doing this was a mistake. Everything was fine in my life until Meghna strolled back into it again, and now she's the one making things complicated once more. "But maybe you're right. We should just call this off. You can go get your revenge on Zak. Which, by the way, didn't even work."

"What are you talking about?"

"I'm talking about the fact that his rugby championship match was the same week as the European Young Scientist Exhibition. So . . . you just made things easier for him. Now he has more time to concentrate on his project, more time to develop it. He might even win the whole thing thanks to you."

The phone line is silent for a minute that seems to stretch out forever.

"I couldn't have known," Meghna mumbles finally.

"No, but maybe if you had talked to someone before carrying out your plan, you could have considered the outcome," I say. My voice sounds reprimanding, and I expect Meghna to speak back to me in her biting tone. But she doesn't.

"You're right," she says instead. "Maybe I could have thought things out better. But you can't tell me that you think our plan is going any better, Rani. We have completely different ideas for this project, and you are absolutely obsessed with the fact that this project is yours. How am I supposed to contribute to a project that's always going to be yours?"

"You have to let go of the fact that you only see me as a coder," I retort.

"Fine, but this project? It's not going to work for me. I barely even know anything about languages. My project was all about climate change and flooding. Could you have come in and contributed to that?"

I take a deep breath. Meghna may have been frustrating in how she commented on my app, but she's not wrong, either. Maybe the reason why it's seemed like Meghna doesn't care is because this is not one of the things she's passionate about. I spent months researching languages in building this app, and I expected Meghna to come in and have the same knowledge and passion that I did.

"You're right. I haven't been fair," I say. "Maybe we need to rethink this whole thing. Maybe we have to come up with a whole new project, one that makes use of both of our skill sets."

"And one that exposes Zak," Meghna chimes in.

"Meghna—"

"No, listen to me," Meghna says. "You're scared to tell your parents about who Zak is and what he did. So, you don't tell them at all. We show them. We show everyone."

The idea has an appeal to it. "And how do you propose we show everyone?"

"I've been thinking about this. We make an app that's all about cheating," Meghna says. Her voice is higher now, faster. Her words are almost running together, like she's so excited she wants to get them out as quickly as she can. It's almost endearing. It reminds me of the old Meghna, the one who was my best friend. "We could make something that looks into the social media accounts and digital footprint of someone to figure out if they're cheating on you. And maybe there can even be a way to help people who've been cheated on. Give them advice on how to deal with it. Like a . . . digital therapist. What . . . what do you think?" There's a hesitancy to her voice as she asks the question.

It's not something I would have ever come up with myself, but as she lays it out, I can already picture the app taking shape in my mind. It's a far cry from my language app, but there's something exciting about the idea of it.

"Okay, I'm in."

EUROPEAN YOUNG SCIENTIST EXHIBITION

Group Proposal

Student #1

Name: Meghna Rahman

Age: 17

School: St. Catherine's Secondary School

Student #2

Name: Rani Choudhury

Age: 17

School: Sacred Hearts International School

Project category: Technological and Mechanical Sciences

Project Title: "C.A.T." app

Project details:

C.A.T., or "catch a two-timer," is a phone app that'll help anyone in a relationship figure out if their partner is cheating on them.

This app will track a person's digital footprint and comb any data they have available online in order to provide details about their activity. Through this, *you* can determine whether your partner has been lying to you, and if they have been seeing someone else behind your back! Better yet, if you download a version of this app into your partner's phone, it will give you access to even more of their data. The app will be discreet (on both their phone and yours), and won't show up unless it's specifically searched for, which means your partner never has to know.

The app also aims to provide psychological help. If you suspect your partner is a cheater, or if you discover that they *are* a cheater, our digital therapist will help you come to terms with all of this.

Both of us have been cheated on in our relationships—by the same guy. We only found out by a fluke, and we had to go out of our way to confirm that he really *was* cheating on us. We know that if an app such as this was available to us, things would have been much simpler.

This app is one that can help revolutionize relationships!

APPROACH:

Step one:
We will design a clean, simple, and extremely user-friendly UI. We will code the basics of finding and retaining data, which is what the basis of the app is.

Step two:
To showcase the usability of our app, we will focus on our case study: Zakkariyah Sardar (also known as Zak, also known as our cheating boyfriend, soon-to-be ex). We will use the app to find data on him which shows that he has been cheating on the both of us. All the evidence we provide will be found through the use of our app.

Step three:
We will research into cheating and psychology in order to build a digital therapist which will be able to help users. For this demo version of the app, we will be using research to create digital therapist scenarios, but a real version of the app could go further. It could consult a large pool of therapists to help create in-depth digital therapist scenarios.

22

MEGHNA

"I don't get the name," Rani says in an infuriatingly calm voice as I type out the last line of our proposal on my laptop. It's Friday afternoon, a week since we decided on our new idea, and the two of us are in Café Nightingale once more. But I've been so focused on our project that the rest of the world has barely registered to me until now. It's just been a little bubble of me, Rani, and our proposal.

"What's not to get?" I ask. "It's brilliant, if I do say so myself."

"It just seems confusing," Rani says. "Should it not be something that tells the judges exactly what it is? It seems . . . gimmicky."

I frown and try really hard not to glare daggers at Rani. When I came up with the acronym C.A.T. last night while tossing and turning in bed, it had been a sheer stroke of brilliance. It took everything in me to not text Rani right at that moment, at 3:00 a.m. on a school night, to tell her about the genius of this name. The fact that she doesn't even get it? It says a lot about who Rani is—not that I don't already know her to the bone. "It's not gimmicky, it's clever and creative." Not that she would know much about that; I have to bite my tongue to keep from saying that out loud. "Think about it, if you have an app on your phone which you've specifically downloaded to catch your boyfriend cheating on you, you wouldn't want it to be called 'cheater finder' or something, would you? Then everybody and their mother would know what that app is for, when you're really trying to be discreet. Especially if the app is going to be downloaded onto your partner's phone as well."

"But for a mock-up of the app, which is what we're going to be presenting, I feel like we need to be clear and concise," Rani says. "I know you didn't think my language app was particularly creative, but it *was* clear and concise, and it was getting the message across. That's what the judges are looking for."

I hate the condescending note in her voice, like she knows better than me about what the judges want.

"The name is part of the appeal, it's part of the pitch. The app has to be discreet, and the name helps it to be discreet."

"But—"

"And it's nonnegotiable," I say, cutting Rani off and pulling the laptop close to me just so I don't have to continue this ridiculous conversation.

"Fine," Rani says finally. "I guess I see your point, and we can keep the name, for now."

"Great." I choose to ignore the *for now* as I place the laptop on the coffee table between us and take a long sip of the coffee I ordered. It's become lukewarm, but it still tastes amazing. Nobody does coffee like Café Nightingale, and I'm a little miffed at myself for avoiding it for so many years. "Now, on to the last thing. One of the important things we need for our presentation is collecting data on Zak. How fast do you think you'll be able to code that part of the app?"

Rani sighs. "I'm not sure. I've been looking at similar apps—mostly spy apps—and the code doesn't seem too complicated for an app that would store and share the data on your phone. Your phone is already storing most of that data, so it's just about making a code that enables it to be shared and stored for an indefinite amount of time. The code that might take longer is scouring someone's digital footprint when the app isn't downloaded onto their phone."

"That's fine," I say. "I mean, with that part of the app we'll have all the time in the world, right? But if we can get a basic app up and running, install it onto Zak's phone and—"

"How are we going to do that?" Rani asks.

"We'll find a way. We're his girlfriends; we can ask him to make a call or a text on his phone, or change his lock screen or . . . I don't know. That's going to be the easy part, Rani," I say, waving her concerns away.

"We'll have to change the permissions on his phone, as well as install the app," Rani says. "And if he finds out what we're doing, everything will be over before it's even begun."

"So, we'll just make sure we're being covert about it all," I say.

Rani glances at me thoughtfully for a moment.

"What?"

"Nothing, it's just. You're not very good at being covert," Rani says matter-of-factly.

I try to ignore the tingle of anger that the comment sends through me. I don't think Rani means it in a mean way, but it annoys me all the same that Rani somehow thinks she has me pinned down when we haven't been friends in years. She doesn't know me at all. If she did, she would know exactly what I was planning.

"I can be good at being covert. I've been hiding a boyfriend for the past three months, haven't I?"

That makes Rani shut up, and I try not to paste a smug smile on my face that, for once, I'm right and Rani Choudhury is wrong.

"And you think you'll be okay spending time with him like nothing's wrong?" Rani asks after a moment. Her voice is softer now, like she worries she will upset me. I guess considering how I was last time we saw each other in her house, it's not a wrong assumption to make. But I know that if I want to do this—if I want to get back at Zak for everything he's done to me—I need to suck it up.

"No big deal." I shrug.

Rani takes me in for a moment, something contemplative behind her eyes that I can't quite figure out. "If you want, I can be the one to do it. When I spend time with Zak, my family is always there, so . . . it might be easier to distract him."

"I can do it," I insist.

"Meghna, you don't have to. Look, I'm going to be seeing him next week, anyway. If I can get that part of the app running by then, I can do it."

"Why are you seeing him next week?"

"Because it's my dad's birthday, and we usually celebrate with Zak and his family," Rani says.

"Oh." I try not to think about how that used to be me and my family. How these intimate dawats between our families were filled with nothing but joy, laughter, and good food. Now my parents never get invites like that to anywhere. They barely get invites at all. No wonder Ammu had jumped at the chance to go to the dawat at the Bhuiyans.

"Okay, fine. I guess you have your coding work cut out for you until then."

"I guess I do," Rani says. "I'll keep you updated."

I nod slowly, trying to put all thoughts of the past behind me. I know that we'll never go back to that place, so there's no point dwelling on it. No matter how much I sometimes miss it.

23

RANI

I SPEND THE WHOLE WEEK PORING OVER THE CODING FOR OUR APP, though mostly it's through headaches, sleepless nights, and a barrage of texts from Meghna. Coding, and science in general, has always been a solitary task for me. When I close the door to my bedroom, I shut out all the noise and just get down to it.

But working with Meghna changes all of that. Even though she knows very little about code, she wants constant updates. I'm in the middle of homework on Wednesday night when my phone lights up with a message.

Meghna: so once the server is up and running that's it, right?
Me: not exactly
Meghna: what else is there to do?
Me: I still have to figure out some errors with the code so far, and we have to apply for an Android developer account so we can actually privately launch the app so it's possible to test it out and to download it onto Zak's phone. we could use the one I opened for my own apps, but it's probably best if we get a brand new one so it's easy to access for both of us.
Meghna: and how much does the android developer account cost?

Me: once our project is accepted, we'll get reimbursed by the EYSE.

Meghna: but until then, we have to pay how much?

I don't get a chance to reply before my phone rings. And I know technically it's not possible for a phone to vibrate aggressively, but this call definitely seems to.

"Can you stop beating around the bush?" Meghna says, as a way of greeting.

"I wasn't, I was just saying it's not a big deal because we'll be reimbursed. It's only €25, anyway, and I can cover it if you want," I offer.

"I don't want. I can pitch in *my* fair share of it until we're reimbursed," Meghna says. "Anyway, are you working on the app right now?"

"I have to finish my physics homework first, and then—"

"And when is your dad's birthday party?"

"Friday."

There's silence on the line for a moment, and I can almost see the frown on Meghna's face, even though I can't actually see her.

"That's only two days away, Rani," Meghna says gravely. "And we still have so much to do to get the app working. Maybe we should postpone when we download it onto Zak's phone."

"It's going to be fine," I say, even though thinking about all the work ahead of me doesn't make me feel like it *will* be fine. "I think I can get it all done before Friday night. And anyway, we'll need the rest of our time to gather data, not to mention coding the rest of the app."

"And designing the UI so it's not, you know, so ugly."

I try to ignore the bite of irritation I feel at Meghna's easy insult and concede. "Yes, and the UI. It's less than two months until the exhibition in Europe, so we have our work cut out for us."

"You know what might help?" Meghna asks, in such an offhanded way that it makes me wonder if whatever she's going to say next is something she's been thinking about for some time.

"What?"

"If you talked me through some of the stuff you're doing. The coding, the software you're using, all of that. Maybe I could help you out with it all," Meghna says.

"I don't know, it's a lot to go through," I say.

"I mean, when we're at the exhibition in two months, I just don't want it to seem like I have no clue about any of it. That would make us both look bad, right? I may not be a techie like you, but I can at least learn some basics."

I glance at my computer screen, where my coding software is open. It had certainly not been an easy task to learn all of it. Other than a brief tech summer camp I went to a few years ago, I'm completely self-taught. That's part of the reason why it usually feels like such a solitary activity. Part of why it feels like mine.

But I can hear the desperation in Meghna's voice, and it's not like she's wrong. It would be helpful in the competition if she had a basic knowledge of coding and applications, more than just the design elements.

"Okay. Why don't you come over after school tomorrow? I have all the software on my desktop, so—"

"Okay, I'll be there!" Meghna says a little too brightly.

I can tell Ammu isn't too happy about Meghna coming back to our house when I tell her about it after school. But all she says is, "Make sure you clean your room before she comes."

Between catching up with homework, student council, and trying to code our app on a time crunch, I've definitely let my bedroom fall into shambles. There are empty tea and coffee mugs all over my desk, papers and folders scattered across the bedside tables, and I've been piling my dirty laundry from the week into one dedicated corner of the bed. I change out of my school uniform and start cleaning up as fast as possible. I shove the dirty laundry into our laundry basket, somehow manage to stuff all the papers and folders into drawers, and barely manage to set down the cluster of mugs into the kitchen sink when the bell rings.

I cast a glance at myself in the hallway mirror. I'd changed into the first outfit I found that was clean: a deep-brown cable-knit sweater and pants. My hair is a mess—I quickly run my fingers through it as if that will help—and I can see the lack of sleep in my red-rimmed eyes. But I know there's nothing much to be done about my appearance now, especially as an impatient Meghna rings the doorbell once more.

"Hey!" I say brightly, throwing the door open.

Meghna doesn't even feign a smile as she nods a greeting. "Hi." Unlike me, she looks put together in a tweed collared dress and matching black leggings, with her hair neatly parted to one side.

"So, have you made any more progress on the app?" Meghna asks as the two of us shuffle up the stairs.

"I've been in school all day," I point out.

"Well, I've been brainstorming ideas for our digital therapist during my breaks from class," Meghna says proudly. "But we can't implement anything *I've* been working on until we have the basics of the app coded."

"Right," I mumble, throwing open my bedroom door and waving Meghna in while trying to contain my irritation. Working on Meghna's schedule is somehow more taxing than the overwhelming schedule I set for myself when I'm coding. For my language app, there were too many sleepless nights I spent going over my code, trying to find the parts that I had messed up and fixing them.

"Well, when you help me figure out coding a little better, hopefully things will be easier." Meghna shrugs, like learning to code is as easy as anything.

"Let's see how much you can pick up," I say, slipping into the computer chair by my desk and motioning for Meghna to sit down on the folding chair I'd gotten out of storage for her.

I open the software I use and the window where the code I've been working on has been inputted. I click to the display phone so I can show Meghna exactly what I have so far.

"I've been keeping the UI really simple, and we can go in and figure out the specific design elements of everything later on," I say as the display phone turns on and shows the home page of the app.

"That's all the code?" Meghna asks. When I turn around, she's staring at the screen with confusion in her eyes.

"Yeah. I'm using Python—that's the one I used for my language app, so I'm a little more familiar with it," I say, hovering over the code. "There are still a few things that aren't executing properly, and I basically have to figure out exactly where I went wrong with the code. And once I have that, it would be helpful if we could test it out on an actual phone before we go to the trouble of installing it on Zak's phone."

"And after that we can work on my part of the project," Meghna says with a flickering smile. "I don't want to slow you down. Why don't you just talk me through things when you're doing them?"

"You won't really get it unless you already understand what I've done," I say.

"I'm a quick learner, don't worry about me." Meghna smiles for real this time and sits back in her chair, watching the screen instead of me.

"Okay . . ." I say, closing out of the app preview and clicking back to my code. "So I've been having trouble figuring out the exact code for the app to store incoming texts and messages. I thought I could just alter the outgoing one, but something is broken in the code . . ." I scan the code thoroughly, to find where I've messed up that is stopping the algorithm from being executed properly. It's not exactly rocket science; I feel like this is coding I should be able to do in my sleep. But sometimes even the most basic coding principles will go over my head if I have a lot going on. And Meghna has been occupying my mind a little too much since we agreed to do this thing together.

It's even harder to think now with Meghna's gaze trained on my computer screen and occasionally wandering over to me.

I sit back after a few minutes of this, trying to ignore the heat rising up my cheeks from how close Meghna is hovering.

"Do you want, like, a cup of tea or something?" I ask.

"No, I'm okay. You keep . . . doing you," Meghna urges.

"It's just a little difficult to concentrate with you here," I say. "I thought you wanted to learn the basics of coding, not just watch me as I try to figure this out."

"I'm learning while watching you," Meghna insists, though I really don't know how much she could be learning from watching me just stare at my code.

"I don't think I can work while you're watching me," I counter.

Meghna frowns, and my heart sinks a little. She's been so hard to read ever since we started talking again: happy one second and angry the next. I'm not sure exactly what about me keeps setting her off.

"How did you learn to code?" she asks finally after a moment. "I mean, back when we used to hang out, you weren't exactly interested in this stuff. So maybe it would help me learn if I knew how you learned."

"I don't know. I went to a summer camp for coding where I got my head start," I say.

"So, one day you just woke up and thought, hey, you know what would be fun, going to a summer camp for coding like a massive nerd?" Meghna asks, tilting her head to one side. Even though the question is a little abrasive, from her playful tone, it almost sounds like she's teasing me.

"Well, takes a massive nerd to know one," I point out.

Meghna rolls her eyes. "Seriously, why did you decide to go to that camp? It couldn't have been an out-of-the-blue decision."

"I don't know. It was silly, I used to spend a lot of time online, and it seemed like fun, the idea of being able to make something from scratch. I've never been creative like you, but, you know, I always liked numbers and figuring out how one thing leads to another. So, I saw this summer camp and decided I would try it. It was really great," I say. It was the summer when everything had fallen apart, when Meghna and I went from talking every day to never talking. When she ignored all my calls and texts, and it felt like life as I knew it had suddenly vanished from existence. Like I had stepped into some kind of a parallel universe. That summer camp felt like a bubble away from everything else. Like a chance to build myself into something different—without Meghna, or my parents, or anything else being part of the equation. Just me and simple computer codes, learning how to create something out of nothing.

"And I suppose there's no two-day intensive coding boot camp?" Meghna asks after a moment of silence.

"None that I know of," I say. "But if you really want to learn, it's not that difficult, I promise. You probably already know a lot more than most people. And this software is free. If you download it and fiddle around with some tutorials, you can probably get somewhere pretty fast."

Meghna nods. "I'll do that. You should send me your file, and maybe I can break it down and figure it out like that."

"Yeah, I can do that," I say. I turn back to my desktop, at the code on the screen, and as I get back to work, Meghna watching me over my shoulder doesn't seem so distracting anymore. At least, not distracting in the worst possible way.

24

RANI

Birthdays are rarely a big deal in our house—unless, of course, the birthday is Neel's. Being the babu of the family always means special treatment.

Still, Ammu will make sure we do at least something to celebrate birthdays. So, when I wake up on Friday morning, the house is in chaos because Ammu is preparing for Abbu's birthday dawat this evening. Despite it only being us and Zak's family, Ammu is going all out and making multiple dishes, including biryani.

I have half a mind to ask Ammu if I can invite Aarti to dinner, too, but because I don't want her to have a fit about portion sizes, I decide against it. Instead, I duck out to catch the Luas to school with as little noise as possible. When Ammu is preparing for dawats, there is no telling what will set her off.

At lunchtime, Mrs. Quinn calls me into the physics lab to talk about the EYSE, so I ditch Aarti at the cafeteria and head over to see her.

"Rani, come inside," she says, unlocking the door and pushing it open to let me through. All the labs are usually locked when not in use since the school spent so much money getting high-tech equipment into each one. Mrs. Quinn leads me to one of the lab desks at the front and sits, patting the chair next to her.

As soon as I sit, she flashes me a grin. "The European Young Scientist Exhibition at last!" she exclaims, clapping her hands together. "I know you've been eager to get in for a long time. So, let's talk about your project."

"I already have a proposal," I say. I reach into my bag, pull it out—I printed it last night in anticipation—and submit it for Mrs. Quinn's approval. She smiles like she always does when I'm overprepared and takes the papers from me. There's silence in the lab for a few minutes as her eyes flicker over the pages. I can't read her expression.

"Hmm," she says, putting the pages down on the empty desk in front of her. "Very . . . different from your language app."

"Right . . . I wanted to do something different. Something more . . . ambitious?" I don't know why, but not having Mrs. Quinn's immediate approval sets my teeth on edge. What if this project isn't good enough to win? What if I let Meghna talk me into something that would lead to us losing the EYSE altogether?

"It's a lot of work, and you don't have a long time to complete it all," Mrs. Quinn says.

"Well, I've got a partner this time. She's at another school, but we're pretty sure between us we can do it," I say.

Mrs. Quinn finally turns to me, a smile apparent in her eyes. "It'll be hard work, but honestly, Rani, I think this is what's been missing from your projects."

"This?" I ask, not sure what exactly she's referring to. This app is different from my other work, but not so completely out of my wheelhouse.

"A personal connection," Mrs. Quinn says. "It makes all the difference in competitions like this. When the judges see that it's not just science for the sake of science, that it's real to you, that helps make it real for other people."

Zak . . . Being cheated on . . . *That's* what's been missing from my project. Not my hard work or research, but the fact that suddenly I have a story to tell. Because I guess Mrs. Quinn didn't think my language app had a personal connection, even though I had started it because of how Ammu and Abbu always tell me just how important language is for Bengalis. But it's not like people who aren't Bengalis really understand the extent of it. Ammu and Abbu have brought me up telling me never to forget that Bangladeshis fought and died because of our language. And it's fighting for that which eventually led us to become an independent nation in 1971.

"You're right," I say to Mrs. Quinn instead of all of these stormy thoughts in my head. "I hope this personal connection gets us far in the competition."

Mrs. Quinn's smile widens. "If this Meghna is as bright as you, I'm sure you have nothing to worry about. Maybe this could be the year Sacred Hearts finally brings back an award from the European Young Scientist Exhibition."

And even though Mrs. Quinn's dismissal of my previous work as not personal enough hurts a little, I can't help that her approval now fills me with a kind of confidence I haven't felt in a long time.

YOU BETTER HAVE A GOOD GAME PLAN FOR TONIGHT. THE SLIGHTLY THREATENING text from Meghna scares me as much as it makes my heart flutter. Because after years of silence, Meghna and I are on texting terms. Even if it's texting about the guy who cheated on us both.

Me: I was going to pretend my phone is broken and that I needed to use his to make an important call.
Meghna: seriously? you're at your house, with an abundance of other phones
Meghna: you need a better game plan
Me: what's your clever idea then?

The dots indicating she's typing appear and disappear over the next few minutes. The message she finally sends takes me by surprise.

Meghna: what are you wearing?

I glance in the mirror at my off-white salwar kameez with printed flowers decorating the torso. I had thought nothing of it when Ammu insisted this be my outfit for the dawat, but Meghna's question suddenly makes me feel self-conscious.

Me: why does it matter?
Meghna: because he's a stupid boy and he's more likely to not think anything if he's busy thinking about how nice you look. think, Rani!

I guess her logic makes sense in some convoluted way, but considering he's been more than happy to date Meghna while seeing me, I don't think her plan stands much of a chance of working.

Me: Meghna, I don't think anything I can wear to the dawat can distract him from me . . . stealing his phone? he's usually glued to that thing.

Meghna: you're right.

Meghna: plus, it's a family function.

Meghna: use your sisters, then.

I thought of trying to use Pari and Neel, but considering just how chaotic they can be sometimes, I wasn't sure if getting them involved was the best idea.

Me: I don't know if they're trustworthy . . .

Meghna: Rani, if you mess this up . . .

I take a breath. Meghna has always been intense, but she is somehow even more intense about this than anything else. I guess on some level I understand; she's had her heart broken, and this is her way of trying to get over that.

Me: I won't mess it up.

The doorbell ringing, shrill and loud, interrupts our conversation. Downstairs, I can hear Ammu telling Abbu to get the door while yelling at Neelam and Parisa to clear their things from the sitting room.

They're here, I text Meghna quickly before adjusting the white urna across my shoulder and slipping out the door.

Downstairs is as chaotic as you might expect from any Bengali dawat. Abbu is shaking hands with Sardar Uncle and launching into a discussion about Bangladeshi politics while Ammu has already dragged Aunty into the kitchen to show off the new outfit she bought Parisa for her piano recital next week. I catch some of their conversation as I walk down the stairs and note that Ammu has conveniently left out Parisa throwing a fit about how she's not wearing the outfit.

"Hey." Zak is by the door, hanging his winter coat on the half-overflowing coatrack. "Where have you been?"

"It's been about five minutes since you guys arrived," I comment.

"Right, just usually Aunty makes you greet us at the entrance," Zak points out. And he isn't wrong. Ammu often cajoles me into getting ready early and staying by her side to greet Aunty and Uncle. Unlike Pari and Neel, who are still upstairs in their respective bedrooms, doing who knows what.

"It's a weekday; I was working on my homework," I say.

"Homework like . . . your European project?" Zak cocks an eyebrow, and for a moment I wonder if he knows. But then I realize he's just teasing, trying to get info about my project, probably so he can brag about his own.

"I haven't started yet," I say. "Have you?"

"You haven't started yet?" Zak's eyes almost bug out of their sockets, but I can tell he's doing it as hyperbole. "Ms. Overprepared hasn't started overpreparing? Seriously?"

"There's time." I shrug.

He narrows his eyes like he doesn't quite believe me, but then he shrugs, too, and says, "I have finally had a chance to get started now that we're out of the rugby championships. It's just going to be difficult to top the project I put forward in the Ireland fair."

"So you're doing something new?" I press.

"Thinking about it." If he's suspicious of how curious I am about his project, he doesn't act like it. Still, I figure it's best to change the subject altogether. After all, I still have to figure out a way to get his phone away from him, but it's not like there's an easy segue into that.

"Let's get away from the door," I say instead, and lead him into the empty sitting room. We can hear the drone of Uncle and Abbu's conversation from the closed double doors leading into the kitchen and dining area, so it's not like we're totally alone. But it's still probably the most privacy Zak and I have had in a long time.

I sit on the couch on the far side of the room and—to my surprise—Zak sits himself down right next to me. Not on the opposite side of the long couch, nor on the other couch by the double doors. But right next to me. So close, in fact, that if he inched a little closer to me, our hands would be touching.

I try to ignore the fact that blood rushes to my face at his proximity and gulp down the discomfort raging in me.

"So, I wanted to ask you something," I say.

"I knew you were being nice to me for a reason." When I turn to face Zak, he's giving me a cheeky grin that doesn't help endear him to me.

"I'm always nice to you," I say.

"You always put up with me." Zak says this as if I'm some kind of mathematical problem that he's got all figured out.

He's definitely not wrong, but I quickly change the subject. The last thing I need is to get into an uncomfortable conversation about *us* when I know he's been lying to me and my parents for months now.

"Look, I didn't really get a chance to look into your app during the exhibition a few weeks ago, and I was hoping to now." I hold out my hand for his phone expectantly.

But Zak just considers me with a frown, making no move to hand his phone over to me. Maybe this will be harder than I thought.

"Trying to steal my ideas?" Zak asks finally. He asks it like a joke, but I can tell there's a seed of doubt there.

"Please. I just thought it was a cool idea, and I never got a chance to see what the judges clearly saw in it," I say.

"You didn't have an interest in my app until tonight," he points out.

"Well, you said you were doing a brand-new project for Europe, so it's not like you're exactly sharing sacred secrets with me." I smile at him, trying to look as innocuous as possible. But Zak doesn't budge.

"If it was anyone else, I would let them play with my app for hours. But you can probably figure out how I did everything within seconds and replicate it," he says.

I finally retrieve my hand, feeling foolish for trying this ploy at all. Maybe I'm not as good at subtlety as I made myself out to be to Meghna. I just didn't think Zak saw me as real competition—I thought he would take any opportunity to boast about himself.

"Fine. I was hoping I could join in when my parents sing praises about your app, but I guess I'll just have to keep telling them it's not as good as mine."

He sighs before slipping his hand into his pocket and taking his phone out. I try to ignore the rush of excitement that prickles my skin, the thunder of my heartbeat at success being so close. I'm already imagining Meghna's look of approval when I tell her about this tomorrow.

But then Zak hesitates, holding the phone just a little out of my reach.

"You show me yours, and I'll show you mine," he says.

"Seriously?" I ask.

"Hey, it's only fair," Zak says.

"Fine, I'm doing a new project, too, so . . ." I shrug, holding out my phone to him. He sighs and types out his password on his phone before handing it over to me and taking mine out of my hands. I try not to let my emotions show on my face as I bypass his athlete app on the home screen and click into Google Play. I already published our app privately last night after making sure the basics of it were working. I even gave it access to Zak's Google account. I quickly scroll to find the app now and hit download.

I glance over at Zak as the download percentage goes up, but he's too engrossed in the narrative portion of my app to notice me. Still, it doesn't stop how quickly my heart thuds. It would only take a glance for him to find out exactly what I'm up to.

I glance back at the screen and realize the app has finished downloading. I quickly click out. Just as I'm about to hit Settings, though, Zak's voice interrupts me.

"So, thoughts?" he asks. He's turned toward me, though my app is still open on my phone.

"It's, um, good," I say quickly, clicking the lock button so the screen goes blank. "I can see why the judges chose it."

Zak smiles, and for a moment there's none of that smugness that he usually carries around in him. He almost seems sincere. Like he's genuinely pleased I've given him a compliment.

"Thanks," he says. "I mean, it means a lot that you think it's good."

"It does?" The words tumble out before I've thought them all the way through.

"Of course it does. You're like . . . the only other person who gets all this stuff. And you know coding better than a lot of people. That's why I'm glad we're, you know. Together. I like that we can share this with each other."

His words confuse me more than anything else. In all the time that our families have known each other, in the year that we've been in a "relationship," he's never spoken to me like this before. Most of the time it feels like we're all in the Zak Sardar show, and the rest of us are just playing extras. Especially me.

"I'm not sure we're really sharing this with each other," I say. "I mean, aren't we just doing this because of our parents?" The question doesn't come out with the exact eloquence I would have liked it to, but it's out there now. Zak's expression shifts into a frown, but I can't tell what he's annoyed at—the question itself, or the situation that we're both in.

"Is that how you feel?" Zak asks.

"Isn't that how you feel?"

"Look, I . . ." Zak begins, heaving a sigh and running his hands through his black hair. If it was someone else, I may have found this charming. "I guess I said yes to this arrangement at first because it seemed like the right thing to do. For my parents, but also for us. I mean, we're kind of the perfect fit on paper, right? We're both into science, we're the same age, we're here. It was just . . . easy. And maybe before I would have been looking for an out, but I'm not anymore."

"You aren't?" I try to read something in the thickness of his voice, the strange sincerity of his expression. How can he really believe everything he's saying when I know the truth?

"My parents always told me that you have to make sacrifices to build the life you truly want for yourself. They sacrificed a lot to come here and to give me the life that I have. So did your parents, right?"

"Right." I nod. "So, you think this is a sacrifice? You and me?"

"No . . ." Zak shakes his head. "I'm not explaining myself right. I thought it was. But Rani, we're kind of the best things to happen to each other, aren't we? We're friends, we get each other. I mean, how many people can you sit next to at a dawat and swap apps you've coded, knowing if they say it's good or bad that actually holds some kind of merit? How many people know what you're talking about when you talk about tech or science? We know each other. We know each other's families. We're like family already. How many people are that lucky?"

"Not many," I say. Because he's right in a way. We are lucky, and maybe if we were two very different people, this would be a love story instead of what it is now: a farce.

"I like yours, too, by the way," Zak says finally. "Your app. I mean, it's definitely not an app I would have made, but it's good. Unique."

He hands my phone back to me, and while it's the last thing I want to do, I slip his back to him, too, suddenly not so sure about Zak and exactly what he wants out of our relationship.

25

MEGHNA

"I CAN'T BELIEVE, AFTER ALL YOUR BOASTING, YOU COULDN'T DO it," I say when Rani fills me in about what happened at the dawat last night. The two of us are in a secluded corner of Café Nightingale.

"I just couldn't really ask for his phone again without looking suspicious," Rani says. "At least the app is on his phone now. We just need to find a way to get his phone and fix the accessibility settings, and then—"

"I'll do it," I cut in before Rani can launch into her family's next plans to frolic with the Sardars.

Rani seems to hesitate before speaking. "Are you sure? Because I don't mind trying again. I'll just have to figure out how best to approach it without making Zak suspicious and maybe I can—"

"You had your chance, and you failed. I'll figure it out."

Rani eyes me with a look that seems a little bit too much like sympathy. "Okay," she says, though it sounds like she's trying to appease me more than anything else.

Her sympathy makes my anger flare up somewhere deep in my gut, but I guess her feelings are not exactly misplaced. I've barely spoken to Zak since that day at the park. I sent him a quick text a few days ago about being too busy with school to hang out, which he ignored. But that's the only conversation we've had in the past week. The idea of seeing him in person again, acting like everything is normal, like *we're* normal, makes my stomach twist.

But this was all my idea, and I know it has to be done. Rani's tried, and now it's my turn. I just have to figure out how to do it.

"So, what's your plan?" Rani asks.

"I don't know. I guess I'll ask to meet up like usual and . . ." I stop when my ideas run dry.

Rani raises an eyebrow. "Not such a simple task, is it?"

"I'll just a find a way for him to leave his stuff with me and go off somewhere," I say with as much confidence as I can muster. I'm not giving Rani the satisfaction of being right. "I'll figure it out."

"You should take a friend with you," Rani suggests, instead of rubbing my incompetence in my face. "For support."

It takes everything in me to not send a death glare in her direction. "I don't need support. You were fine on your own with him, so I'll be fine, too."

"I had support," Rani says. But I don't remember her mentioning any friends in the vicinity when Zak went over to the Choudhurys'. "My sisters. My parents. Yeah, they may all be obsessed with Zak, but it made it easier having them there. There was a way for me to get away from him if I needed. If it . . . felt difficult, or something." She's saying it as if she anticipates *I'll* have difficulty with it even when she didn't.

"I'll be fine. Zak and I always meet up on our own, so it'll be weird if someone's there," I say.

"What about your friends?" Rani asks. "Hasn't he met them? You could make up an excuse that you were hanging out with them when—"

"He's never met them, he wouldn't go for it," I cut in. Rani blinks at me in surprise, but I brush past it as quickly as I can. Sure, I always thought it was strange that Zak wanted us to live in this bubble that was just us. No parents, no friends. Just the two of us, secret meetings, trying to avoid any places where he would know anyone or I would know anyone. In a country as small as Ireland, that's difficult to do, but we found a way.

Now it all makes a lot more sense, but I don't want to admit to Rani—or anyone—that I should have clued into it much earlier. That I chose to overlook the red flags that were waving right in front of my eyes.

"I'll just come up with a few different ways that I could get his phone away from him, just to be on the safe side and not leave anything up to chance. All I have to do is go into his settings and give our app access, right?"

"Right," Rani says. "And the sooner you can do it, the better. We want enough time to gather data so we're ready for Amsterdam by the end of November. You should probably set something up this week."

"Right, this week," I say, trying to ignore how even the thought of texting Zak makes my mouth dry.

"So, maybe you should text him, then," Rani says with a raised eyebrow.

"Now?" My voice comes out more shrilly than I thought possible, and I quickly clear my throat, trying to get my heart to stop beating so fast. "I can do it later."

"No time like the present," Rani says in her grating voice. "We can plan to meet again to discuss next steps once you've managed to enable access. It's kind of what's going to set a majority of our project into motion."

"Right." I slip my phone out of my pocket and unlock it, going to my messages with Zak. This is probably the longest we've gone without seeing each other or speaking on the phone in our entire relationship.

"Do you want me to do it?" When I glance up, Rani is giving me that pitying look I hate so much.

"I can do it," I say with a lot more confidence than I feel. I type out the words faster than my brain can think and hit send. "There, done." I flip the phone around to show Rani.

Me: meet at our spot after school on monday? You can tell me all about your young scientist project.

Rani nods her approval, so I tuck my phone back into my pocket and shut my laptop, slipping it into my backpack. "I should probably get home before my parents start wondering where I've gotten off to."

"Oh, right. Okay," Rani mumbles. She actually seems a little disappointed at having to break up our meeting. "So maybe next weekend we can go over everything."

"Sure." I stand up, swinging my backpack behind me. "I'll see you later, I guess."

THE PROBLEM IS, DESPITE ALL MY BRAVADO, THE THOUGHT OF meeting up with Zak makes me feel slightly nauseous. I may have somehow pulled off acting like everything was okay that day at the park, but that was before everything had really settled. Before I had told my friends and made everything a reality: Zak wasn't the guy I thought he was, and everything between us was a big fat lie.

Now, until this project is over, I have to keep pretending, even though it's the last thing I want to do.

"I'm proud of you," Janella tells me at lunchtime on Monday when the three of us are sitting by our lockers, eating. She beams at me. "It shows real growth to put aside your differences with Rani to work on your project together."

"Thanks." I shrug. I half want to tell Janella and Yemi about what the project entails, but I also know that if I do, they'll try to talk me out of all the aspects of it I'm not proud of. Like how it means I'll have to face Zak again. And that one of our main aims for the project is to humiliate Zak, and the science comes after that.

"I thought last time you two tried to work together it was a no-go?" Yemi asks, almost like they can smell the lie on me. They know me a little too well for my liking.

"We just came up with a brand-new project that caters to both of our interests," I say. I leave it there, and given that both Yemi and Janella are probably tired of hearing me talk about my science projects all day long, neither of them presses me any further about it. And just to make sure they really can't ask any more questions, I also take a massive bite of my tuna sandwich.

"Next thing you know, we'll be coming to Amsterdam to see you presenting," Yemi says excitedly. "You think Ms. Ennis will approve of that?" They turn to Janella questioningly, like she has an in with Ms. Ennis.

"If it means missing school, I highly doubt that," Janella says.

"Not to mention the funding for taking you all to Amsterdam. She said it's a good thing the EYSE pays for travel and accommodation for me, because our school definitely can't afford it," I say. It's not that our school is poor, exactly. It's that no public school can really afford the funding that a school like Rani's has. Sacred Hearts is known to be one of the wealthiest schools in all of Ireland. While we go on field trips to Airfield farm, they go to various European countries, fully funded by their school. While we sit around our lockers having packed lunches, they get a full lunch menu served in their state-of-the-art cafeteria.

Before Abbu's company went bankrupt, I was ready to join Rani there, ready to live a life of luxury. Now it seems like some kind of a fever dream.

Janella and Yemi launch into a conversation about all the pros and cons of a private versus public education while I chew on my sandwich slowly, willing the Zak-related nausea to leave me alone. To distract myself, I slip my phone out and scroll to the YouTube tutorials I've been watching about coding since being at Rani's house. No matter how many I watch, though—and I've watched at least a dozen all the way through—coding doesn't seem as easy a concept to grasp as Rani made it sound. I'm about to click into a video titled "Coding for Dummies" when my phone buzzes with a string of texts.

Rani: hey, happy monday!
Rani: I mean, how are plans for today?
Rani: are you okay to meet Zak?
Rani: sure you don't want me to come?

I roll my eyes before quickly typing back a thumbs-up emoji. I expect Rani to leave it at that, but the texts keep coming.

Rani: if you need anything just let me know
Rani: I'm here

Rani: I mean, figuratively speaking

Rani: I'll be available

Rani: I'll be by my phone

Rani: you can call or text

"Someone's popular," Yemi says. I glance up to see both of my friends looking at me with questioning expressions.

"It's just Rani," I say, quickly typing back everything fine, talk later, turning my phone to silent, and tucking it back into my pocket. "She's excited about our project, I guess."

Janella and Yemi share another one of their unreadable glances. "You've gone from archnemeses to texting buddies pretty fast."

The use of the term *buddies* offends me more than anything else. "Hardly," I scoff. "She's just annoying and overeager. She has a lot of strong ideas, which makes her very difficult to work with. But I'm figuring it out." My friends still look a little too invested in my apparent "friendship" with Rani, so I quickly change the subject, making a mental note to keep my phone turned off during lunchtime from now on. There's already enough Rani in my life right now without her having to dominate even my school days.

26

MEGHNA

Zak is nowhere to be seen when I get to the park where we usually meet, which I'm happy for because it gives me a chance to take a deep breath and prepare for what lies ahead. But as I'm breathing, I spot a familiar face in the corner that completely ruins any semblance of preparation.

"Rani?" I ask. She tries to duck behind the tree like she did last time we were here, but I've already seen her.

Looking around to make sure Zak isn't here yet, I march over to her.

"I can see you. What the hell? You really couldn't trust me to do this on my own?" I ask.

Rani peeks out from behind the tree trunk, a guilty look on her face. "You weren't supposed to see me."

"Clearly." I cross my arms while looking at her with disdain and waiting for some kind of explanation.

"I was just . . . I wanted you to have moral support. I thought I'd come here and see your friends or something, and then I could be on my way. But, it's only you," Rani says. Her eyes cast around the park like she's hoping my friends are also hiding behind the bushes or something. But obviously Janella and Yemi aren't here, because they have no idea this is even happening.

"Well, you could have ruined everything. If Zak sees you here, how would we explain?" I ask sternly. I want to be angry at Rani, and I try to keep the anger in my voice, but it's kind of thoughtful that she came here to make sure I had support. Even if she's definitely in the wrong for doing it.

"I know," Rani says. "I'm sorry."

I let out a huff of frustration, but even that doesn't come out half as angry as I want it to. If I'm being honest with myself, having Rani here feels comforting in a way. She's been through this—she's done this before. Her presence makes it feel more doable.

"Look, there's a café down the road from here where Zak and I sometimes go for food. There's a corner booth that's super secluded. Why don't you go wait there? I'll find you after I've met up with Zak," I say.

"Okay." Rani nods, her hands nervously pulling at the straps of her backpack. From her heavy backpack and the Sacred Hearts uniform, I realize she must have come here straight from school. "Text me if you need anything."

"Sure," I say. If I had properly answered her texts before, I could have probably kept this whole situation from happening. But maybe it's good that it did.

Rani gives me a wave over her shoulder as she exits through the back gate, and I shuffle toward the swings and sit down. When I check my phone, I realize that Zak is a full fifteen minutes late. There's not even a text to apologize or let me know that he'll be late. It's not exactly out of the ordinary for him, but today it makes anger seep into my bones.

Tardiness is not high on the list of Zak's bad behaviors, but it does make me wonder how much I've been letting slide simply because I was looking at him through rose-colored glasses. He's never met Yemi and Janella, and nobody in my family knows him outside the context of being Sardar Uncle and Aunty's son. It was so easy for me to dismiss Zak's every bad quality simply because it seemed worth it to keep the secret.

That feeling of shame blooms in my chest again, mixing with the anger I feel at Zak.

And that's exactly when he decides to make his appearance, with his hair tousled, the school tie around his neck loosened. Just a few weeks ago, the sight of his carefully disheveled look would have made my palms sweaty, but now it sets me on edge.

"Hey, stranger," Zak says easily, taking the swing beside me and giving me a grin. "Long time no see."

"Hey," I say. "Not really my fault."

Zak's grin falters, and I immediately take a quick breath, trying to let go of my anger so I can at least pretend that everything is okay.

"Sorry," I say, shaking my head and turning to him with what I hope is a convincing smile. "School has just been so crazy. All of our teachers are giving us a million tests because of the Leaving Cert, or whatever. And it's like, there's still a year and a half until then. And my parents are already obsessing over university applications and worrying about grants. And . . ." I sigh. "It's been a lot."

"Sounds like it," Zak says, his smile returning slightly.

"I think my parents thought that if I got through to the European Young Scientist Exhibition, maybe the money and connections from that could have helped. But since I didn't . . ." I shrug.

"I'm sorry you didn't," Zak says. And he actually sounds like he means it, even though I know he doesn't. I know he doesn't care at all. "But, hey. I brought something to cheer you up!"

He stands up, and I notice the tote bag he's been holding all this time. He pulls out a familiar picnic blanket—one we used during our first-ever date—and lays it out on the ground.

I remember how the two of us ran into each other at the library, at the start of summer, both combing through the science section for ideas for our Young Scientist Exhibition project. I almost didn't *recognize* him at first—it had been years since the last time we'd seen each other at a dawat—but he'd recognized me almost instantly. We connected over science, and reminiscing over when he was the intruder in my friendship with Rani. We talked about how much things had changed, skirting around the uncomfortable subject of everything that had happened with my family. He asked for my number then, and it didn't take him long to ask me out. I was hesitant, but I had felt a spark of something at the library, a connection, so I said yes.

Now, he gives me a grin, almost like he's checking to make sure I'm appreciating the fact that he's gone to all this effort to actually arrange something for today. But on our first date, he was nervous and sincere, making sure that we were on the same page and peppering me with questions about what we had missed in each other's lives rather than being concerned about whether I was appreciating his efforts.

Zak pulls out two Tesco meal deals—two sandwiches, two packs of Taytos, and two bottles of Coke.

"I would have made something, but I did come straight from school," Zak says, waving his hand over his makeshift picnic like he's presenting something grand.

"Have you ever cooked in your life?" I ask. It's meant as flirtatious banter, but my tone comes across a little too abrasive. So I move across to the picnic blanket, open up a bottle of Coke, and take a huge gulp in the hopes Zak doesn't notice something is definitely off with me.

"You okay?" Zak asks, sitting down next to me. He places his phone on the blanket and links his fingers with mine. It takes everything in me to not pull away. I think about Rani, and somehow that helps. She did this before, so I can, too. I'm not going to let Rani be better at one more thing than me.

"I guess, just still annoyed that I lost to Rani at something else," I blurt out.

Zak nods knowingly. "Her project was honestly pretty basic, but I guess it had the right stuff to appeal to the judges. They probably liked that it had that Irish element in it. You'll get them next time." Zak gives my hand a squeeze, and I try to shoot him a normal-looking smile even though it pains me a little. I quickly glance at the phone still resting on the picnic blanket. It's within reach, but there's no way Zak won't notice if I grab it.

"You know what would make this perfect?" I ask.

"What?"

"Some ice cream," I say with a smile, as convincing as I can make it.

"Really? It's ten degrees," Zak points out.

"But it's sunny, and I've had the worst week. Please?" I plead. "You owe me, you were late again."

"What about what you owe me for ignoring me all week?" Zak asks.

"What about what you owe me for not even coming to see my science project during the exhibition?" I ask.

Zak sighs. Something about the science exhibition must tug at his sense of morality, or maybe he's just trying to avoid talking about that day, knowing how quickly he could have blown everything up. "Okay, okay. I'll get you your ice cream." He stands up, brushing bits of dust off his pants. "Anything else for your highness?"

"Nope, that will be all." I flash him a grin while sliding his phone toward me and out of his line of sight.

"I'll be right back," Zak says. He turns toward the gates of the park, making a right at the sidewalk toward the corner shop at the end of the street.

I grab his phone as soon as he's out of sight, but his lock screen stares me in the face. I half wish Rani were actually here now. With all her computer expertise, I'm sure she would have some way of getting into his phone and bypassing his password. Knowing Zak, though, it's the most obvious password. I try his birthday, and then his birthday backward, but neither of them works. I try the number on his rugby jersey, then the number of his favorite rugby player's jersey. Still nothing.

I glance up at the entrance to the park. Still no sign of Zak.

Sighing, I pull up Rani's contact on my phone and hit call. She picks up on the first ring, as if she's been waiting for me to ask for help.

"Everything okay?" she says, instead of *hello*.

"Fine, I've got his phone, but I don't know his password. I tried his birthday and the number on his rugby jersey, but—"

"It's his mom's birthday, December twenty-ninth," Rani says. I try to ignore that gnawing of annoyance that Rani knows him better than I do. That at some point they became the kind of people who shared their passwords with each other.

"Thanks," I mumble. "I'll talk to you later." I'm already typing the password into the phone. It unlocks easily to the green-and-white background of the Irish rugby team, and I quickly navigate to his settings, then give our app every single permission possible, feeling a rush of satisfaction at being able to pull off a task even Rani couldn't. It's not exactly something my parents would be proud of, but one step at a time.

I've only just tossed the phone back on the picnic blanket when Zak appears, two Calippos in his hands. He holds one out to me and, as much as I want to end this date right here and now, it's not like I can do so without rousing his suspicions. So, I accept it with a smile and tear off the packet as he takes his seat beside mine. This time, he searches for his phone with a frown and pockets it as soon as he finds it.

"Do you ever think about how we barely have any photos together?" I find myself asking a few moments later. When this is all over, all I'll have to remember Zak by is my memories. And those have definitely been tainted now.

"We have photos together," Zak insists.

"We do?"

"The one you added to my contact on your phone." He nods, though I remember he hadn't exactly been thrilled when I'd taken that photo, mentioning that any proof of our relationship could end up getting us in trouble with our parents. It made sense then, but I kept the photo. Now it seems he just didn't want proof of me because of Rani. "And I'm sure there's also photos from dawats when we were kids."

"Even if those exist, they don't count," I say. "I mean, of us together. Now, like this. You know, memories of our dates, us being together."

Zak sighs. "Is this why you've been ignoring me?"

"What?" I blink at him slowly, confused at how the two things have linked up in his head.

"I figured something must have happened, but I thought you were still just mad about the young scientist competition, not that that's my fault."

I swallow down my angry response about what I really discovered at that exhibition, and say, "Nothing's happened. I'm just saying that—"

"You want us to be public?" Zak asks.

That's what he's worried about? Of course that's what he's worried about.

"I don't want that. But I mean, would it really be that bad if we were?"

Zak shakes his head. His fingers are a little too tight around the wooden stick of the Calippo, like he's trying to tamp down his anger, too. "I thought you understood, Meghna. My parents wouldn't be happy about it. Your parents wouldn't be happy about it."

"My parents would understand. They'd be annoyed, sure, but they'd get it. I mean, you're an appropriate guy. You're Bangladeshi and you're Muslim, and honestly it could be a lot worse."

"Gee, thanks." Zak frowns. "Well, my parents wouldn't understand at all."

"Why?" I ask, trying to understand his logic. I'd gone along with it for so long without ever really questioning it. "Our parents would get along, I think, and—

"You know what happened with your parents, Meghna," Zak says in a grim voice.

"*You* know what happened. My dad didn't do anything wrong. All the stuff about him being corrupt and committing fraud were ridiculous rumors," I say. "It was just a business deal gone horribly wrong. It could have happened to anyone."

"I know, but image means something to my parents," Zak says.

"And it means something to you. I'm not the right image for you," I say.

"What? No!" Zak's frown deepens. "I don't care about any of that. I just . . . I want this to be a secret for ourselves. So we have none of the stupid pressure that our family would obviously put on us. Do you really want our relationship to constantly be under a microscope? Our parents wanting us to get married at the drop of a hat? My parents wanting you to go into a career that they deem successful and appropriate? Because that's what things would be like if we told them."

"So, we're hiding our relationship because we don't want to be under a microscope?" I ask.

"Well, that's one of the reasons," Zak says huffily, though he doesn't launch into any one of his other purported reasons.

"I just sometimes feel like it would be easier if everything was out in the open. Even if we had to deal with some pressure and some scrutiny," I say. "Then . . . we could go on proper dates to anywhere. And you could hang out with my friends, and I could hang out with yours. And when we have a really busy week like I did, we could still figure out times to see each other."

"Is that really what you want?" Zak asks. His voice is somber in a way that worries me a little. What if I say yes and he agrees to it? I can hardly tell my parents about him when I'm only using him for my science experiment and plan to break up with him as soon as we're done with it. "Because I really thought we were on the same page here," Zak finishes before I have the chance to answer. He actually looks disappointed when he finally meets my eyes. Like he expected better from me—like he expected me to be the girl who would always be happy to be his secret.

I guess that *is* what he expected from me. The dutiful, secret girlfriend. It dawns on me that that was my role to perform all along. There was no scenario in which I would ever get to fill the position of Rani.

27

RANI

No matter how much I try to concentrate on my homework and studies, I can't help but keep looking over at the glass front door of the café, waiting for Meghna to make an appearance.

The café owner, a woman who looks to be in her fifties, with graying hair and a frown for a mouth, keeps casting me curious glances from the front counter as she sorts everything out. It's 4:00 p.m. on a Monday, so not exactly peak hour for any café, but it seems to be especially empty in this one. Apart from me, there's one other person who is hidden in the other corner of the café, having what seems to be a pretty terrible virtual job interview.

"Anything else for you, hon?" the café owner asks after I've been cradling my coffee for an hour too long. Her words are kind, but the frown is ever present.

"Um, I'll have another cappuccino?" I ask, though more caffeine is definitely not something I need.

I glance away from the door and toward my open math textbook. We have been studying algebra in class, and earlier today it seemed easy enough. But now my brain can barely make sense of the questions that Mr. Cook assigned us for homework.

I solve for *x*, but when I check the back of the textbook, I realize my answer is completely wrong. Letting out a breath of frustration, I cross out my entire solution.

"I'm pretty sure you just added something wrong." Meghna's voice comes from above me. When I look up, she is already sliding into the seat opposite me while shooting a grin at the café owner, who smiles back like her and Meghna are old friends.

"You can't even see what I'm working on from over there," I say.

"I have better eyesight than you think," Meghna says. "And anyway, the simplest answer is usually the correct one. I know you know how to do algebra, so instead of crossing out all your work, just try to figure out where you went wrong."

I look down at my notebook and trace back my work before finally finding where I added things up wrong. I draw an arrow from there to the bottom of my notebook and get the right answer.

"When did you become such a good teacher?" I ask, putting down my pen and closing my notebook. Even Mr. Cook, who is an actual, qualified teacher has no patience when someone gets the wrong answer. It doesn't help that Leaving Cert math is usually going a mile a minute and he can hardly afford to slow down just for a handful of struggling students.

Meghna just shrugs. "I help my friends with their homework sometimes. I'm kind of the math genius in our group. Or . . . the genius in general."

I let out a small laugh while the café owner brings over two cups of coffee. She sets down the cappuccino in front of me and a cup of black coffee in front of Meghna.

"Thanks, Aoibheann," she says, picking up the mug and taking a long swig. I study her instead of picking up my own mug, trying to gauge how things went with Zak. She doesn't look angry, really. She looks almost as she did that first day she showed up at my house: tired, defeated. Though definitely less determined and heartbroken.

"What?" Meghna asks, once she's put her drink down.

"Nothing." I shake my head and quickly glance away from her and toward my closed notebook. "How did it go?"

Meghna sighs. "It's done. Now I guess we just wait for our app to do its magic."

I thought she would gloat about how she succeeded where I failed. Maybe even tell me all the things I could have done instead that would have led to us succeeding even earlier. But she doesn't do any of those things. She just looks sad, even when we're right where we want to be.

"Was it weird to be around him again?" I ask.

"Yes," she says. "And it's going to be weirder because . . . I don't think either of us can break up with him yet."

"Why? We have what we needed him for, right?"

"Sure, but I was thinking about the digital therapist. Wouldn't the first thing someone wants to know about their situation be why they were cheated on in the first place?" she asks. "I mean, that's what I wanted to know. At first, I blamed you. Now I blame Zak, who I should have always blamed, obviously. But after talking to him, I feel like I understand it better."

"You do?" I can't help but wonder what actually happened during their date. What conversation they had that's making Meghna appear so somber.

"Yes, and I think that it should be part of our research. People are going to want more from our app than just to see why their partner is being super suspicious. They're going to want answers along with their support," Meghna says.

"How do we give them answers?" I ask.

"Well, for one, I think we need to add more depth to our story," Meghna says, sitting up and meeting my eyes. She's talking excitedly again, her previous moroseness slowly dissipating. Her eyes are alight with the possibility of our project, instead of our doomed romances. "Our story is what's going to push this project forward. You said your teacher liked that our project had a personal touch, so let's tell them everything. Not just what our app can do, but tell them the full story of its origin."

"Isn't that going to get too personal?" I ask. I can already imagine what people might think about my situation with Zak. People already have such narrow ideas of arranged marriages—not that our situation is even an arranged marriage in the traditional sense. But people never realize that there can be more nuance to marriage than their Western perception of it. That arrangements can look different. That there are so many instances where arranged marriages work, where people are happy. Zak and I just don't happen to be one of those instances.

"Maybe a little. But I think we can go broad, too. We should find statistics of cheating. Making it as broad as we make it narrow. Make it about everyone, but also about us," Meghna says. Everything she's saying makes sense, I'm just not sure how comfortable I feel about the whole thing. About sharing such intimate things with a panel of judges. With strangers. But I can tell that Meghna's been thinking about this. And we do need to flesh out our project if we want to have a shot at winning.

"Okay. I'm on board," I say.

Meghna eyes me for a moment, like she half expected me to refute her ideas. But then she nods her head and says, "Thanks." Strangely, I think this may be the most pleasant conversation we've had since we saw each other at Bhuiyan Uncle and Aunty's dawat a few weeks ago. I would feel happy about us kind of getting along for once instead of biting each other's heads off, except I know that the only reason Meghna isn't finding every chance to argue with me is because whatever happened with her and Zak—today and before—has hurt her on some deeper level that I can't even understand. He may have betrayed me, too, but from the look on Meghna's face, the change in her personality after finally spending time with him, it's obvious there's a difference. One that I can't quite understand.

So, instead of going any deeper into it, I decide to go back to the science.

"So, if we want to conduct wider research, we should probably do some qualitative studies," I say.

"I can look up statistics for cheating. See what's already out there," Meghna says.

"That'll be good, but we probably want to do our own research, too," I say. "Maybe . . . we could do a survey. It would make the research a little bit more limited, sure, but also it does narrow things down to people in our circumstances. Teens in Ireland, Irish schools, all of that." I pull out my laptop and begin typing it all up, but Meghna is silent on the other side of the booth.

"I don't know about that," Meghna says finally. "Wouldn't we need, like . . . permission and stuff for that?"

"I'm sure Mrs. Quinn would be happy to give us permission at my school," I say. "Your science teacher wouldn't help you out?"

"She would," Meghna says hesitantly. "But I don't know." She glances down at her half-empty coffee mug. "Wouldn't it be weird talking to people we already know about this stuff?"

"I mean, they don't have to know all the details of the project. Just the basics," I say. "And I think if we really want a proper investigation into Zak and cheating and all of that, we should also talk to other people. We can't be the only ones giving our account. It's biased and one-sided. Ideally we would have Zak's account, but that would prove to be difficult, so our friends and family will have to do."

"It's a case study," Meghna replies. She sits up straight, energy finally seeping back into her voice. And even though it's that familiar annoyed expression on her face, I can't help that it sends a spark of happiness through me to see her like this once more.

"Yes, but we need other things to balance out our case study. We don't want room for error or accusations of not doing our due diligence. I suggest we interview my friends and your friends, to give us a little more depth into romantic relationships in general and their perception of Zak. My friend Aarti is not really a relationship person, so I think she would be a great person to interview. What about your friends?" I ask.

"They're not really good examples. One of them has been in a long-term relationship for, like, forever, and the other one has never been in a relationship before."

"That's perfect!" I say. Meghna glances up with a frown that tells me she thinks this is decidedly not perfect. "I just mean . . . it gives us insight into different people. I think it will help us if we understand their perspectives and get our own data as well. It shouldn't begin and end with Zak."

"I'll think about it," Meghna grumbles. I realize this is probably the most I'm about to get out of her, so I leave it at that.

"I should get going," I say, stuffing my books into my backpack. "It's getting late, and my mom will definitely be annoyed if I'm not home by dinnertime."

"So you guys still love your family dinners, huh?" Meghna asks. There's a hint of a smile on her lips, almost like she's teasing me. I try to ignore the way that makes my heart skip a beat.

The two of us slide out of the booth and wave goodbye to Aoibheann as we head out the door.

"I don't know if I'd say I love it, but I would never turn down my mom's cooking," I say as we hover outside the front door. "Or your mom's, for that matter. Does she still make her famous chingri malai curry?"

"Only when Bhaiya is over." Meghna rolls her eyes.

"He moved out?" I ask. It makes sense that he did, but it's strange to think about Meghna and her family's lives changing in the past few years. In my mind, they've remained the same smiling family of four that always welcomed me into their home and made me feel like their own.

"About two years ago now. He got an apartment closer to town because it's closer to his work, but I swear he spends more time in our house than he does at his place," Meghna says with a sigh. But there's something fond in it.

"It sounds nice. I know I'd miss Pari and Neel if they ever moved out. Or if I did, I guess," I say. I can't imagine a life where Pari and Neel aren't causing trouble everywhere they go. "I should . . ." I motion toward the right side of the road. "My bus stop is just a few minutes' walk."

"I'll walk with you," Meghna says, surprising me. It seems she even surprised herself with the offer, because she hastily adds, "My house is that way, anyway."

The two of us fall into step toward my bus stop. We pass by trees that are quickly changing colors, their leaves a beautiful golden orange. I study those instead of thinking about Meghna and just how close the two of us are as we walk down the narrow sidewalk. In fact, our hands nearly brush. Each time I feel her presence beside me a little too close, I feel like my throat is closing up from nervousness.

"Do you think it'll snow this winter?" Meghna asks after our silence has gone on for a little too long. She's looking at a skeletal tree on the side of the road instead of at me.

I gulp to try to clear the dryness of my mouth and say, in a croaky voice, "I hope not."

"Seriously?" Meghna asks. "I thought you loved snow days." When we first moved here and our parents became friends, Meghna and I bonded over our shared excitement of the snow. And the few times when it did snow enough for schools to close, we found a way to make it to each other's houses, bundled up in warm jackets and scarves, ready for an adventure in the cold.

"Yeah, but it's different now," I say. I want to tell her it's because we're no longer friends. Because snow days now mean having to chaperone Pari and Neel. It means being holed up in the house for way too long under the scrutiny of my parents, with nowhere to go and no excuses to keep me busy. "I . . . don't want to miss out on too many classes for the Leaving Cert," I offer instead.

Meghna frowns but doesn't say anything else. We reach the bus stop finally, and she hovers while I check the timetable.

"It should be here in five minutes," I say.

"Okay." Meghna nods. She glances up the road like she's not sure if she should stay or go. "Well, thank you for coming today."

"I thought you were annoyed at me for coming," I say, trying to bite down a smile at the annoyance that immediately creeps into her face.

"I am, but I still appreciate it, I guess," Meghna says. She doesn't look at me as she does, almost like she hates that she's having to admit any of this. "I'll see you later."

She whips around and hurries up the road before I can say anything else. I watch her disappear from sight, willing my heart to not feel the things it's feeling. Because Meghna has already broken my heart once and she didn't even know it. I'm not sure I can afford to get it broken again.

28

MEGHNA

Somehow, over the course of dozens of text messages and even a few phone calls, Rani convinces me that the next step for our project is interviewing our friends. No matter how many times I try to distract her by asking for updates about what our app gathered from Zak's phone, she keeps insisting that she needs time to pull data and interviewing people is what we have to do in the interim. Which leads to a strange conversation with Janella and Yemi about what our project is actually about, and a few raised eyebrows. Still, they agree to the interviews. And that's how, the next Saturday, I find myself sitting in a café with Janella and Yemi, waiting for Rani to show up.

"I can't believe we're finally about to meet your archnemesis!" Janella says with a little too much excitement.

"She's not my archnemesis," I say defensively, even though I'm pretty sure I have called her that at least a few times throughout the years I've known Yemi and Janella. "We're trying to be on better terms," I admit begrudgingly. It's a little strange just how easy falling back into old habits with Rani has been. As much as I want to be annoyed when she sends me a text about the project or calls me out of the blue, I feel a tingle of warmth every time she does. Like even if I don't want to remember our previous friendship, somehow my body remembers it. Maybe even longs for it.

And it's difficult to stay that pointedly mad at Rani when there's someone much, much worse to focus all my anger on: Zak. Ever since our "date" on Monday, I haven't been able to stop thinking about him. But not in the way it used to be. How I used to think about him fondly, even imagine our futures together. The day I'd finally tell my family all about him.

Now, I think about him with a strange fire in my belly. Anger niggles at me every time he sends me a text, and more often than not I leave it unread for hours, if not days, letting him stew in the silence and hopefully wonder what exactly has changed.

"She's late," I say with a frown, checking my phone to see it's been exactly ten minutes since Rani was supposed to meet us here. The waitress comes around at that exact moment, a hesitant smile on her lips.

"Ready to order?" she asks.

"We're still waiting on someone," Janella responds, shooting back a smile of her own. The waitress doesn't seem too impressed with just how much time we're taking, and from the queue of people standing outside and the filled-up restaurant, I'm not exactly surprised. It's Saturday afternoon in Dublin city center, so most places are booked and busy.

"I'm sure she'll be here soon," Janella says reassuringly to me and Yemi, as if Rani is one of her best friends or something.

"Hm," is all Yemi says. They've been the most hesitant about everything to do with this project since I confided in them and Janella about it all—leaving out a few important details, of course.

"I still don't really understand how this project is good for you when you've just broken up with Zak," Yemi says. "It can't be healthy to think about cheating right after you've been cheated on."

"It's an outlet," Janella offers before I say anything, which I'm grateful for. "I mean, it's like your acting is an outlet for you."

"Yeah, but I'm channeling my emotions into acting. You can't channel your emotions into . . . a science project about cheating," Yemi scoffs.

They both turn to me, as if to solve their argument.

"Yes," I say. "It *is* an outlet. It's fun to figure out the science behind it rather than focus on my own specific situation."

"Fun?" Yemi raises an eyebrow but leaves it at that. "How did Zak take the breakup anyway?"

"Um, he . . . I . . . ghosted him," I say, which isn't a complete lie. I have been ghosting him a little.

"That's how you're going to end it?" Yemi asks.

"Does he deserve any better?"

"I was thinking he deserves worse," Yemi mumbles.

Thankfully, before they can ask me any more questions that make my palms sweat, the door to the restaurant flies open and Rani stumbles inside. She spots us in the corner almost immediately and waves, nearly dropping the laptop in her hands as she does.

"That's Rani?" Yemi asks with a frown. I'm not sure what to read into that question, but they definitely don't sound impressed.

Well, without her school uniform, Rani does look a little worse for wear. She has on an oversize sweater, and her long black hair, which is usually perfectly brushed and left loose by her sides, is tied up into a messy ponytail. Still, Rani pulls off the disheveled look with a little too much poise as she approaches our table. If I had thrown on an oversize sweater and put my hair into a messy ponytail, I'd probably look like a lump of clay.

"Hey," Rani says, sidling into the empty seat next to Janella and giving me a grin. "Sorry I'm late. I got a little caught up with doing work for our project."

"You're only, like, ten minutes late," Janella chimes in. "Hi, I'm Janella. And this is Yemi."

Yemi passes Rani a smile that looks more like a grimace than anything else, though Rani's expression doesn't give away if she's noticed.

"It's nice to meet you both," she says. She places her laptop on the counter between us and opens it. "I hope Meghna's filled you both in on everything, because then we can get started with—"

The waitress clearing her throat interrupts Rani.

"Ready to order?" she asks, her smile a little clipped this time.

"Yes, we're ready," I say, worried that she's about to kick us out, since we've been here for way too long without ordering. "I'll go first." I shove a menu toward Rani as I rattle off my orders. By the time the waitress gets around to Rani, she thankfully seems to have made up her mind about what she wants, too.

"What was her problem?" Rani asks.

"There's just too many people here, and they've been turning some customers away," Janella says.

Rani glances around like she's noticing for the first time just how busy this place is. How she didn't notice as she shoved her way inside is truly a wonder.

"Do you think they'll be annoyed about my laptop?" she asks, looking at the beat-up old device like it's the most precious thing in the world.

"I'm sure it'll be fine," Janella says. "Continue!"

"Okay, so, um. I'm sure Meghna has filled you in on everything, and we're just really looking to interview you, I guess, about your experiences with relationships. Or, like, the lack of." Her eyes flick up for a moment to Yemi, whose eyes narrow into a glare. Thankfully they decide to glare at the table in front of us instead of at Rani or—the person they should be glaring at—me. "It's just to add depth to our project and our case study."

"Case study?" Yemi asks. "What's your case study?"

"Well, it's—"

"Just all the data we're going to be gathering," I cut in before Rani can say anything else.

"You know that's not what a case study is, right?" Yemi asks, turning to me with a frown.

I wave off their question and face Rani instead. "I think you should interview Yemi first. They have to go to rehearsal right after this."

"Rehearsal?" Rani asks, curiosity piqued.

"It's for a theater production of *Hamlet*," Yemi says, with a little too much flair.

"An amateur theater production," I add.

"For school?" Rani asks. "I didn't know schools put on *Hamlet*."

"No, it's a theater group that I'm a part of. We put on two shows a year, so this December we're doing *Hamlet*. And then next May it will be *The Mousetrap*."

"Wow." Rani's eyebrows rise as if she's actually impressed. "That's amazing. I didn't even know amateur theater productions like that existed."

"We don't like the term *amateur*, which I've said many times," Yemi says, shooting me a glare this time. "But yes, it's usually just friends and family in attendance, but they love it. We've kind of outdone ourselves with *Hamlet* this year."

Janella and I quickly nod our heads in agreement, less because we agree and more because we don't want Yemi's wrath focused on us. Not that Yemi's acting is not great, but the rest of their group lacks their commitment, and often trickle in and out of practice as they please.

"Well, we can definitely interview you first," Rani says. She logs into her laptop while I take out my phone to record.

"So, we're working on an app, but it has a digital therapist aspect to it that we're trying to put together," Rani begins. "We're really trying to tell a full story. About us, and also about cheating and relationships. So can you state your age, and maybe tell us briefly about your experience with romantic relationships?"

"Sure," Yemi says, though they still don't look particularly happy about any of it. "I'm seventeen years old, and I'm currently in fifth year. I don't have much of an experience with relationships. I mean, I've liked a few people here and there, and been on a few dates, but it's all been a bit low-key. No long-term relationships or . . . relationships at all, really."

Rani quickly types into her laptop. "So, have you ever cheated on anyone or been cheated on?"

"No, to both."

"Do you know someone who has been cheated on or who has cheated?"

Yemi glances over at me. "Yes . . ."

"Which one?"

"Cheated on, I guess."

"And what was the fallout of that? And why do you think it even happened?"

Yemi frowns. "Because the guy was an asshat? I don't know."

Rani glances up from her laptop, a small smile flickering on her lips as she looks from me to Yemi. I don't know why, but I feel a pull of pride toward them. As much as they hate the idea of meeting Rani and doing this interview, I know they're putting up with all of it because of me.

"Okay, and did you think he was an asshat when you first met him?" Rani asks.

"Well, I never met him, so no."

Rani's eyebrows furrow, but she continues typing. "Did you think he was an asshat from what the person you know told you about him?"

"No. I didn't think he was one until he cheated, I guess. And then I knew for sure he was."

"So, before he cheated, what did you think of him?"

Yemi hesitates for a moment. "I guess it's difficult to say because I never met him, and everything was secondhand information. But he seemed . . . I don't know, like he could be the right person for my friend. He seemed like a good guy."

"So why do you think he would have cheated?" Rani asks finally.

"I'm not sure. Maybe I didn't have the right version of him. Or he was just pretending to be someone he wasn't. Maybe the signs were there that he was a cheater and I just missed it."

Or I missed it, I think, clenching my fists as Yemi continues. If I'm learning anything from this conversation with Yemi, it's that I was the gullible person. I brought him into my life and felt it was okay to keep him at bay from everything I knew— my friends, my family, all of it. And I thought the fact that he was doing it was some kind of a favor to me. When all along, he was just duping me.

And I fell for it all.

29

RANI

Our interview with Janella goes about the same as the one with Yemi. Between our food and the uncomfortable conversation, I wouldn't exactly call the interviews a success, but it's the closest to it that we could get.

After the interviews, Yemi heads to their rehearsal and Janella for a date with her girlfriend, leaving Meghna and I alone to go over everything. As our table is cleared up, we order more coffees while the waitress frowns us down.

"So, how come you didn't tell them everything about our project?" I ask once the waitress leaves us be.

Meghna, for once, looks a little flustered. She glances down at the table instead of at me, and I can see a flush of red on her cheeks.

"I just didn't think it was that important," she says with a shrug. It's clear that she did think it was that important, if she went out of her way to lie to her best friends.

"You think they wouldn't like the whole revenge idea?" I ask.

Meghna looks up at that, with a frown. Almost like she hadn't expected me to be so blunt with my question.

She sighs. "Maybe Yemi would, but not Janella. And I don't know, Yemi and Janella are best friends, so I feel like if I tell Yemi, Janella will find out, too."

"I thought you were all best friends?" I ask, my brows furrowing.

"We are, but . . ." Meghna shrugs again. "Yemi and Janella are closer, kind of. They've gone to school together since primary school, so that's how long they've been friends. I'm like . . . the new one in their midst. Not that I ever really feel it, but sometimes . . . I don't know."

I guess I can understand that in a way. Yemi and Janella are friends the way Meghna and I used to be. When we went to school together, lived in the same neighborhood. When there were no secrets between us, and we were joined at the hip.

They're what we would be if something hadn't wedged its way between our friendship.

"They seem like good friends. To you," I say. "I think even if they had their hesitation, they wouldn't talk you out of doing this. It's what he deserves . . . right?"

Meghna holds my gaze for a moment. "Right. It's what he deserves." She nods. "I should get going." She begins to put away her things and pull on her coat while I do the same.

"Are you getting the bus home?" I ask.

"Yeah, from Bachelors Walk," she says.

"Let me at least walk you to the bus stop. I can finally tell you what our app has gathered from Zak's phone so far."

Meghna's eyes light up at that, and, as much as I wish it was because of my offer to walk with her, I know it's because she's finally getting the data she's been begging me to tell her about.

"Okay, let's go," she says, trying to sound less enthusiastic than she is while I try to ignore the flutter it sends through my stomach.

We fall into step easily. It's almost like hanging out together has become a routine. The silence that washes over us is not uncomfortable anymore. It's almost familiar. Like the days before our parents fell out with each other.

"So, um. The stuff I've gotten from Zak has been things we could have used to figure out he was cheating, if we didn't already know. He texted you about going on another date and was trying to be flirtatious," I say, not mentioning how his texts have been getting further and further apart now that Meghna's have become one-worded, if she even bothers to reply. "And a few texts to me about our families. I've been trying to text back and talk about our arrangement, and he's taken the bait on that."

"That's good. So . . . we have what we needed from the app, right? It proves that you can catch that someone is cheating with it," Meghna says. "All we have to do is polish it. I can get started on the design elements. I already have an idea of what the icon can look like, and I think the interface should be clean but still warm and inviting."

"It would be good to get a little more data. Something that *really* seals the deal about his cheating. And we still have a little bit of work to do with the coding. I've been trying to work on a code for getting data from his digital footprint. I'm thinking anything that is linked to his accounts. That means that even if you can't manage to install the app into your partner's phone, it can still help you. Maybe if you work on the design, I work on this code, and we can meet up next week to—"

"I can't." Meghna cuts me off. She stops in her tracks so suddenly that I'm halfway down the street before I even realize. I backtrack, a frown on my lips as I study the furrow between her brows.

"Why not? I know you're busy with school and everything, but we have to have everything reviewed before we submit it, and we're already in October, so—"

"That's not what it is." Meghna's eyes are downcast as she says it, the furrow between her brow deepening. She takes a sharp breath before she finally glances up at me, like she's made a decision on something.

"Look, I can't . . . keep doing this."

My stomach twists, my heart hammering so loudly in my chest all of a sudden that I'm sure Meghna can hear it. Parisa was right—Meghna is doing this again. Without ever even explaining why she did it in the first place.

"You can't . . . I mean, it was your idea to do this project, and I thought you wanted to get into the EYSE, but if you're not—"

"No, that's not it," Meghna cuts me off yet again, shaking her head. "I can't keep meeting up at these cafés and getting food and dessert and whatever. It was fine before, but now . . . honestly, I can't really afford it. It's been a bit too much."

"Oh." Relief floods me. Meghna isn't ending our friendship again with no explanations. "You could have just said. We could have met at my house. Your friends would have been welcome there."

"Or we could have met at mine," Meghna presses a little defensively, like I dismissed that her home was an option.

"Or yours," I agree.

"I just can't even do the Café Nightingale thing anymore. I know we used to hang out there all the time, but . . . it's just . . . nowadays it's . . ." I can feel that telling me any of this is making her uncomfortable. She's barely looking me in the eyes. I don't think I've ever seen Meghna at a loss for words like this before.

"It doesn't matter. I like your mom's food way better than the food they have at any café." I shrug.

Meghna finally meets my eyes, but it's like she's studying me. Trying to see if there's judgment hidden behind my words.

"So, maybe sometime after school next week, you could come to mine," Meghna says. "And we can fill each other in on what we've been working on and put it all together."

"Sure," I say.

"In the meanwhile, you should keep an eye on the data you get from Zak." Meghna is all business again as she begins walking toward the bus stop once more. Almost like the vulnerable conversation we had just moments ago never even happened. It takes me a minute to catch up with her—both in walking pace, but also in terms of our conversation.

Maybe, all this time, I've been approaching my friendship with Meghna all wrong. Maybe everything that happened and who she is now is less to do with me and more to do with her. To do with all the things in her life that had to change overnight, which I never even had a clue about. And maybe I still don't. I just need her to invite me into those vulnerable parts of herself once again. And maybe today was a glimpse into that.

30

MEGHNA

For some reason, Rani stays on my mind long after I board the bus, waving goodbye to her through the window. Her in her slightly oversize sweater, her long, black hair in a ponytail, a smile lighting up her eyes. I can't get rid of that image, try as I might.

It doesn't help that when we get to school on Monday, the first thing Yemi and Janella want to talk about by the lockers is Rani.

"You know, I had this idea of Rani in my head from all the ways you've described her, but she was really different from how I imagined her," Janella comments thoughtfully.

"Yeah, honestly. I thought she would have devil's horns or something," Yemi adds.

Janella turns to her with a small glare. "Come on, she was nice."

"Yeah, but it was all fake. Right?" Yemi asks. "I mean, you say all the time how fake she is. She's saying one thing and meaning another. It's all about getting the attention on herself."

"Right," I say, though my words sound lackluster. The truth is that for a long time I've thought that Rani must be like that. But so much of it was because of everything that happened with my parents. How we were completely shunned from the Bangladeshi community we knew because Abbu lost his job and rumors of fraud and embezzlement spread around like wildfire. Sometimes, we were invited to places just so people had something to gossip about. Other times, we weren't invited at all. Neither was exactly desirable. Nothing was like it once used to be, when people respected us.

We expected the Choudhurys would be on our side, but suddenly they wanted nothing to do with us, either.

Rani was just part and parcel of that. What made it worse was how everybody held her up on a pedestal, even my parents. Even after everything.

I thought it must have meant Rani was fake. That everything about her perfect life, perfect grades, perfect everything was just an illusion. But maybe I was wrong. Maybe I misjudged her. Maybe the things she says aren't hiding something more malicious underneath.

"That didn't sound very convincing," Yemi says. Instead of looking at them, I open my locker and begin sorting through my stuff, as if I'm looking for a book. Even though all the books I need for my morning classes are already in my backpack.

"I just feel like, she's helping me out with this project. I wouldn't have gotten the opportunity to do it if she didn't agree to let me help her. And she could have called it quits when things weren't working out at the beginning," I say. And it's all true, I realize as I say it. Other than revenge on Zak, what exactly is Rani getting out of this partnership that she wouldn't have otherwise? I guess my science skills are nothing to sneeze at, but I doubt Rani sees it that way.

"I don't know. It seems to me like she has ulterior motives. I don't trust her," Yemi says. When I finally close my locker and glance at them again, they have their arms crossed as if nobody is about to change their mind about it.

Janella just rolls her eyes at Yemi's antics, as she often does. "I liked Rani. And I don't think she has ulterior motives. But also, nobody's telling you to become best friends with her. But if she's working with Meghna, it's good that you two are getting along. That's all I'm really trying to say."

"Yeah, I mean . . . maybe Rani isn't the worst person in the universe, like I once thought she was," I admit hesitantly, as much as I hate ever admitting that I'm wrong about something. "But maybe Yemi's right. Maybe there's still more she's hiding under the surface. Some ulterior motive."

Janella sighs, like she can't deal with the two of us today, but then the morning bell rings. Lockers begin slamming shut as people start shuffling toward their first classes of the day.

Janella and Yemi wave goodbye as they head to their geography class, while I make my way to art. Still unfortunately thinking about Rani.

BHAIYA'S CAR IS PARKED OUTSIDE THE SCHOOL GATES AT THE END of the day. I slip out my phone and see half a dozen missed calls and a few texts from him to say that he'll be picking me up after school. So I wave goodbye to Yemi and Janella and climb into the passenger seat.

"Why are you here?" I ask.

"Nice to see you, too," Bhaiya grumbles as he starts the car up and begins to pull out of his parking space. "I just got off work early and I was going home anyway, so I thought I'd pick you up for once, instead of you taking the bus."

"Thanks," I mumble.

He glances over at me and heaves a sigh. "So, you're doing better? After the whole junior science project stuff?"

I shrug. "Yeah." I wish I could tell him about Zak. That would explain why everything hit me so hard that day. It would make me seem a little less strange. Before I found out Zak was cheating, I had considered telling Bhaiya about him on multiple occasions. I knew he would understand, and he would keep my secret as long as I wanted him to. But Zak talked me out of it each time. I guess he knew it would be a gateway to telling Ammu and Abbu, too.

Now there's no point telling him about Zak, even if it would make everything easier to explain away.

"Good, because you know it wasn't your last shot. You have next year to still make it into the European competition. And even after that, you have countless opportunities to make a difference in science. You know, when you're young it seems like your entire life is contained into these small spaces, like school or the young scientist competition, but . . . when you grow up you see how it's about so much more," Bhaiya says. He's looking at the road and nodding his head like he's very proud of this wisdom he's spouting.

"You're not that much older than me," I say. "I don't think you've seen the big, wide world yet when you've barely ever even stepped foot outside of Ireland."

Bhaiya gives me a quick glare out of the corner of his eye, but I can tell he's not really annoyed.

"I'm just saying, once I went to university, and then started work, I realized the world was a lot bigger than I thought it was before. When I was in school, I would have never thought I could do something like work at a start-up like this, but . . ." He shrugs. "I'm just saying, sometimes you want something so bad, and it feels terrible that you never get it. But . . . usually there's something better out there. So whatever happened with the young scientist project—"

"I'm going to the European competition," I interrupt before Bhaiya can get too high on his own sage advice.

Bhaiya's eyebrows furrow, but he doesn't look at me. He's always been a careful driver. Extra careful when I'm in the car with him.

"I thought that you didn't get a chance at it?" he asks.

"I didn't, technically," I say. "But Rani asked me to help her with her project. Team up. So, we're doing it together."

Now Bhaiya looks really confused. "Rani who?"

"Rani Choudhury, who else?"

"The girl you have despised for the past five years?"

"*Despised* is a really strong word."

"That's literally the word you've used on multiple occasions."

"Maybe she's not that bad," I say with a sigh. "I mean, we're working together. We have been for the past few weeks, and it's been going . . . well, I think."

Bhaiya frowns. "You've been working together for a few weeks? Should I check and make sure she's still alive?"

"I wouldn't ever murder Rani," I say defensively, though I'm sure I've joked about it on a lot of occasions. "She's not *that* bad. And we're older now, and I guess she's different, and not . . . as annoying as she used to be."

"She was never as annoying as you," Bhaiya says.

"You think that because I'm your sister, and she's not."

"She was kind of like my sister. I mean, I saw her enough. She would annoy me enough," Bhaiya says. "Honestly, I'm glad you guys are working together. I never really understood why you stopped talking to her."

"Seriously?" I ask, crossing my arms.

Bhaiya shrugs as our house comes into view and he pulls into the driveway.

"I mean, you two were joined at the hip, and then suddenly you never wanted to talk to her again," Bhaiya says. He turns off the engine but doesn't make any effort to get out of the car. And even though I desperately want to end this conversation and stop talking about Rani, I don't, either.

"Her parents were being awful. And . . . everyone was being awful. And Rani was just a part of that," I say.

"Because of her parents?" Bhaiya asks.

"Yes. And because she . . . never said anything. Or did anything," I say finally. That was the biggest form of betrayal. "She was okay with her parents bad-mouthing Ammu and Abbu, bad-mouthing us. Treating us like we were worth nothing. That's not friendship. It's a friendship of convenience if someone can throw you under the bus so easily."

"She was a kid, Meghna," Bhaiya says. He's looking at me now with sympathy in his eyes, but I don't know if it's for me or for her.

"Yeah, but so was I."

"Not everybody is as loudmouthed as you," Bhaiya says.

I roll my eyes. "Whatever. Point is, I guess Rani is not that bad, and we're seeing how things go. I'm not ready to be best friends again, but maybe I don't constantly think about ways to destroy her anymore."

But even as I say that, a twinge of guilt twists in my gut. If I go through with my plan at the EYSE, maybe I *am* still plotting to destroy Rani. At least, I'm planning to undermine her and win at her expense. But after everything, isn't that what she deserves?

Somehow, no matter how much I try to convince myself of that, I can't match up the Rani Choudhury who exists in my head—the one who deserves it—and the real-life one I've been seeing a little too much of these days.

31

RANI

Ever since last weekend when Meghna admitted that she couldn't keep meeting up at cafés, it feels like something between us has changed. I can't really put my finger on it, but it's like before she didn't trust me, and now she does.

We text back and forth almost every day. Most of it is about the project and her progress—or lack of—in trying to learn to code, but Meghna throws in the occasional tidbit about her brother, or her parents, even Yemi and Janella. It's a glimpse into her life that I wouldn't have been allowed before.

I guess it also helps that the project hasn't hit any snags. Meghna emails me her art for the UI, and I code it all into the app easily. We now have a unique icon, and a landing page that's as beautiful as it is user-friendly. The landing page is simple and efficient; it opens up to a light blue page with a button linking to devices. Clicking on it opens up a list of different apps that are being traced on this device: WhatsApp, text messages, Instagram; and clicking on those takes the user directly to the data, all laid out in an easily digestible way. Below that is a scroll wheel of advice and questions about cheating and relationships, each with a unique icon, courtesy of Meghna. If a user clicks on one of these, they're taken to the digital therapist.

"We need data from surveys for the basis of the digital therapist," I tell Meghna over the phone later that week as I'm on the bus home from school. "I spoke to Mrs. Quinn, and she said that the two of us can go around during last class on Thursday and survey everyone we can within that one-hour period. What do you think?"

"I can do that, I'll just need to get permission from my teacher," Meghna says. "And we'll have to finish up the questions for the survey." We've spent the past few days passing potential questions back and forth, but we definitely don't have anything solid yet.

"I can type them up and ask Mrs. Quinn to make a bunch of copies of them. So . . . you just have to show up," I say.

"To your school . . ." Meghna says a little morosely.

"Are you not a fan of my school or something?"

"No, it's not that. It's just weird, you know. Because I was supposed to go there. Wear your prissy uniform, eat at your prissy cafeteria," Meghna says jokingly, but there's a hint of something behind her words. Regret? Longing?

"Our school uniforms are not that different from yours," I point out. Our colors are a deep violet, while theirs are navy blue.

"Whatever, seems different enough to me. But I guess I'll see you and your prissy uniform on Thursday," Meghna says.

That's how I find myself making my way toward the front entrance of the school when the bell for the last class of the day rings. Meghna is standing by the sidewalk, staring up at the building with a strange expression on her face.

"Hey," I say. Meghna turns away from the school, and her face breaks out into a smile when she sees me.

"Hi." I try to ignore the flurry of butterflies in my stomach as I usher her indoors and away from the October chill in the air.

"Did you find the place okay?" I find myself asking, even though the words sound strange on my lips. Formal. I just don't know how I'm supposed to talk to Meghna here. Before everything blew up with our families, we used to dream about this place. What it would be like, whether we would share classes, how our lockers would be next to each other, and we would spend our lunchtimes hanging out. It's strange to think of that Meghna and this Meghna at the same time.

"It's kind of difficult to miss. It's a big school," Meghna says.

"Right. Well, Mrs. Quinn said she's informed all the teachers we might be coming around and they'll help us out. We just have to go in, introduce ourselves, and tell them why they're doing the survey," I explain, digging into my backpack and pulling out a stack of papers. I hand half of them to Meghna.

"I would suggest splitting up, but I feel like private school kids might throw their pens at me or something if they see my disheveled public-school uniform," Meghna says.

"We'll go together, don't worry," I say, leading her into our first classroom.

Doing the surveys is easy, thanks to Mrs. Quinn. We knock on the doors of each of the classrooms, and the teachers pass our surveys out to be filled. It's going through all the answers after school that's the problem, as we realize when Meghna and I are sitting with stacks of papers in one of the empty classrooms.

"I think all the answers this person gave are from the plot of *John Tucker Must Die*," Meghna says, pointing to one of the survey sheets. Sure enough, the answers about cheating do seem to have an uncanny resemblance to that movie. I throw it into our discard pile, which is growing a little too large with all the movie references and joke answers that people have filled their surveys in with.

"Maybe we'll have better luck with your school," I say with a sigh. I've just picked up another survey when someone drops into the chair next to me.

"Need help?" Aarti asks with a grin.

"I thought you didn't want to hear about my science project," I say. "And shouldn't you be on your way home?"

"I couldn't pass up the chance to meet the famous Meghna," Aarti says, glancing at where Meghna is sat.

Meghna just considers her coolly. "I'm famous?"

"No!" I cut in before Aarti can say something that exposes a little too much. "I mean, she just knows you because I mentioned we're working on this project together."

"Right. It's nice to meet you . . ."

"Aarti," Aarti offers.

"Right. Rani mentioned we could interview you for the project," Meghna says, and from her grin I can tell she's eager to get started on that.

"I can go through the data, if you want to talk to Aarti," I say. "It might be easier, anyway. It will save us from having to set something up later."

"Okay." Meghna squares her shoulders like she means business and whips out her phone to take notes. "So, did you meet Zak?"

"Unfortunately," Aarti deadpans.

"You didn't like him?" Meghna asks.

"You can't ask leading questions," I interrupt, even though I'm supposed to be typing up the answers from the surveys.

"This is not a courtroom, Rani," Meghna says with a scowl.

"Yes, but you can't lead your interview, either. It creates bias."

"I won't ask leading questions if you'll stop backseat interviewing," Meghna says.

"Fine," I say.

Meghna shoots me a satisfied smile before turning back to Aarti. "So, what were your initial thoughts about Zak?"

"Well, I can't even remember the first time I met him. I think it might have been before Zak and Rani had their whole setup going. I don't remember ever liking him. He's too . . . full of himself, always was," Aarti says.

"And your final thoughts on him?" Meghna asks.

"After what he did?" Aarti scoffs. "Is there a stronger word for hate?"

"Detest? Loathe? Abhor?" Meghna asks.

I have to stop myself from interjecting. Instead, I glance down at the survey that has been in my hand for the past few minutes. Thankfully, it was filled by one of the students who actually took it seriously.

Still, even as I type up the rest of my answers, I can't help but be pulled into Meghna and Aarti's conversation. I've never known Meghna to be so focused before. She asks Aarti question after question—about Zak, Aarti's own relationships, even questions about me, which make my face flush with embarrassment. Meghna quickly types the answers into her phone.

It seems like, ever since her date with Zak, something has shifted in Meghna. It's different from the usual fire that fuels her, the one that makes her into the passionate person that she always has been. There's a sadness hidden underneath it all, or maybe it's a thirst for revenge that she's never had before for anything else. I'm not sure if it's a good thing or a bad thing, though. I'm not sure what I should think of this new Meghna.

Aarti almost looks impressed by the time Meghna is done with her.

"I have to get going," Aarti finally says. "It's getting late, and I think the after-school activities will be ending soon, and they'll be kicking us out at that point. But it was nice meeting you, Meghna." And she actually seems to mean it. I have to stop myself from beaming at Meghna—Aarti is not exactly the easiest person to impress, and there are not a lot of people she would consider her friends.

"I'll text you later, Rani," she says before getting up and heading out of the classroom. Meghna turns to me as soon as Aarti's out of sight. "I like her. Finally, someone who had the right idea of Zak all along."

"We can't use a lot of her interview," I say.

"Sure we can. It's part of our case study—part of your personal story. She's your best friend," Meghna says as she begins to pack up. I try to ignore how strange it feels to have Meghna refer to someone else as my best friend.

"Thanks for coming today. I know it was a little weird being here," I say instead.

Meghna shrugs like it's no big deal, but from her tone before, from her expression when I saw her today, I know that it meant something to her. That she was thinking of how the two of us used to talk about coming here, too. "It was good that I came. I mean, I feel like we finally have basically everything we need to submit our project. I can probably get Yemi and Janella to help me do the survey in our school next week. Then we just gather up the data from all the surveys, get some more from Zak. Input everything into the app to create a demo presentation. And then Amsterdam." Meghna grins.

"And then Amsterdam," I say with a smile.

"WHY ARE YOU IN SUCH A GOOD MOOD THIS WEEK?" PARI ASKS while we're getting ready for a dawat at Mehreen Aunty and Hasan Uncle's house that evening.

"Just having a good week." I shrug nonchalantly while applying a coat of pink liquid lipstick.

Pari frowns. "Normally, this is the stage of the night when you're annoyed that Ammu's making you dress up and wear all that makeup."

I shrug again, because for once I'm not bothered by the makeup or the fact that the salwar kameez Ammu asked me to wear is a little too light for the cold weather we're having, while also too itchy because of all the gems embroidered on it. And it's definitely not my style of salwar kameez.

"Things with the science project are just going well, and . . . I guess I just feel like maybe we have a real shot at winning," I say. And it's true. With our data, all the research we've already done, and Meghna's charm and passion, I'm sure that we can awe the judges at the competition. We just have to sit down and pull everything together.

"The one you're doing with Meghna?" Pari asks.

"Yes, but . . . she's just my partner in it," I say, trying to keep the smile off my face.

Pari just sighs, shaking her head. She finishes her own makeup—a light layer of foundation, a touch of blush and lip gloss that's barely visible—makeup that Ammu definitely won't notice.

When we get to the dawat I'm surprised to see Sardar Uncle and Aunty pulling up in their car but no sign of Zak.

"Assalamu alaikum!" Sardar Aunty exclaims when she sees us. We all greet her with our salams.

"No Zakkariyah today?" Abbu asks as we approach the front door. I'm glad I'm not the only one thinking it.

"No, he says he has to work on his science project," Aunty says. "He's obsessed with it, it's all he's been working on for the past few weeks."

"I just don't understand why he can't do it at home. You would think doing coding and apps, he just needs his computer," Uncle complains, though it doesn't sound like he minds it too much.

"But he says he has to be in the lab at school, getting help from his teachers to do it," Aunty says with a sigh.

I frown, exchanging a glance with Pari, though from her confused expression it doesn't seem like she understands why I don't believe a word of what Zak has been telling his parents. There's no way his school lab is open *now* on a Thursday evening, and no way that his teachers would stay behind so late to help him with a science project that has very little to do with the school directly.

So where exactly is Zak tonight? And why is he lying to his parents?

I make a mental note to ask Meghna about it later, feeling a little thrill run through me that I have a legitimate reason to talk to her again so soon. Maybe I can even excuse myself and text her about it during this dawat instead of entertaining the aunties all night long.

My dreams, though, are short-lived. As soon as we're invited inside, Pari and Neel rush upstairs to find the other kids, but Ammu pulls me into the sitting room to greet the other aunties, and once they start launching questions at me, it's difficult to find a reason to excuse myself without coming off as rude.

"We heard that you got into the European science competition," one of the aunties says, though she doesn't sound impressed so much as annoyed, which I don't quite understand.

"Yes," Ammu says, beaming at me with pride for once. I feel a strange glow of warmth at that. At least there's something that makes my parents proud of me, other than being with Zak. "She's been trying to get in for so long. And if she wins, she gets to shadow some real scientists."

The aunty who asked the question purses her lips, like this may be one of the worst things she's ever heard. "Ammara Bhabi," she says, addressing Ammu. "You know, those competitions are full of boys, no? You're really going to let her go off to some European country with no supervision? Do an internship with no supervision? All surrounded by men?"

My stomach drops at her questions. I feel a pinch of anger making its way through me but don't let it show. Instead, I keep my smile intact even though I don't even know who this aunty is. If I've ever even met her before, it's been brief exchanges of salam. And now she thinks she can tell my parents what I'm allowed to do or not do?

"Well, there'll be teachers with her," Ammu says, though her beam of pride has completely dropped. "And so many other students. There are girls there, too. And Zak will be there, he's competing, too."

"You have to think about these things early on, Ammara Bhabi," the aunty continues like Ammu hasn't even spoken. "Rani isn't a child anymore. She's almost an adult."

Bhuiyan Aunty, who has been quiet until now, nods in agreement. "Rani has always been such a smart girl, but you know, working in technology and surrounded by men . . . that's something you have to discourage her from doing."

They're all speaking about me like I'm not even in the room. Like I'm not sitting right here in front of them.

I clear my throat to get their attention, but nobody even bats an eyelash in my direction.

"Um, Aunty?" I say. Finally everyone turns to look at me. My face is heating up, and I hate how meek I sound. "There's a lot of women in tech now, and the European Young Scientist Exhibition is like . . . a once-in-a-lifetime experience. Some of the kids who have won have gone on to work in amazing things: developing new technology, medical breakthroughs, one of the winners from five years ago just joined the UN as part of the Environment Programme. And Zak will be there, too, competing."

"That's all great, Rani," Bhuiyan Aunty says, though her firm voice doesn't make it seem like it's very great at all. "But how can you be a part of the UN Environment Programme and raise a family?"

"Have you even talked to Zak about all of this?" the other aunty asks. "How does he feel about you competing with him? How will he feel if you win, and he loses? How will that affect your relationship?"

My face is red-hot now, though I'm not sure if it's from anger or embarrassment. "I mean, Zak isn't—"

"We'll definitely have to think a lot more about all of this," Ammu interrupts before I can say anything else. "The Sardars have always been happy about Rani being so dedicated to her education, but nobody wants a girl who is *more* educated than her husband."

The other aunties nod in agreement, clearly happy Ammu is taking their ridiculous suggestions seriously. I want to say more, but I don't even know what to say. What might convince them that there's so much more to me than a comparison to Zak, or any man, really. That Zak shouldn't be the barometer for my success, and he definitely shouldn't stop me from going after what I want.

But the conversation moves on swiftly to other topics—upcoming weddings, pregnancies, and how Bhuiyan Aunty got snubbed from a dawat last week. I just sit there, hoping that these aunties didn't just ruin my shot at everything I've been dreaming about for years.

32

RANI

Ammu doesn't mention anything about the European Young Scientist Exhibition on the car ride home or the next morning. I don't want to get my hopes up, but I'm optimistic that her silence means that she didn't really pay as much attention to what the aunties were saying as I thought.

It's the last day of school before the midterm break and the day of Halloween, which means everybody comes to school dressed up for the costume contest. There are costumes ranging from Marvel characters and Disney princesses, all the way to cat ears. Aarti is dressed in all black with her long, black hair tied up into pigtails on either side.

"Wednesday Addams?" I ask, inspecting the goth makeup that she's applied a little too heavily to really fit Wednesday.

"Of course, and I had to throw it in the teachers' faces that for once I can wear as much makeup as I want and they can't say anything about it," Aarti says haughtily. "And you're dressed as . . . ?" She looks me over with a frown.

"The first thing I could find in my wardrobe?" I say hesitantly. Halloween and dressing up have never exactly been my thing. Unlike a lot of people in this school including Aarti, the school uniform is a welcome reprieve from having to think about how to dress and what people will think about me depending on what I wear.

"Seriously?" Aarti asks with a sigh. "That's what you came dressed as last year."

I shrug. "I'm supposed to go to Meghna's house after school anyway to work on our project. I didn't want to go in costume and make a bad impression with her parents. It's going to be the first time I see them after our parents fell out."

Aarti raises an eyebrow. "I didn't know you and Meghna had so much history."

"Just a little," I say, shrugging again and fiddling with my locker combination. There's too much history there to fill Aarti in on, and I'm half-afraid to confide in her too much. Aarti and I may be best friends, but we've never been close the way Meghna and I were.

"Well, I had a feeling you wouldn't dress up, as always, so . . ." Aarti digs into her backpack and after a moment produces a tiny, black headband with a little witch's hat attached. "It won't win you the costume contest, but at least you won't be the total nerd not dressed up for Halloween."

"Thanks, Aarti," I say, taking the headband and securing it on top of my hair.

She smiles. "Perfect."

I STAND IN FRONT OF MEGHNA'S HOUSE FOR A FEW MINUTES, TRYing to figure out if this really is the place. I check and double-check the address she sent me, and then the gold-plated number on the house. It's only when the door flies open, and Rahman Aunty waves at me, that it registers that this really *is* Meghna's house.

I wave back, feeling my face flush as I wonder how long she has seen me standing here before heading to the front door. It's not that the house is small—it's a two-story terraced house, so definitely *not* small. But it's so much smaller than the place they used to live in before—only a few minutes down the road from ours. That house was like a palace compared to this.

"Assalamu alaikum, Aunty," I say, stepping through to the narrow corridor while she beams at me.

"Walaikum salam. When Meghna told me you were coming over, I thought maybe she was joking," Aunty says, looking at me like she's still not sure I'm real. I wouldn't blame her if she thought that.

"Because I love pulling pranks on you?" Meghna's voice comes from somewhere behind me. When I turn around, I find her standing in the doorway to the kitchen, arms crossed. She's wearing heart-patterned pajamas. Her hair is loose and messy, and she's not wearing any makeup for once.

"Meghna, I told you to get changed before Rani came," Aunty says disapprovingly.

"I'm at home, I'm going to be comfortable after being at school all day," Meghna says in the voice of an irritable child. "Come on, Rani. We have work to do." She gives her mom an aggrieved look before leading me up the stairs to her bedroom.

It's strange, because almost everything about her house is different from before. The place is smaller, the decorations are different. The place even smells different than her old house did; more homely and less manufactured. But Meghna's bedroom, while a completely different room, is so distinctly *her*.

It's not as messy as my bedroom often gets, but there's kind of an organized chaos to it. Her pink-and-purple bed is made, but it's creased where she's tossed her backpack and schoolbooks on it. Her desk has a few scattered papers alongside her silver laptop. There's a corkboard on top of her desk, with photos of her with Yemi and Janella, as well as reminders written on scraps of paper, which have been loosely pinned to the board. I notice two in pink, crinkled paper: The first says, *Halloween fancy dress contest at school next Friday!!!!!* And the second, *Rani meeting afterschool @ mine—31st October.*

I try not to be insulted at the amount of exclamation marks she put for the fancy dress contest compared to how the note about our meeting has absolutely none.

"You can sit anywhere you want," Meghna says, plopping herself down on her bed.

I pull out the chair from under her desk and sit down, putting my backpack on the ground and trying to tuck it away a little. I don't want to mess up her clean bedroom.

"So, were you with Zak yesterday?" Meghna asks before I can start to even take out my things.

"No . . . were you?" I ask.

"Are you lying?" Meghna asks, narrowing her eyes.

"No . . . are you?" I ask.

"Stop repeating everything I say," Meghna says.

"Stop asking me silly questions, then. Why would I be with Zak and then lie to you about it?"

"Well, he was being kind of weird. I asked him to hang out because I thought it would help with the data we were collecting from the app, but he was barely responding. I asked about his project, and he barely said anything. It was not like him. I have thousands of texts where he was telling me about his Irish project," Meghna says.

"He told his parents that he was working on his project at the school lab last night," I say. "But I'm pretty sure that was a lie. His school lab wouldn't be open after school, definitely not that late."

"So, he's lying to everyone. You, me, his parents . . ." Meghna looks away from me, her eyes unfocused like she's deep in thought. "Do you think he suspects us?"

"No." I shake my head. "There's no way. How would he ever know what we've been up to?"

"The same way that I discovered what he was up to. Maybe he saw us together. I mean, as far as Zak knows, I hate you with the heat of a thousand suns, so it would definitely be pretty suspicious if he saw me with you," Meghna says.

I want to press in on the fact that as far as Zak knows she hates me, and ask what she thinks of me now, but I know now's not exactly the time. "Wouldn't he say something if he did have suspicions? Why would he avoid us and lie to us?"

"I don't know," Meghna sighs. "But I think we need to find out what he's up to."

"I don't think there's been any unusual activity on his phone, but I haven't been checking it regularly," I say. Pulling out my laptop from my backpack, I set it down on Meghna's desk and open up the test version of the app. The messages that he had exchanged with Meghna pop up on the side. It's exactly as she said: him acting evasive and strange. I scroll through some of his other texts, but they're mostly about homework, school, or teachers. Nothing that feels out of the ordinary.

"What about his social media?" Meghna's voice is a little close to me. When I glance up, she's hovering by my shoulder, her eyes glued to my laptop screen. I try to ignore that tingly feeling on the nape of my neck from her closeness and go back to the screen.

I click into what the app has stored from Zak's Instagram page, but there's nothing here that seems strange. There are messages with his friends from school and his teammates. There are a few messages about a Halloween party they're all supposed to attend tonight.

"Maybe he's just been busy," I offer. Meghna frowns, like she's unwilling to accept that as an explanation.

"What about his Snapchat?" Meghna asks.

"He's never really used it much, so I haven't been monitoring it . . ." I say, heading to where the data from Snapchat is stored. It notes a flurry of activity over the past two weeks, including an ongoing streak with an account that he doesn't seem to have interacted with before.

"That's not you, is it?" I ask.

She turns to me with a frown. "You think my username would be Irish!Muffin? And you really think I'd be Snapchatting that asshole?"

"So, who do you think it is?" I ask, glancing back at the activity.

"Can't we see the photos they've shared?"

"I don't think so. The way Snapchat works means that the data isn't stored on the phone, which means that it isn't stored on our app. I would have had to code something entirely different, and probably work it into the Snapchat app somehow."

"Shit," Meghna mumbles. She stumbles onto her bed with a sigh, flopping onto her back and staring up at the ceiling forlornly. "What the hell is Zak up to?"

"Meghna, I think this is good. This shows that even with us being so deliberate with our app, there's things that we've missed," I say, typing it into our project document. "Science is full of human errors. I think we can definitely add this into our final presentation."

"But we have to find out what Zak's hiding from us. This is important, Rani," Meghna says. I think this is the first time she's said my name in a way that didn't feel like she completely hates me. She says it like it's the most natural thing. I hate that something as simple as Meghna saying my name can sway me more than anything else. I sigh. "Okay, let's figure out a way to find out what he's up to. But after that, we have to focus on the project. We have to submit everything for approval right after midterm break and the trip to Amsterdam is just a few weeks away."

"Yes, fine," Meghna says. "You think you can maybe find out where this party Zak's going to is?"

I sigh, turning back to my laptop. "In the texts, they're talking about going to Eoin's. They're both getting a lift from Brian at six p.m., which means they should already be there. I think that's the most I can gather from this." When I turn around, Meghna is frantically scrolling through her phone, her eyebrows scrunched together in concentration.

"What are you doing?" I ask.

"Just trying to find . . . aha!" Meghna exclaims. She faces her phone out to me. It's an Instagram story from one of Zak's teammates. It's not the guy Zak mentioned in his texts, but I recognize him from a few of his matches. There are a bunch of photos: from his Halloween costume to the drive all the way to the Halloween party.

"There aren't exactly any notable locations in the photos," I point out.

"Rani, sometimes, all you have to do is ask," Meghna says with a smile as she types into her phone. Just a moment later, her smile widens to a grin. "There. I've got the address. Just had to tell him that I was from Sacred Hearts and a bunch of us were looking for the best Halloween party tonight."

"You *really* want to go to this party?" I ask.

"We have to, if we want to find out what's going on with Zak," Meghna says. She's already running a brush through her hair and putting on eyeliner, too busy to see the panic in my eyes.

"I don't know if our parents will approve of us going. I told mine that I was going to a friend's to study," I say. I can't imagine my parents would have been too thrilled if I'd told them I was going to Meghna's house, but I can imagine they'd be even less thrilled to know that Meghna wants to take me to a Halloween party where we barely know anyone.

"Rani," Meghna says with a sigh. "Please. I'd go by myself, but . . . I can't." She turns to me with pleading eyes, and there's no way I can say no to that.

So, against my better judgment, I nod. "Okay, fine. Let's go to this party. I'm going to need something to wear, though."

Meghna smiles in a way that makes a fresh flurry of butterflies erupt in my stomach. "Don't worry, I've got you covered."

33

MEGHNA

Somehow, between my wardrobe and the nearest two-euro shop by my house, Rani and I manage to put together passable Halloween costumes. She is wearing one of my black dresses—though it's a little short on her. With the witch headband Aarti apparently gifted her this morning, and a little black eyeliner and dark red lipstick, she makes the perfect witch.

I would have changed into the costume I wore to school this morning, but Yemi, Janella, and I decided to go as The Powerpuff Girls. And I can't really go as Blossom without my other Powerpuff Girls. So instead, I put on a pink dress and some old fairy wings I wore for Halloween years ago and throw some glitter into my makeup routine.

As we get off the bus and make our way to the party, we pass by kids going door-to-door for trick-or-treating, dressed as superheroes, princesses, and everything in between. It's strange to think when we were kids, Rani and I used to dress up and go trick-or-treating together. One year it would be my parents taking us, the next Rani's. And when Bhaiya got old enough, he even took us at the promise of some of our sweets. The party is in full swing by the time we get there. I recognize a few girls I saw at Rani's school when I was there, but most of the people here are complete strangers.

"We should split up and search the party," I say, taking a look around.

"No," Rani objects quickly. "What if he sees you? He'll be suspicious. It's better if he sees you with me. I could have been invited to this party. There are a few girls from my school. We could say you came with me."

"Which wouldn't be suspicious?" I ask.

"Less suspicious than you being here on your own," Rani says. The idea of splitting up is not exactly fun for me, either, even if we'll cover more ground that way. And anyway, Rani looks so out of place here, and she has such a deer-in-the-headlights expression that it would feel cruel to abandon her in the midst of all these people.

"Fine, let's not separate. But we do have to walk around to see if he's here," I say. The two of us weave through people, avoiding eye contact and ignoring pickup lines from guys from Zak's school. From the main hallway, we search the kitchen, the sitting room, the dining room, and even take a peek at the downstairs bathroom. Zak is nowhere to be found.

"Maybe he's upstairs?" I shout over the loud thump of the music.

Rani says something back, but I can't hear her over all the noise.

I sigh. "Let's go out back, away from this loud music." We weave through people again, opening the sliding glass doors of the kitchen. And that's when I finally spot him—Zak.

He's sitting in the distance, in a group of what I assume are his friends. But his chair is pushed back, almost like he's part of the group, but separate. And when I step forward just a little, I realize why—he's holding hands with the girl in the seat next to him. The shock of it makes me freeze in the middle of my step, and Rani bumps right into me. The two of us topple forward, though I find my balance at the last minute, catching Rani by the shoulders, too, so we don't go crashing to the ground. Now is definitely not the time to get caught.

I stand, pulling Rani up with me, and motion for her to follow me into the shadows and away from the party. She gives me a questioning look but follows.

"Are you okay?" she asks in a concerned voice.

"Zak is here," I say, pointing to him in the distance. Rani spots him finally, her lips turning down into a frown.

"He's with a girl," Rani says, making the same connection that I did a moment ago.

"Yeah," I sigh. "I guess we found Irish!Muffin."

"We have to do something!" I say as Rani ushers me through the back gates and out of the party. We were only in there for a few minutes before everything fell apart. I hadn't expected a lot from Zak—but I never expected that he would cheat on us *again*. "I don't understand. How does he even have the time? Between rugby practice, his science project, the two of us, his family . . . where is he fitting all this in?"

"It must be new," Rani says. She sounds a lot calmer about this whole thing than I feel. Though, surprisingly, I'm not as angry as I would have thought. I already knew Zak was cheating on me—what does it matter if it was one girl or two? What matters is that he's been lying to me and playing me for our whole relationship. That he never really cared about me in the way that he pretended to. And weirdly, I think I'm starting to get over it. "I mean, logically, he wouldn't have had the time to have three relationships at once on top of everything else. But now he doesn't have rugby practice, and he hasn't been spending any time with either of us recently."

"That's true, his weird excuses about being busy have only cropped up in the past two weeks," I say in agreement. "So it's a two-week-long relationship so far."

"Give or take." Rani nods.

"We have to talk to her. We have to tell her what he is before she gets sucked in too deep," I say. If there's one thing I've learned from this whole thing, it's that being cheated on sucks. And whoever this girl is, she definitely doesn't deserve to find that out when she's past the stage of infatuation.

"How do we do that?" Rani asks. "I don't know, maybe we should just stay out of it."

"Rani," I say, giving her a small glare. "You know we can't do that. We have to find a way to tell her. She deserves to know."

As we make our way back to the bus stop, I pull out my phone. The girl hasn't exactly made herself difficult to find—her Instagram username is the exact same as her Snapchat. I can tell it's her because Zak follows her, and she follows Zak.

"This is her," I tell Rani as we get off the bus. "Julie Walsh." She's pretty, with a heart-shaped face, porcelain-white skin with just a sprinkle of freckles dotted around her nose, and blond hair that seems to fall perfectly around her shoulders.

"So how do we get in touch?" Rani asks.

"I could send her a message and tell her about Zak," I say.

"What if she tells him?" Rani asks. "What if she asks him to tell her the truth? And also, why would she believe us? We're strangers."

"So, we need proof," I say. I scroll through my phone until I find the one photo that Zak and I have together, from one of our very first dates. We look so effortlessly happy in it, but now I know that even then he was seeing Rani. Everything with us had been a lie from start to finish.

I turn my phone screen to Rani. "I can send her this photo, some texts between us. Send me a photo you have with him, too. She can't pretend that it's not suspicious. And if she asks him . . . we already have a lot for our project. So, we'll be okay."

Rani studies me closely for a moment. I'm half-afraid she's going to say no. Logically, it makes more sense to protect our project and not jeopardize it so late in the game, and Rani is all about logic. But then she surprises me by nodding.

"Yeah, okay. Let's message her," she says.

I have to fight to keep the grin off my face. To stop myself from throwing my arms around Rani in excitement. "Okay, you send me your photos and then we'll message her tonight and see what she says. You could come back to mine and stay over?"

"I can't." Rani shakes her head. "Ammu might be weird about me staying over at yours, and I think it's just easier if we meet up tomorrow instead. We have the entire midterm break, right?"

"Right. So, you'll come tomorrow? I won't text her until you approve it," I say.

"Okay, I'll be over tomorrow. First thing in the morning, except it takes me like an hour and a half to get to yours, so maybe second thing in the morning," Rani says. "And I'll wash your dress and bring it back."

I give her a once-over. "You can keep it, it suits you. I have other black dresses."

Rani smiles, and weirdly it sends a flutter through my stomach. "Thanks, Meghna. I'll see you tomorrow."

"See you." I turn around, pocketing my phone, and begin the walk back home. When I'm far enough away and in the shadows, I turn around, watching Rani as she stops the bus with an outstretched hand and climbs aboard. That familiar feeling of warmth returns as the bus pulls away. But surely it must be this weird night. Or a Halloween sugar rush.

There's no way I have a crush on Rani Choudhury.

34

MEGHNA

"Another girl? There is something seriously wrong with Zak!" Yemi says over the phone so loudly that I have to close the door just in case Ammu and Abbu are paying attention.

"Just when you think he can't get any worse," Janella chimes in. "Are you doing okay?"

"I'm fine," I say, tugging at the ends of my bedsheet so it lines up properly. Rani texted me earlier this morning to say she was already on the bus, on her way over. When I informed Ammu, she beamed like this was the best news she's gotten in forever and immediately rushed to the kitchen to start making lunch. I can already smell the creamy chingri malai curry she's making. I know Rani's going to be over the moon about it—Ammu is famous for that dish specifically. "Are you *fine* fine or just saying you're fine because you think it's what we want to hear?" Yemi asks. "Because we can come over there with ice cream and rom-coms, and we could have a sleepover and talk about just how much Zak sucks. You just say the word."

"I'm really fine," I insist, for once actually meaning it. "And you know, Rani's on her way over. We're going to text this girl and work on our project. And I don't know, weirdly I think being occupied with all this stuff has been helping. I didn't even feel that angry when I saw him with this new girl."

"Good!" Janella says enthusiastically. "He doesn't deserve your anger!"

"And hey, maybe when you go to Amsterdam, you'll meet someone new there. There's going to be loads of guys from schools all over Europe, and they'll be just as nerdy as you," Yemi adds.

"Right," I say, though in reality I'm thinking about Rani. Maybe the person I need to get over Zak is not someone new, or even a guy. Maybe it's someone I've known for pretty much my whole life. "Can I ask you guys a question?"

"If you're going to ask about grilling me with more questions for your project, I'm going to have to decline because we are seriously amping up the rehearsals for our show over midterm," Yemi says.

"No." I chuckle. "I was just wondering, I guess, how . . . I mean . . . if . . ." I don't know how to ask the question or if I really want an answer. For most of my life, I've been pretty sure about exactly who I am. The only time that was thrown off-kilter was when Abbu lost his job, rumors spread, and we became ostracized by a community we thought had our back. But now, for some reason, I'm questioning things. Like, maybe the reason I was so adamant about separating myself from Rani when everything with our parents happened was because I already thought of her as more than my friend. Maybe Rani was actually my first-ever crush, the first person I trusted and loved, and I was scared of being rejected and hurt. So I just did it first. And now that we're working together, it's old feelings resurfacing, not new ones.

That maybe I might not be the token straight person in our group like I thought I was.

"Hello? Meghna?" Yemi's voice pierces through my thoughts, as does the resounding sound of the bell ringing.

"Sorry, I think that's Rani. I'm going to have to go," I say, feeling a wave of relief. I guess I really didn't want answers. "I'll talk to you both later, bye."

"Keep us updated!" Janella gets in before I hang up.

A knock on my bedroom door sounds, and when I open it, Rani is standing in the doorway.

"Hey," she says, her smile a little too bright. I try to tamp down the way it makes my heart beat a little too fast. "Aunty let me in and told me to come up to your room."

"Yes, come on in." I wave her inside, trying to ignore the way the room feels warm now even though we're approaching winter and it's drizzling outside.

"So, did you think about what we should text Julie?" Rani asks, taking a seat by my desk once more.

"I even typed it all up, and it's ready to send," I say, nodding. I approach my desk, leaning over Rani and opening up my laptop. She smells citrusy and bright—like she's just stepped out of the shower. I nudge my laptop a little to the left, just to avoid her smell and what it's doing to me. If Rani notices that I'm acting strangely, she doesn't say anything. Just smiles in a completely unhelpful way.

"Here." I open up to my Instagram profile where I have a message typed to Julie. Rani looks over the message, her eyebrows furrowing as she reads.

"I think this is good," she says finally.

"And I have photos of me and Zak, and the photo you sent of you and Zak. So, I'll hit send and then . . ." I press enter on the message before quickly loading up the photos and sending those, too. I wait for a moment after, watching the little icon that shows the photos are loading until it turns into the little tick to show they have been delivered.

"And now we wait, I guess," Rani says, taking a deep breath.

"Now we wait," I repeat. I close my laptop and move away from the desk while Rani begins to dig through her bag.

"It would be good if we could finish preparing our project today. So we can submit and hopefully have everything ready soon," she says.

"Okay, yeah. No point waiting around doing nothing," I say with a shrug. My phone vibrates by my bedside table, and I freeze. So does Rani, with her laptop half-open. We catch each other's gaze before Rani tilts her head to the phone.

"Do you think it's her?"

"Maybe."

My heart is beating fast as I grab my phone, but it's just a message from Yemi, informing me about the dates of their show in December.

"It's not her," I say, putting the phone down.

"Well, okay. So, our project," Rani says, turning back to her laptop. "I've been doing a lot of data analysis from our survey over the last few days, and I've basically drawn up a bunch of charts and graphs, which will be really good for our presentation, I think. A lot of the research out there supports the data we found and—" Rani cuts herself off as she glances over at me once more, frowning. "Are you going to come over here to look at it?"

"I can see it from here," I say, even though I'm all the way by the bedside table, standing awkwardly and like this bedroom doesn't even belong to me.

"Meghna, I know you're angry about this other girl, and I know you're anxious about what she's going to say," Rani says with a sigh. "But it's going to be fine. No matter what happens, our project is coming along well. I think, in a way, it helps that Zak is seeing someone else as well, right? He's undeniably a huge asshole. And pretty soon a lot of people are going to know it."

"Yeah," I say. "Pretty soon we're going to be getting our revenge and showing everyone his true colors."

"So, come over here so we can finish and make that happen," Rani says, waving me over again.

I sigh. If only Rani knew that I was less concerned about Zak and Julie, and more concerned about me and her. "Okay."

THERE ARE A FEW THINGS I LEARN ABOUT RANI AS WE WORK SIDE by side going over the data for the project and agreeing on how we're going to present it: She uses rose-scented perfume, which layers amazingly with whatever citrus shampoo she's using, and I can kind of see why she's always gotten into the Ireland Young Scientist Exhibition every single year. She's pretty amazing at and dedicated to what she does. Maybe it doesn't have the flair or creativity that I try to put into my projects, but the science is solid.

She's constructed multiple graphs that showcase the data from our research, percentages from our surveys compared to other research done on cheating and relationships.

By the time we're done going through the numbers, using them to construct the basis of our digital therapist, and adding our own ideas to the presentation, Ammu is calling us down for lunch.

"I've been smelling her chingri malai curry since before I even stepped in the door," Rani says excitedly as soon as Ammu's call comes. It's the first time I've seen her eager to leave her science stuff behind.

"She's been cooking for you ever since she heard you were coming. I think you guys are on the same level. Come on." I close my notebook while Rani puts away her laptop and both of us bound down the stairs.

Lunch is strangely familiar. Ammu and Abbu pepper Rani with all kinds of questions about her school, the science project, even her parents. Rani answers everything with a polite smile while accepting multiple servings of the chingri malai curry and even firing back questions of her own about Abbu's new job and exactly what Ammu puts into this dish. It's like everything that happened in the past has been completely forgotten.

It's just as we're finishing up lunch that my phone buzzes again. I exchange a quick glance with Rani before picking it up. There's a message.

Julie: I had no idea about any of this. can you meet me? I could really use someone to talk to about this right now.

"We have to go," I tell Rani when I show her the message in the hallway, away from my parents.

"We don't even know this girl," Rani says. "And we still have our work to finish."

"Talking to her will help with it," I insist. "Getting her perspective of her relationship will help balance out everything that we have. And plus, we kind of had each other to talk to about Zak. She doesn't have that."

Rani sighs. "We're not her friends, Meghna. If we meet her, we have to be objective about it."

"Okay, we'll be objective," I say with a smile before leaning into the kitchen doorway. "Ammu, Abbu, Rani and I are going to go out for a little bit, okay?"

Ammu smiles, like she's all too happy about letting me go off anywhere as long as I'm with Rani. "Okay, Ammu. Just don't be home too late."

"Okay, Ammu," I repeat, quickly messaging Julie about a time and place to meet. "Let's go."

35

RANI

I'M NOT SURE HOW EXACTLY MEGHNA KEEPS CONVINCING ME TO do things I would never consider doing in a million years. It's something about her smile, and how her pleading gaze makes her look like a kicked puppy. It's very difficult to say no to.

That's how we find ourselves in town thirty minutes later, sharing an umbrella to protect ourselves from the rain as we make our way down a busy O'Connell Street. We turn right down one street and left down a narrow alleyway I haven't walked before, then finally duck into the café that Meghna suggested meeting up in.

I spot her before Meghna does. She's sitting in a corner by the window, cup of coffee in her hands, a somber expression on her face. As if she realizes someone is staring at her, she looks up and her bright blue eyes find mine. She doesn't smile exactly, but when a flash of recognition lights up her eyes, her face softens. She waves a hand toward us while Meghna closes the umbrella, trying to shake off some of the excess water on it.

"Ready?" Meghna asks.

I shrug. "Sure."

"Hey," Julie says as soon as we're within earshot. Meghna and I take seats opposite her.

"Hi, I'm Meghna, and this is Rani," Meghna says.

"And I'm Julie. It's nice to meet you, I guess?" Julie says. I suppose *nice* is not exactly the word to use when you're meeting the girls that your boyfriend is cheating on you with. "I have to ask. How did you find me?"

Meghna shrugs. "Zak was acting weird, so we had an idea that something was going on. A little bit of online sleuthing led to you."

Meghna is smart for leaving out the part about our app, and following Zak to a party. We don't know how Julie would take all of that.

"Wow," Julie says with a sigh. She glances out the window as if she's digesting the information. "We met, like, two weeks ago. We're both in the same class for English grinds and he was helping me out."

I exchange a quick glance with Meghna. Zak definitely never said anything about taking grinds, though I guess that goes with everything else I know about him—he likes to act like he's the best at everything. Like he's better than me, and better than Meghna, too. It wouldn't fit his image to tell us he needed extra lessons in English for the Leaving Cert.

Julie continues, clearly not catching the silent communication between me and Meghna. "He was *so* nice. We got coffee afterward, and I felt like, I don't know, I'd met someone who really understood me. And who I really liked. We've been hanging out constantly these past few weeks. He always makes time for me. His friends are so nice, and even *my* friends liked him, which is honestly an anomaly."

She sighs, turning back to us sadly. "I saw a photo of you on some Instagram post he was tagged in," she says, holding my gaze with a frown. "I asked him about it, and he said you were his cousin. I didn't doubt it, but I probably should have."

"He's pretty good at playing the boyfriend," Meghna chimes in before I can respond. Not that I have much to say, anyway. Maybe

Meghna and Julie have more in common than I do with either of them. Both of them had actual feelings for Zak. They look like it hurt when they learned he cheated. The only reason it hurt me is because he disrespected my family and lied to us all for so long. Feelings were never in question for me.

"We were together for three months. I thought he was the perfect guy for me during that time, but once I realized what he was doing, I think I started seeing the cracks in our relationship," Meghna continues.

I nod in agreement. "We were kind of set up by our parents, so we didn't spend a lot of time alone. But he still found ways to charm everyone. My parents and my sisters are definitely all over him. They're ready to accept him into the family with just how much he's charmed them."

"Wow," Julie says. "Yeah, he would take me to my favorite restaurants. He always paid; I felt like he was seriously treating me like a princess. He told me that maybe his parents wouldn't be super happy about the whole thing, but once he tells them he can convince them to come around. He said he was working up to it."

"He was going to tell them about you?" Meghna asks, like she can't quite digest it. I see her hands clench beside mine, and there's something that's tugging at me to put my own hands over hers. To comfort her.

Obviously, I don't.

"He was probably lying," I say. "I mean, if he did, he would have had to break things off with me, and his parents would have to tell my parents. I don't think he would have risked it."

"I don't know, it felt like he was maybe working up to it," Julie says. "But I guess it doesn't matter now. I'm going to have to break things off with him. I just don't even know what I'll say."

"Just . . . maybe don't mention us?" Meghna says. "We don't want him to lash out at us."

"Sure." Julie flashes us a smile. "So, how long were you with him?" she asks, tilting her head toward me. "You're the person I actually saw evidence of before you guys even messaged me."

"Like a year," I say.

"Wow," Julie mumbles.

"Yeah," I sigh. It's strange to think that one guy got the best of all three of us, that we're all connected by him when he clearly never cared about us at all.

After a few hours of exchanging notes on Zak and our relationships—one long, one medium, and one very short-lived—one thing is very clear.

"Zak treated Julie way better than us!" Meghna says as soon as we're out on the street again and out of Julie's earshot.

"I don't know . . ." I drift off, even though from the way she described things it did sound like it. She got expensive dates at restaurants, promises to meet the parents. She even met his friends, and vice versa. The only reason Zak ever met Aarti was because she's Bengali, too, and would sometimes go to the same dawats as us.

"He was doing everything in his power to keep me from his parents, even though they would have probably been more okay with me than with Julie. At least I'm Bangladeshi," Meghna says with a glare at an upcoming puddle in the street. If looks could kill, that puddle would have definitely evaporated.

"Look, maybe it was all just a lie. I mean, Julie isn't Bangladeshi, so she probably understands less about our culture, and maybe he was just trying to appease her."

Meghna turns to me, her face stoic. "They were together for two weeks, Rani. What girl wants to meet her boyfriend's parents after only two weeks?"

I guess she's right about that. We walk in silence for a moment, though I can tell that there's a storm going on in Meghna's head. She's probably cursing Zak out in her mind.

"At least the whole thing helps us, right?" I offer after a few minutes of silently walking down O'Connell Street.

"What do you mean?" Meghna asks.

"I mean, there's a lot we can do for our project with the information Julie gave us. Why was he treating her better? Was it because it was a new relationship? Because her being from a different culture meant that he felt he had to treat her differently? What factors went into how he treated each of us? What about each of us is different or similar? And what does the data on relationships say about these differences and similarities?"

"Race, color, class," Meghna says simply. "Think about it: Julie is white, and he treated her better than either of us in just two weeks. I've been begging to meet his friends and for him to meet mine, and he always found excuses not to. But with her, it's no problem. He didn't want me to meet his parents because they wouldn't approve of the fact that we don't live in a big, fancy house anymore and that we take welfare money, live in social housing, and I go to a public school in the north. And you . . . maybe it's colorism." She pauses in the middle of her speech, her eyes drifting over to me—looking at me in a way that feels almost intrusive. It sends a chill down my spine. "He couldn't see how great he had it with you. Everything could have been perfect. His parents' approval, a beautiful girl. But we're not exactly the same skin tone, and you know how Bangladeshi people can be about that. You're not beautiful unless you're forsha, bullshit that Zak must buy into." She holds my gaze for a moment too long—a moment in which I'm pretty sure I lose my ability to breathe—before turning away and beginning to walk once more. "Anyway, you're right. If nothing else, it shows Zak to be the asshole that he is. But . . . we're going to need . . . something. Something that's really going to expose him in front of everyone."

"He needs to admit what he's been doing," I say.

Meghna looks at me again. "I think we need to break up with him."

36

MEGHNA

When I text Zak to meet up to talk the next day, he responds almost immediately. I wonder if Julie's already broken up with him, and he's scrambling. Either way, it's good for us.

Rani and I aren't exactly rolling in surveillance equipment, so we have to make do with what we have. Zak and I will be going to our café near my house. I'll be recording our conversation the entire time on my phone.

Rani will sit in a booth on the other side of the café and try to get as much of our "date" as possible on her phone. The voice recording is much more important than the video, but both of them will help with our presentation, at the end of the day.

On the morning of the breakup, as I'm applying finishing touches to my makeup, Rani calls. I pick up on the first ring.

"Hey, how are you feeling?" she asks.

"Weirdly nervous, and excited," I reply while swiping my eyeliner to draw in wings. "I'm kind of glad to finally be done with the charade."

"Yeah, just a few more hours and it'll all be over." She doesn't sound half as excited as me, but I guess for her it doesn't matter when she breaks up with Zak. It's telling her parents that's always been her biggest concern. I want to reassure her. Tell her that when she does break the news to them, everything will be okay. But Rani starts speaking again before I can form any words of reassurance.

"I should get going. I'm almost at the café, and I'll try to get the booth opposite your regular one. I'll see you soon?" she asks.

"Yeah, see you soon, I guess."

IT'S THE MIDDLE OF THE DAY ON A WEDNESDAY, SO THE CAFÉ IS pretty quiet. I go in, sit down at our usual booth, hitting record on my phone and laying it face down on the table. Spotting Rani on the other side, I give her a wave and a smile, trying to ignore the way her smile back makes my stomach flip. *One messy relationship at a time,* I remind myself. First, I have to deal with Zak.

Then maybe sometime in the future, I can deal with whatever the hell is going on with my feelings for Rani.

"Hey." Zak sounds strange when he approaches me, giving me a stilted smile and sliding into the seat opposite me. He looks more somber than usual. Julie must have dumped him, and this is the result.

"Hi," I say, trying to match his serious tone. I definitely don't want him to get the wrong idea about what this is.

"Have you been here long?" he asks.

"Just a few minutes." I shrug.

"Ready to order?" Aoibheann appears at our table unnoticed, her usual friendly smile on her face.

"I'll just have an Americano," I say.

"Same," Zak agrees, shooting Aoibheann his signature smile,

which used to be able to make my heart slow down but now just gets under my skin in a way nothing else ever really has.

"So, I think we should talk," I say as soon as Aoibheann is out of earshot.

"Yeah, I think so, too," Zak says, surprising me. "Things have been kind of weird lately. And I don't know, something's been up with you." Zak meets my gaze, and I can see sympathy behind his eyes. Even though it seems feigned. "I feel like ever since the Young Scientist Exhibition, when you lost and I won, you've been angry at me. Resenting me." I have to stop my jaw from dropping open at that. Is he really trying to turn things around on me?

He doesn't wait for me to respond before barreling on. "It just feels like we're not on the same page anymore. I get it, it must be hard. I get in every single year, and you never do. And this year I'm going to Europe, and, with my project, I probably have a great shot at winning. I just feel like I can't be with someone who's acting jealous the way that you have been. I've been wondering: Is this what it's always going to be like? I'm going to feel guilty about my success if I'm with you?"

It takes me a moment to realize what he's doing. *He's* breaking up with *me*. That's why he was so quick to agree to this meetup today.

"Hang on a second. I'm *not* jealous of you. I haven't been angry about you getting through to the European competition. It's great that you did, and I'll support—wait!" He's spun such a tale that I've forgotten the real reason we're here. "You've been cheating on me!"

At this accusation, Zak finally looks a little taken aback. Some of the color drains from his face as he takes me in. "What . . . what are you talking about?"

"I'm talking about the fact that you've been cheating on me with Rani Choudhury for our entire relationship, and now you're cheating on me again with a new girl, Julie Walsh," I say. "I've spoken to both of them, so there's no point denying it."

Zak just blinks, dumbfounded for a moment. I'm glad something's finally stopped him from lying and manipulating me. But then Aoibheann comes around with the coffee, putting each cup in front of us, and somehow that seems to wake Zak from his stupor.

"Look, yeah, maybe I was seeing Rani while I was seeing you. But you can't exactly blame me," he says.

"Why can't I blame you?" I say, trying not to let the red-hot anger that's currently coursing through my veins seep into my voice. I just know he's going to find a way to use even that against me.

"Because you've said it yourself. Rani is, like, perfect. Her family is great. She's pretty, smart, she's top of her class. She'll probably get six hundred twenty-five points in the Leaving Cert, get into a great university, and go on to have an amazing career. The two of us just make sense together. You and I . . . I tried to make it work, but we don't make any sense," Zak says matter-of-factly. He coolly picks up his coffee, taking a sip.

I know that I shouldn't let his words get to me. He's saying whatever he can to turn everything on me. To make himself into the good guy in this breakup. But it hurts to think about how easily Zak can throw my worst insecurities back at me. He's one of the few people who understands how I've gone my whole life being compared to Rani, how I've loathed that she's better than me at everything. At least, I thought he understood.

"Rani and you don't make sense," I say, trying to keep the waver out of my voice. "She's way too good for you."

Zak gives me a questioning look. "You're really standing up for her now?"

"I'm just saying—you're not the catch that you think you are, Zak. You've lied and cheated on three girls, and now you're trying to pretend that anything can justify it."

He purses his lips. "Look, Meg. I didn't mean for our relationship to go on as long as it has. Things with Rani are too serious because of my parents. Things with you were supposed to just be fun. Rani's no fun about anything, but you are."

"And Julie?" I ask.

Zak shrugs. "It's new, and it doesn't really matter. What matters is that I think that it's best if we stop seeing each other."

"At least we agree on something," I say.

"I'm sorry, Meg, I know that—"

"Don't call me that—you know I hate it when you call me that," I say.

He gives me an awkward smile, but I know he doesn't really care. He isn't apologizing for cheating, for lying, for stringing me along. He isn't apologizing for hurting me, manipulating me, for trying to make this breakup seem like my problem.

"I should get going," he says, pushing his mug aside and standing up. He doesn't say anything more, doesn't say *goodbye*. I don't look up at him, I just stare down at my coffee, the steam rising off it. Feeling the anger still boiling in my blood and that bitter aftertaste of sadness.

"Hey, are you okay?" Rani's voice is somehow right beside me.

When I look up, she's hovering over me. "Zak left, and you didn't come over."

"He's such an asshole," I say. "I can't believe I actually thought he was a good guy. Like we could have some kind of a future together."

"I know," Rani says, sliding into his seat. She pushes away his mug and gives me a sympathetic smile—a real one. "I'm sorry."

I shake my head, trying to get rid of Zak and all the horrible things he said to me. Picking up my phone, I hit the button to stop recording. "At least we got it all. And people will see his true colors soon. There was one weird thing, though. He said things with Julie were new. You think she still hasn't broken up with him?"

Rani glances down instead of at me. "I think maybe she's not planning on breaking up with him. I don't know, Zak texted me this morning. He broke up with me."

"What?" I can only stare at Rani, though she's still not quite meeting my eyes.

"Yeah, when I called, I was going to tell you. In case that's why he was agreeing to meet you, but you already sounded nervous. I didn't want to freak you out or throw you for a loop, so I didn't."

"He *did* want to break up with me," I say. "So he wanted to end things with both of us. But he says things with Julie are new."

Rani shrugs. "Something must have changed for him to break up with us."

I nod in agreement. And I'm betting the change is Julie. I pick up my phone, typing out a message to Julie before I lose my nerve: what did you say to Zak, exactly?

"What are you doing?" Rani asks.

"Trying to get to the bottom of it." I show her the message.

She purses her lips like she's not happy about how impulsively I acted but doesn't say anything more. Julie's reply comes after only a moment.

Julie: what do you mean?
Me: Zak and I just broke up, and he broke up with Rani too. did you say something to him?
Julie: kind of
Julie: look I feel bad about how everything went down but after talking to you both I realised that maybe Zak just needed a push to make a choice. I told him that he couldn't keep doing this. he needed to choose one of us and that was that. I guess he made his choice.
Julie: I'm sorry but I think when we started dating, he must have already known that this is how things would go down. we just started dating and I don't even think it really counts as cheating that he didn't break it off with you two first. just a slightly delayed breakup.

I glance speechlessly at Rani, who looks just as dumbfounded by Julie's reasoning.

"I don't even know how to respond," I say.

"I know." Rani takes my phone before I can say anything else and types out a quick reply:

Me: good luck.

I give her an appraising look when she gives me my phone back.

"What?" she asks. "She's going to need it. I'm thinking maximum one month before he finds some other girl."

“Probably less. He’s going to the Netherlands soon, and I don’t think he’d pass up the opportunity to meet someone there,” I say.

Rani lets out a giggle, and, after a moment, I join her. Until we’re in peals of laughter in the middle of a nearly empty coffee shop. Like we haven’t both just been dumped by the most eligible Bangladeshi bachelor in Dublin. Like we couldn’t care less about any of it.

37

RANI

WITH ZAK OFFICIALLY OUT OF THE PICTURE, SUDDENLY EVERYthing seems easier. By the time our midterm break is over, Meghna and I have spent hours poring over our project and getting everything ready. On the first day that schools open, we submit it to both our science teachers. I expect that it'll take a few days at least to hear back, but Mrs. Quinn calls me into the physics lab during lunchtime.

"So, obviously this app is very different from your language app in many ways," Mrs. Quinn says. I can't tell if she means it as a compliment or an insult, so I just flash her a smile.

"I just wanted to diversify, I guess," I say.

"Honestly, Rani, this is strong. The app seems easy to use—the interface is great. And it's clear that you two have done a lot of research into various aspects of this, too. I'm just not so sure if you really want to base it *all* around your personal story," Mrs. Quinn says. There's a pink flush in her cheeks, and she doesn't quite look me in the eye. "I gather that whatever happened was . . . unpleasant, but science should be objective. That's what the judges want to see. I'm worried that all your good work will go to waste because you've brought too much of the personal into the science."

"But you told me that I needed to bring *more* personal things into my science. That's why I was having trouble at the Irish Young Scientist Exhibition. Judges couldn't get a sense of who I was," I say.

"And so, now I've done that. I've brought myself, and you're saying it's too much?"

"That's not . . ." Mrs. Quinn sighs, finally meeting my gaze. "You're right. When I first saw your proposal for this project, I thought it was perfect. You would be bringing something personal to appeal to the judges, to help you stand out from the crowd. Everything needs a story, some kind of a personal connection. But I worry this is going too far. You and Meghna's story might be overshadowing the science. The judges might not see it as personal, but as trivial."

"Why?" I ask with a frown. "Isn't this something that a lot of people can relate to?"

"Yes, but you have to think about your target audience, Rani. The judges at the competition are mostly going to be middle-aged men, and most of the people competing alongside you are going to be boys. A project from a female-led team about an app to catch a cheating partner, with a focus on how your own experiences shaped the app and your presentation of it? They'll undermine it," Mrs. Quinn says with a sigh. "The project is good, but that doesn't mean there aren't areas that need a little more thought. There's also the issue that a major part of this app is invasive. You will be showing how your app specifically taps into someone's data without their consent. The judges might question that, too. I think the work here stands up as tough competition against everyone. But I don't want you to go in and be surprised by the reception it gets. It's better to think about these issues *now* than be blindsided by them later."

"Okay," I say with a nod. I guess I can understand her issues with the ethics behind the app, but I'm not sure I grasp what exactly her problem is with our personal experiences being brought into it. I wonder, if a male-led team did the same project, would she be having this same conversation?

"So, you think, other than this, we're ready to go?"

Mrs. Quinn sighs. "All I need is for you and your partner to get your parents to sign the consent forms allowing you to go to Amsterdam in two weeks."

I take the forms and stick them into my backpack.

When I call Meghna on the way home to tell her about what Mrs. Quinn said, she scoffs.

"I can't believe she actually tried to pull that. Like the competition being sexist is our problem!" Meghna says. "Like, they cry about how we need more women in STEM, but we only get to be there if we do things on *their* terms? How's that fair?"

"I don't think she wanted us to change anything. I think she was just warning us," I say, trying to defend Mrs. Quinn. "And there's also what she said about how our app looks into people's data without their consent."

"Every app is looking into people's data without their consent. *And* they're selling it to major corporations who are then trying to sell us their products. How is our app more unethical than any of those?" Meghna asks.

"Well, for one, I'm guessing those app developers didn't steal our phones and download their app into it without our knowledge," I point out.

Meghna grumbles something incoherent under her breath before finally sighing. "Okay, fine. Maybe the ethics of our app are a little bit fishy. But isn't that kind of the point? Isn't that what happens when you suspect your partner might be cheating on you? You become a little unethical."

"I think we just have to make sure we address this during our presentation," I say. "Mrs. Quinn just wants to make sure that we anticipate problems that might come up."

"Well, Ms. Ennis—my science teacher—loved our project. And she thinks we have a great shot at winning," Meghna says.

I slip out of the bus as it reaches my stop and begin walking the short road up the hill to my house. "I guess that's the important thing. We're done, and in two weeks we'll go to Amsterdam, present, and hopefully win."

"Right. And then . . . we'll be done," Meghna says.

"And we'll have gotten our revenge," I agree, though I know my voice sounds dull instead of excited. I hadn't thought about what the end of this project really means: Meghna and I won't have an excuse to see each other anymore.

"And hey, if we win, we'll probably get to shadow together," Meghna says.

"Yeah, that's true," I reply. At least it's something. "I think I have to tell my parents about Zak. Before we go to Amsterdam, I mean."

"That makes sense. You don't really want them to find out through the news getting out," Meghna says. "Do you want help figuring out what to say?"

"No," I say. "I think I just have to tell them the truth. I think it helps, the whole Julie thing. He hasn't broken up with her, and that kind of helps my case." Zak has really dug his own grave here, especially if he decides to introduce Julie to his parents. I can't imagine they'll be too happy about it. After all, our relationship was just as much a result of his parents' insistence as my parents'.

"Well, you can call if you need help. I'm pretty good at talking to parents," Meghna says with an air of confidence.

"Talking to *my* parents?" I ask while rifling through my backpack for my keys. I find them and stick them into the front door lock, turning until I hear the click. I can already smell the aroma of the chicken curry Ammu is cooking.

"Okay, maybe not your parents," Meghna admits.

"Ke ashlo? Rani?" Ammu's voice calls out, interrupting my conversation.

"Ji, ami!" I call back. "I should go, I'll talk to you later."

I hang up the phone and shuffle to the kitchen, where Ammu is busy preparing a lavish dinner. She's got all four cookers going at once, and even the oven is turned on.

"Are we having guests over?" I ask.

"The Sardars are coming for dinner," Ammu says, not looking up from stirring the chicken curry. "Can you get me the morich from the fridge?"

I set down my bag on one of the chairs, trying to ignore the rock suddenly lodged in my throat. How am I supposed to face Uncle and Aunty? How am I supposed to face Zak? Worse, what if they're here to break the news to my parents before I can? I already saw how good Zak is at manipulating the truth to make himself into the good guy. Ammu and Abbu are already too ready to believe everything good about him, and everything bad about me. I have to get ahead of this.

Opening the fridge, I grab the box of chilies and hand it to Ammu.

She cuts a bunch of them, sprinkling them into the different dishes. I'm trying to think about how to tell her, but my throat is dry.

"How come Zak's parents are coming?" I ask finally, after it feels like I've been hovering for a little too long.

"Just visiting for dinner," Ammu says, totally ignorant to the internal crisis I'm currently having.

"When are they coming?"

"In a few hours, Rani." Ammu finally looks up with a frown. "Go get changed and get ready so you can help me. Don't just stand around here."

"Ammu, I kind of have to talk to you about something," I blurt out. When I imagined telling Ammu and Abbu about Zak, I thought I'd have at least a week to plan it out properly. I thought I'd sit them down when they were both relaxed—maybe right after lunch on the weekend when they sit with a cup of tea to watch something on TV—and I'd break the news to them. They'd be in too good a mood to be angry about it.

But now Ammu is looking at me like I'm already stressing her out, and I haven't even said a word about Zak and the breakup.

"I have to finish cooking, Rani," Ammu says.

"This is important," I insist.

She sighs but puts the lid on the chicken curry and shuffles to the kitchen table to sit. I follow, trying to think up words to explain everything, though I can barely think over the loud thumping of my own heart.

"Ammu, you know how you had this plan for me and Zak?" I ask.

Ammu frowns but nods slowly.

"Well, Zak kind of had other plans. I found out that he's with someone. Another girl. Her name is Julie," I say quickly. "They're together, so, Zak said *we* can't be together anymore."

Ammu doesn't seem surprised or in disbelief like I thought she would be. Her expression doesn't change at all. "This is not a time for jokes, Rani," she says finally.

"I'm not joking, Ammu. You can ask him, if you want. It's true."

Ammu's frown deepens. "Did you say something to him? Zakkariyah wouldn't just do something like that."

"No," I mumble. "We barely even talk outside of our dawats. I haven't seen him in a while and—"

"It must be that silly science contest of yours," Ammu says, shaking her head. "I knew I should have listened to those bhabis when they warned me about it. But I thought: Rani is good at it, Rani wants to do it, I'll let her."

I feel like I can barely breathe. My words are stuck in my throat, but, somehow, I manage to get them out. "Ammu, this has nothing to do with the science competition, I promise. It's Zak. He does what he wants to do, and he doesn't have the same plans for our future that you and his parents do. That's all that it is. Isn't it better in some way? We don't even know each other that well."

Ammu is full-on glaring now. There's a kind of anger in her eyes that I don't know if I've ever seen before. "If not Zakkariyah, then who?" she asks, like I'm already all out of options.

"I don't know." I shrug. "Maybe for now I just do my Leaving Cert, try to win the European science competition, go to university, try to get a good job, and—"

Ammu shakes her head, like that's unheard of. "I know what things are like here, Rani. You want to go to study technology in university with all boys? You think I don't know what'll happen?"

I don't know how to tell her how little interest I have in that. I know that she wouldn't believe me if I tried.

"Ammu, Zak lied to me. He lied to us all. Why would you ever want things to work out between us?" I ask finally.

That, at least, seems to rid her of some of her anger. She heaves a sigh and stands up.

"Go get changed. I have to finish up here," she says, shuffling back to the cooker.

"Ammu, if Aunty and Uncle—"

"Rani, we'll figure it out," Ammu says. I'm not sure if it's supposed to be reassuring, but it doesn't do much to make me feel better. I nod before heading up the stairs, the well of tears that has been building in my chest breaking free.

38

MEGHNA

Zak and his parents are coming over tonight. so, I told my mom about the breakup. she didn't take it too well. should have gotten the permission form for Amsterdam filled out before telling her, ha.

I read and reread Rani's text. I can tell she's trying to make light of the whole thing, but I can sense the upset between the lines. How could she not be upset? How could her mom take Zak's side over hers?

I know there's no logic to it, but instead of texting Rani back or even calling her, I find myself on her doorstep an hour later, considering if I should ring the doorbell or not. If Zak and his parents are really here, at least I can speak up for Rani. Tell them that Zak was cheating with me. I have the proof. They can't possibly keep supporting him.

But the house inside is quiet. You would hardly think anybody is even home.

I ring the doorbell, and after a few minutes a breathless Parisa opens the door. Her smile drops into a frown as soon as she sees me.

"What are you doing here?"

"I'm here to see Rani. Is she here?"

Pari nods. "Upstairs, in her room," she says begrudgingly.

I move past Pari, taking off my shoes at the bottom of the stairs. I look for Aunty and Uncle, but they're nowhere in sight. So, I climb up the stairs and head straight to Rani's room. I have to knock a couple of times before I hear any kind of a response.

"Pari, I told you to leave me alone!" Rani says. She sounds more disgruntled than I've heard her in quite a while.

"It's not Parisa, it's me," I say.

A moment later, the door flings open. A disheveled-looking Rani is looking down at me.

"Meghna. What are you doing here?" she asks.

"I saw your text. I was worried, I guess," I say, even though it feels intensely weird to admit that. "Are you okay?"

She definitely doesn't look okay. Her eyes are red-rimmed like she's been crying, and her cheeks are puffy. Her clothes are ruffled, and her hair is a mess, like she's just woken up from sleep.

"I guess, come in." She leads me into her bedroom, which is even messier than the last time I was here. Her bed is unmade; there are books and clothes everywhere. Rani clears a space on the bed, and the two of us sit down.

"Look, you don't have to worry," Rani says with a sigh. "My parents are mad, but there's no way they'll really say no to Amsterdam after all this time. If anything, I can probably try to convince them it's a chance for me to win Zak back and then—"

"I'm not worried about you going to Amsterdam," I say. I can't believe, after all this time we've spent together, she'd really think that would be my number-one concern. "Just . . . if my parents took Zak's side over mine, I'd be pissed as hell."

"Yeah," Rani says. "It's not . . . they're not horrible people." She glances at me with a worried look, like I might believe they are. "They think of Zak like he's their own son, you know. They've gotten used to the idea of us. It's just a lot to take in."

"Yeah, but you're their *actual* daughter," I point out. "Isn't it their responsibility to take care of you before anybody or anything else?"

Rani just shrugs, like she's really not sure. Like she thinks it's normal for her parents to support Zak over her. And I realize something—all this time my parents may have been comparing me to Rani, I may always come second to Rani, but maybe Rani comes second sometimes, too. Maybe sometimes she comes last. And maybe it's to the people who should always put her first.

I know that Ammu and Abbu think that Rani hung the moon, but I also know that when it comes to anything that really matters, they would put me first. They would choose me over anybody else.

"I'm sorry, Rani," I say after a moment that seems to stretch out forever. Where I feel like everything I've thought about Rani for most of my life has suddenly shifted. "But you deserve a lot better than this. You deserve better than Zak, and you definitely deserve better than what your parents are doing right now."

Rani glances at me again, and I can see the shine of unshed tears in her eyes. She's keeping them at bay—I know from the way she's blinking too fast, the way her jaw is slightly clenched. Like she's afraid of anyone seeing her vulnerable, even me. Maybe especially me.

I sidle forward until there's barely any space left between us on the bed. I raise my arm, resting it on her shoulder in what I hope is a comforting gesture. "It's okay to admit that all of this is not fair," I say softly.

That, at least, elicits a response from Rani that's more than a shrug.

"Thanks," she says with a sniffle. Finally, a few tears escape from the corners of her eyes. Before she can rush to wipe them away and pretend that she's not that upset, I lean forward. Brush them away with my own thumbs.

"You know how many times I've cried because my parents have acted ridiculously?" I ask. "And they're not even that ridiculous. I can just sometimes be a crybaby."

Rani laughs a little at that. "I remember you would get all teary-eyed whenever you were really angry about something."

"Right, I'm definitely an angry crier." I nod in agreement.

"Meghna, can I ask you something?" Rani asks. She holds my gaze, and I'm suddenly too aware of how little space there is between us. How my one hand is on her shoulders, the other hovering over her face. It would only take one of us leaning forward to close the gap between us.

"Anything," I say.

"How come we stopped being friends?" Rani asks.

I knew I'd have to answer the question at some point, but somehow, I'm not prepared.

"I don't know," I say. "I was stupid about it, I think. I thought it was better if we weren't, after everything that happened."

Rani nods, like she understands, even though I haven't really explained anything. "I really missed you these last few years."

"I missed you, too," I admit. "Probably more than I even realized."

My eyes flicker down to Rani's lips automatically. I'm trying not to think about the heady scent of her perfume, the thudding of my own heart against my rib cage, the warmth of Rani so close to me. Because I know that it will only take a moment for me to give in. For me to lean forward and kiss her.

Downstairs, the front door makes a loud click as it opens. Rani looks elsewhere, sliding away from me on the bed. Putting space between us. There's a rush of cold air where she was just a moment ago, and I try not to seem too crestfallen at the sudden interruption.

I move away, too, glancing at the door to her bedroom. I can hear the sounds of her parents shuffling around.

"I should probably go," I say.

"Yeah, probably," Rani says unenthusiastically.

"Are you going to be okay?" I ask, glancing over at her.

"Yeah, don't worry about me."

"Okay. I'll see you later?"

"See you," Rani says softly.

INSTEAD OF GOING HOME, I FIND MYSELF OUTSIDE BHAIYA'S APARTMENT that evening. Normally, when I realize I have a crush on someone, the people I talk to are Janella and Yemi. When I first thought I liked Zak, that's who I went to, regaling them with everything I knew about him and all the reasons I liked him. I always knew how they would react: Janella would be supportive in an ecstatic way. She would squeal at all the right times and tell me just how excited she was for me. Yemi would be supportive, too, but in a more suspicious way. They'd ask a lot of questions, want to find out as much as they could.

But I can't go to them about Rani. Because it's not just a crush, and it's not just some person. And I'm a little scared of how anyone will react.

"Meghna." Bhaiya does a double take when he opens the front door to me. "Did you tell me you were coming?"

"No, I was just passing by," I say.

"Passing by?" Bhaiya raises an eyebrow before shaking his head. "Okay, come in. You want tea?"

"Sure," I say, following him into the kitchen.

Bhaiya's apartment is small. There's one bedroom, and an open-plan kitchen which extends out into the dining and sitting rooms.

Bhaiya boils the kettle while I sit down on the couch.

"Remember how you're supposed to be the best brother ever?" I ask when Bhaiya sets a mug of tea down in front of me and sits on an armchair opposite me.

"Your only brother ever, but sure," he says.

"Well, I have a confession that I haven't shared with anyone else," I say.

"Please, do not confess to a murder right now," Bhaiya groans jokingly.

"Bhaiya, I'm serious," I say, though I'm not sure how to actually say the words I want to say out loud.

Bhaiya frowns, studying me closely. "Okay, I'm listening."

I take a deep breath. "I think I may like Rani. As more than a friend."

"Rani . . . Choudhury?" he asks.

"How many Ranis do you know?" I ask.

"I mean, there's Rani Mukerji," Bhaiya says.

"Yes, Bhaiya. I think I am in love with world-famous Bollywood actress Rani Mukerji, who is almost thirty years older than me. Would you help me find a way to share my love confession with her, please?"

"Sorry," Bhaiya says. "I was just confirming. So, okay. You're in love with Rani Choudhury, wow."

"No, I'm . . . I think I like her," I say. "I mean, I don't know. She's so annoying sometimes." I sigh. "But I guess I don't mind that she's annoying. And I think maybe I liked her even when we were kids. Maybe she was, like, my first crush?"

"She definitely was," Bhaiya agrees with a nod.

"What?"

"You two were joined at the hip. You were obsessed with each other," Bhaiya says. "And I didn't think anything of it then, but you were so weird when you stopped speaking to her. The fact that you stopped speaking to her at all was weird."

"So, you knew?" I ask.

"No," Bhaiya says. "I just . . . I'm not surprised, I guess. But you two are friends now, right? So what's the issue?"

"I thought I knew who I was, and now I don't!" I exclaim.

Bhaiya lets out a laugh, which annoys me more than anything else. "Look, Meghna. You're seventeen years old. You're definitely the most self-assured seventeen-year-old I know, but nobody at your age knows exactly who they are. I'm twenty-five and I don't know who I am. I'm pretty sure even Ammu and Abbu aren't sure who they are half the time, they're still figuring it out."

"So you could show up at home tomorrow and come out to me?" I ask.

"Is this your coming out?" Bhaiya asks with a smile. "Because honestly, so far it's just been you confessing feelings for Rani and not a lot about yourself."

"I don't know, I guess it is. Is it bad if me coming out is tied up with how I might feel about Rani?" I ask. I had never thought past Rani or the feelings I suddenly seem to have developed for her. Have there been other girls, and I've just never really thought about it? Besides Zak, it's not like I've had any other relationships, but there have been other guys that I've liked. Maybe all this time, there have been other girls, too, and I've just dismissed those feelings the same way I've dismissed everything about Rani. Shut them down somewhere deep where they weren't supposed to matter anymore.

"I don't think so," Bhaiya says. "But you should probably talk to your very gay group of friends."

"I should," I say. I know that they'll be understanding—more than anyone else. It's just scary to think that overnight the way that I think of myself can change. That there can be another whole identity that belongs to me that I'd never even realized before. "I will talk to them."

"Good," Bhaiya says. "And what about Rani? Does she feel the same way?"

I hadn't even thought that far ahead. I lean forward to pick up my tea and take a long, slow sip instead of responding immediately. "I'm not sure."

Earlier today it felt like maybe the two of us were on the same page. That maybe there was something between us that neither of us had spoken aloud before. But then I think about Amsterdam. The science project. How I've spent the past few weeks trying to figure out how to one-up her at the science competition. If my plans go as I want them to, I will finally beat out Rani and win first place at something.

But what would that mean for me and Rani?

39

RANI

THINGS AT HOME ARE STRANGE FOR THE NEXT WEEK. I DON'T know if Pari or Neel notice it, but I feel like I'm walking on eggshells around Ammu and Abbu. The Sardars didn't come that night I finally broke the news to Ammu. In fact, they don't come over at all, and we don't go over to theirs. Ammu and Abbu don't ask about Zak, and when I ask about signing the permission slip to Amsterdam, they sign it with barely any comments. I don't know if that's a good thing or a bad thing.

With everything done with the project, things with Meghna are strange, too. We barely text or talk, and we definitely don't meet up. Not since our weird moment in my bedroom. I wonder if I've finally done it—pushed Meghna away further than I had before. If my feelings are getting in the way of our friendship like I was always afraid they would.

Finally, the day before the trip to Amsterdam, as I'm packing my suitcase with all the necessities, Ammu and Abbu knock on my bedroom door.

"Your passport," Abbu says, handing me the red passport. "Make sure you text us when you get to your hotel tomorrow and call us every day."

"I will," I say, taking the passport out of his hands and sticking it into the pocket of my backpack.

"Rani, we spoke to your Sardar Uncle and Aunty," Ammu says finally. "And honestly, they're concerned."

My stomach drops, and a rock lodges in my throat. "Concerned?" I ask.

"Yes, about Zakkariyah," Ammu says slowly. "They said you were right. He is with this girl called Jillie."

"Julie," Abbu corrects her softly.

"July, yes." Ammu waves her hand dismissively. "He is with this girl called July. Thinks he has a future with her, all of these things you said. They don't blame you."

I don't know why his parents would ever blame me, but I don't say that. It's a relief that they're finally seeing Zak for who he is.

"They blame her," Ammu says. "Obviously, this girl has some kind of a grasp on him. They think you should talk to him, try to talk him out of this. He's young, still. You can still have a future with him. We want that, they want that. I'm sure once Zak really opens his eyes, he'll see."

"It's difficult here, Rani, you know that," Abbu says. "Young boys see pretty, young, Irish girls and forget about the Bangladeshi girls."

"And she is pretty, prettier than you," Ammu says. "She's so forsha. So I understand, but you have a lot to offer that this July can't."

I shake my head. "I don't want to be with Zak," I say.

"I know it hurt you that he didn't want to be with you and wanted to be with her, but—"

"No," I cut Ammu off, my voice louder than hers. Both Ammu and Abbu look taken aback. I stand up from where I was sitting cross-legged on the floor, packing up my suitcase. I stand taller than Ammu, I realize suddenly. I have for a few years now, but it never felt like I was taller than her. Like I had a voice, and more to say than I was being allowed to say. "I don't like Zak. I never have, and we don't have a lot in common. He's cocky and rude. He likes it when I wear makeup, but I don't like wearing makeup. He thinks that I need to be less than him to succeed. He wants me to do well, but only if it's helping him. That's not even friendship, let alone a relationship."

"Rani, sometimes sacrifices—"

"Ammu," I cut her off again, and she frowns. "I'm not going to Amsterdam for him. Please don't make this be about him. I've been working hard for this for years. I can win the competition, *over* Zak. And that'll be a good thing."

Ammu and Abbu exchange a glance.

"Okay," Abbu says.

Now Ammu turns to Abbu with a questioning look. Like Abbu has broken the carefully considered script they'd worked on for this competition.

"You go to Amsterdam, try to win," Abbu says. "If nothing else, maybe it'll show Zak what he's missing out on." He gives me a smile, like we're on the same page. My heart sinks, but I know this is a win I might not have otherwise. Maybe with my parents everything has to be a step at a time. And maybe this is the first step.

MRS. QUINN IS OUR CHAPERONE FOR AMSTERDAM. SHE'S WAITING outside the doors of Dublin Airport when I step out of Abbu's car.

She waves at me, and I wave back while Abbu hands me my suitcase from the trunk of his car.

"Don't forget to text us when you get there," Abbu reminds me. "And call us every day."

"Okay, Abbu, I will," I say, slipping on my backpack and grabbing the handle of the suitcase. I'm already turning around, ready to go, when Abbu stops me.

"Rani," he says. "Have a safe flight, and good luck. Your ammu and I are proud of you."

I turn back, a wave of emotions running through me. I don't think Ammu and Abbu have ever told me that they're proud of me before. No matter how many perfect report cards I get, how many medals or trophies I win. Sometimes it almost feels expected.

"Thanks, Abbu," I say. "Khodahafez."

"Got everything?" Mrs. Quinn asks when I finally reach her.

"Yep!" I say while patting my pockets to double-check my passport.

"Great, so I think we're just waiting on your partner," Mrs. Quinn says, looking around in search for Meghna, even though I'm pretty sure she has no idea what Meghna looks like. I spot her, though, out of the corner of my eye. She's getting out of a car on the other side of the road, grabbing her own suitcase and backpack. Even though it's six o'clock in the morning, Meghna looks like she's been up and ready for hours. Her hair is neatly brushed and hanging loose around her. She's wearing just the perfect amount of makeup—I can see a hint of pink around her cheeks and a swipe of black eyeliner. She's dressed in jeans, with a black undershirt and a pink vest on top.

She looks more put together than I do on my best day. She catches my eye from across the road, and my heart jumps into my throat. But she doesn't act weird. She waves, her face breaking out into a smile, which doesn't help my heart rate go down.

"She's over there," I say to Mrs. Quinn, nodding over at Meghna, who's now hugging her dad goodbye.

She crosses the road quickly; her eyes are alight as she approaches us.

"Morning," she says.

"Good morning, you must be Megna," Mrs. Quinn says.

"*Megh*na," Meghna corrects, though the difference in pronunciation is so subtle that I don't think Mrs. Quinn picks up on it.

"Right, I'm Mrs. Quinn, Rani's physics teacher. I'll be your chaperone while we're in Amsterdam. I've been in contact with your school and Ms. Ennis," she says. "It's nice to meet you."

"Nice to meet you, too," Meghna says. "Should we get going?"

We get through check-in and security quickly and walk to our gate. Mrs. Quinn goes off to buy coffee, leaving Rani and me alone at the gates—the first time we've been alone since that day in my bedroom.

"So, I made a list of places I want to go in Amsterdam," Meghna says as soon as Mrs. Quinn is out of earshot. "I know we won't have a lot of time, but it's our first time there and we should be able to fit some of it in." She shows me the notes she's been taking on her phone—full of tourist places in Amsterdam. Top of the list is the Van Gogh Museum.

"You know, it's my first time really being away from my parents," I confess.

"Same," Meghna says. "Other than, like, sleepovers at your house when we were kids, and even then Ammu and Abbu were, like, a few houses away."

"It's going to be weird seeing Zak again," I say.

"What did your parents say?" Meghna asks. "They did say something, right? I know you said things were weird around the house, but . . ."

"Yeah, they did. Yesterday," I sigh. "They think Zak's just lost his way, and I need to bring him back to the right path again."

"Because that's your responsibility?" Meghna scoffs.

I laugh. "Yeah, well. I may have convinced them it's not, but . . ." I shrug. "It's not always easy to talk to my parents. Sometimes I feel like they hear what they want to hear, even if I'm saying something completely different."

"Well, for these couple of days at least, you can be parent-free," Meghna says.

The flight to Amsterdam is only two hours long, and the taxi from the airport to our hotel is only fifteen minutes. Mrs. Quinn checks us in while we scope the place out for all the other schools and students. It seems everybody is coming in waves. With us are students from France, Croatia, Estonia, and Sweden checking in, too.

"If you're here for the young scientist competition, please wait by the seating area of the lobby," one of the receptionists announces. "And teachers checking in, please line up by the front desk."

Meghna and I follow the other students to the seating area, but we notice the strange looks that it gets us.

"This is for the European Young Scientist Exhibition," one of the guys from the French group says haughtily.

"We're here for the European Young Scientist Exhibition," Meghna says with a smile.

"Oh yeah? Where are you from?" he asks.

"Ireland," Meghna says. His eyebrows rise into his hairline at this. He exchanges a glance with all the other guys in the seating area.

"I thought Irish people were—"

"What's your project on?" One of the other guys cuts in, presumably before the French guy can spout something racist.

"We created an app that helps catch a cheating partner and also offers a digital therapist as you work through everything," Meghna says proudly. But it doesn't have the effect that she expects. The guys exchange another look, this time with sly smiles.

"Seriously, of all the apps you could have made, that's what you created?" the French guy says. "*Our* team is doing a study into synthetic food and its future sustainability."

"We created an app that helps you track and lower your carbon footprint," the guys from the Croatian team add.

"Our project is studying the physical impact of different sports on the body," one of the guys from the Swedish team says.

"Good luck with your cheating project," the first French guy says with an unfriendly grin.

Before we can say anything else, the guys turn to each other, talking more about their projects, exchanging names and schools, sharing their excitement about the competition. We've effectively been shunted out.

"What assholes," Meghna says, turning back to me, though she doesn't seem deterred. I feel my heart sink again, though. To think, after all our hard work, we're being dismissed just like that.

"Mrs. Quinn did say things might be like this," I point out.

"Whatever." Meghna rolls her eyes. "We don't need them. Our

project is good, and we have just as much a shot at winning as anybody else."

But suddenly I'm not so sure about that.

"Maybe we should rethink the Zak components," I say.

"What do you mean?" Meghna asks as she turns to me.

"I mean, I don't know. The project is good, but maybe the whole Zak stuff makes it too personal? Too melodramatic?" I ask. "If these guys are already making fun of the whole cheating aspect of it, what do you think the judges will say when they learn about how personal it is? They might just think it's a ploy for revenge and nothing else."

Meghna's brow furrows, her lips turn to a frown as she takes me in. "Rani, you're being ridiculous. These guys are just acting like sexist pricks. If *they* did a project like ours, it would have merit, I bet. Don't buy into their whole shit."

"I'm just saying, we want to win. Sometimes winning means playing their game."

"And allowing them to be sexist to us?" Meghna asks, crossing her arms.

"I'm not allowing them to be anything. Meghna, you know how STEM is a male-dominated field. Sometimes that means, I don't know, tamping down our femininity," I say.

Meghna's lip curls like that's the most horrendous thing she's heard in her life. "Rani, don't let weirdo guys like this tamp down anything. I'm definitely not letting them affect our project."

Thankfully, just at that moment, Mrs. Quinn comes back with two key cards. She hands one to each of us, along with an itinerary of our stay. "You have all day today free, but individual interviews are tomorrow morning, and then presentations are after lunch, so you might want to get some practice in. You have my phone number, right?"

"Yes." I nod, alongside Meghna.

"Great, call or text if you need anything before then," Mrs. Quinn says. With that, she turns around and begins to make her way to her own hotel room.

Meghna glances down at her key card. "Room 301," she says. "You?"

I glance at my own. "335."

Somehow though, despite our room numbers being so far away on the numerical scale, we find that they're right opposite each other in actuality.

"Should we meet in my room to practice?" Meghna asks, hovering by the door to her room.

"Okay, give me fifteen minutes and I'll be there."

Meghna nods once more before disappearing into her room with a swipe of her card.

I take a deep breath before entering my own, rolling my suitcase after me. The hotel room is a little clinical, but there's something peaceful about walking in here. Away from home, where everything was tense, away from the sexist guys downstairs. Even away from Meghna and her expectations of this project. Expectations of me.

I plop down on the perfectly made bed for a moment, closing my eyes and letting the silence wash over me. Whatever happens, Meghna and I need to get on the same page. That's the only way we're going to have any shot at winning this thing.

It's just that we're running out of time to figure it all out.

40

MEGHNA

Dumping my backpack on the floor and my carry-on suitcase in a corner, I toss myself onto the bed. At least I can get fifteen minutes of comfort before Rani and I have to discuss our project again.

This past week has been hellish. Since I had the conversation with Bhaiya about how I might have feelings for Rani, I've spent more time avoiding Rani than anything else. It's difficult enough figuring out who you are, much more difficult when there's someone who makes those questions about yourself rise to the surface constantly. I've even successfully avoided telling Janella and Yemi, changing the topic whenever Rani and our project came up. It's just easier this way for a while, until I've really figured things out.

I reach for my backpack, taking out the notes I handwrote about what I was going to say to the judges during my interview. My throat clogs up at the thought of sitting in front of them and telling them all these things about our project, about Rani.

The note cards detail all the ways that I contributed to this project: How I was the one with the idea for the app in the first place. How it was my design elements that made the app shine. How I pushed for the digital therapist, and for using our own personal experience to influence the app. There's no Rani in these cards, almost like she didn't help me at all.

I close my eyes, tossing the cards onto the desk beside the bed. I know it would be wrong to use these note cards. It would be wrong to go ahead with my initial plan and try to win this contest by throwing Rani under the bus. But now Rani is reconsidering our plans to begin with, just because of some random guys. If she can throw away everything we've worked hard for so easily, why shouldn't I throw her under the bus for my own sake?

A knock interrupts my thoughts. I crawl out of bed and open the door. Rani is standing in the doorway with her laptop, a notebook, and a folder.

"I figured we could make a demo of our presentation. Do a proper practice run," she says as she walks into my room and sets all her stuff down on the desk.

"Sure, let's do a practice run," I agree. "And maybe we can do it two ways, one with the Zak stuff. And one without. And we can see which one comes out stronger." I give her a smile, though I know it comes out as more of a challenge than a genuine, good-natured smile.

Rani sighs. "Meghna. The stuff about Zak is good—solid. But you know that's not what the issue is."

"Right, the issue is that you'd rather listen to random guys whose names we don't even know than me, your partner in this project."

"I *want* to listen to you. But Mrs. Quinn warned us that sexism could be an issue. While I was in my room, I looked up the other teams for this year's competition. There are a few girls, but most of them are in groups with boys. There are no other all-girl teams, Meghna. We're the only one. There's not even an individual girl presenting. And there's no other women of color at all. Don't you think we're already at a huge disadvantage? Do you really want to take this risk?" Rani asks.

I can see the logic behind everything she's saying, but it doesn't stop the anger seeping into my bones. I don't want Rani to be right about this.

"We're here because we want to take revenge on Zak. That was the point of all this to begin with. We do the project, we show everyone who Zak really is. That was our deal. And now you really want to go back on that?"

"Meghna, think about it properly. Put aside your emotions for a moment and—"

"You're being a hypocrite!" I cry. "I don't want to put my emotions aside. You want to be a scientist in male-dominated STEM, but what does it matter when you're going to put aside everything that makes you a woman just to fit into what they want? Isn't that the problem? Isn't that what we're fighting against?"

"We can't do it all at once," Rani says softly. "If we win this, that's a big deal."

I hate that while I'm getting more frustrated, Rani is becoming more soft-spoken. I remember this is one of the things I've always hated about her. She's never been good at showing her emotions. Even when we were kids, when we would get into fights, she would rarely raise her voice. She would rarely even show her anger. It was another part of her perfection that I hated.

"Look, let's just do a test run, and then you'll be able to see just how . . ." Rani picks up her notes and begins to thumb through them, but her expression suddenly darkens, and her words dry up.

"Rani, you can't just pretend that we're not having a major

disagreement right now. Before we do any test runs, we need to figure out what—"

"What's this?" Rani interrupts. She holds out the note cards. Not hers—mine. The notes I wrote up for my interview with the judges.

"Just . . . nothing," I say, trying to get them back from Rani, but she holds them out of the way, out of reach.

"Nothing, which tells the judges that you're the person who did all the work on our project?" Rani asks. There's a quiet anger in her voice now. It's unsettling.

"I wasn't going to use them," I say, even though I had still been considering it.

"Then why are they out on the desk?" Rani asks.

"I don't know. I guess with you wanting to leave the stuff about Zak out of the project, I was considering it," I say.

"Are you serious?" Rani asks. Her voice is trembling now, and I realize that all this time I've actually been lucky to never really experience an angry Rani. I can see the hurt and anger flashing in her eyes with every word. "You wouldn't even be here if I hadn't won the competition in Ireland. In case you don't remember, your project didn't win, but mine did. I should have never invited you to work with me."

"That's not fair," I say, my voice quiet. "This project wouldn't be what it is if it wasn't for me."

"No, it wouldn't," Rani agrees. "And it would probably be better off for it. This plan to take revenge on Zak? It's pathetic. Why is everything about him? Yeah, he cheated on you, he cheated on me. He's a terrible person, but it doesn't mean everything has to be about him. You don't want to get over him with this, you just want to take your anger out on someone by exposing him. It's not good science, and it's not going to win the competition. At the end of the day, it just makes everything about some guy who neither of us should have ever even been with. Zak will probably love it, seeing us make him the subject of our project."

I hold back angry tears threatening to seep out now. "Just because you don't have any feelings, Rani, doesn't mean the rest of us don't, either. I had an *actual* relationship with Zak; maybe you just don't know what that feels like. And honestly, I'm tired. I'm tired of always being one-upped by you. Of always feeling like you're better than me at everything. So yeah, I was going to tell the judges that I did most of the work and you did nothing so that for once I can actually beat you at something. So for once I would actually stand a chance against you. So for once my parents would see that I could win something that you couldn't, and they wouldn't compare me to you. I'm tired of not measuring up to you, tired of feeling like I have to do things differently just so I stand a chance against you. I thought it was bad before, but do you know how much it hurt to have to measure up to you even with Zak? To find out that he wasn't just cheating, he was cheating with *you*?"

Rani purses her lips. "Meghna, you're ridiculous. Zak cheated on you, and the worst thing about it was me. Really?"

"I didn't say—"

"*I* never asked you to measure up to me. I never asked you to be anyone that you aren't. I'm sorry you feel the way you do, but I didn't do anything to cause that. I'm just trying to live my life, and guess what? I feel like I have to measure up to people, too. I feel like I have something to prove all the time. But I don't take it out on you. I don't take it out on Zak. Because I'm not that kind of a person."

"You might think you know what it feels like to always be compared to someone, but you have no idea," I say.

"You might think you know what it feels like to be me, Meghna, but *you* have no idea," Rani says. She gathers up her things silently, letting the words hang there. "I'm going to go. You tell the judges everything you've done. You get your win, Meghna. I hope that makes you feel better about yourself."

With that, she swiftly leaves the room, leaving behind an emptiness that seems to take up the whole space.

CRYING OVER RANI IS SOMEHOW A MILLION TIMES WORSE THAN crying over Zak. And the most horrible thing is, I've been here before. Years ago, when I made the decision that we shouldn't be friends anymore. When I ignored her calls and texts. For months, I pretended that it was better for everyone, better for me. That I wouldn't have to measure up to her anymore. But it still hurt like hell to lose her.

And now the hurt is fresh again.

I know that I have to talk things out, but there's so much I've been hiding from people that I don't even know who to call or what to tell them. But I know that it's time.

So, I find myself starting a group call with Janella and Yemi.

They both pick up after one ring, almost like they've been waiting by the phone.

"Meghna!" Yemi's voice is ecstatic. "Are you already there? Tell us all about Amsterdam! Have you been outside, or are you just holed up practicing for your project? You *have* to go out at least for a little bit, please promise you won't spend your whole time there in your hotel room."

"Yemi, give her a chance to actually answer your questions," Janella says, reprimanding them. "Go on, Meghna. Tell us everything."

That's all the prompt I need. Because just like that, everything pours out of me: our revenge plan, my intention to undermine Rani in our project so I could win, my feelings, our fight.

After I talk for what feels like hours and my voice is hoarse and my throat is dry, everything is out there. Silence washes over our call for a minute. I'm afraid of what my friends are going to say. I don't know what I would say if either of them confessed all of this to me.

"Meghna, you're ridiculous," Yemi finally says with a sigh.

"What?"

"You realize from everything you've told us that you've probably been in love with Rani since you were kids, right?" Yemi asks.

"That's a strong word," I say quietly.

"Okay, sure, let's not use that word, then," Yemi says, their voice heavy with sarcasm. "But I think you've been self-sabotaging for a long time. I mean, I always thought it was weird how much you talk about her considering she's supposed to be your mortal enemy, but this definitely puts everything into perspective."

"It does," Janella agrees after a moment. "And I think you've been pretty unfair to her. I mean, sure, it must suck to always be compared to her, but it's not really her fault. She's just doing her thing. And from what it sounds like, she's right. She has her own stuff, too. The stuff with her parents? I mean, her parents would rather support some guy that cheated on her than their own daughter. Isn't that weird? Your parents would never do that. Think about how that must make her feel."

I *had* thought about it, but I guess I had never thought about it enough to imagine the reality of it. Sure, my parents may say, "look at Rani, she got straight As," or "look at Rani, her science project is all about languages, the most important thing to any Bengali," but they've never made me feel like they're not still proud of me. They complain and they annoy me, but at the end of the day, I know they love me. That they would show up and support me even if they had no idea what they were supporting.

I don't think Rani can say the same thing.

"It sounds to me like you've always been trying to take the easy way out," Yemi says. "You stopped talking to Rani way back then because it was easier to do that than face dealing with your feelings, or even face fighting for your friendship when everything else was falling apart."

"And now it's easier to throw her under the bus and act like she's the villain than admit that you might have real feelings for her. That the two of you could have something."

"And also, Rani is right," Yemi adds. "As much as I hate to admit it, all the stuff you have on Zak might embarrass him for a little bit. But at the end of the day, he'll feel like he's the center of your world. Getting revenge might feel good for a moment, but I don't think it's been helping you get over him."

"But I'm over him," I say. But I don't think it's because of our project or because of the promise of revenge. If anything, the revenge aspect of our project has only made it harder to get over Zak. It's made the hurt fresher with every interaction I've had to endure because of him. What's made things easier is Rani. "Though I don't think it's because of the project," I admit. "You're right . . . maybe I have been self-sabotaging."

"Oh, you one hundred percent have been," Yemi says. "Also, Janella, you owe me lunch this weekend."

"Ugh," Janella groans.

"What?" I ask.

"I bet Janella that you would confess your feelings for Rani during this Amsterdam trip, and I was right. You finally told us."

"I was sure it would be after Amsterdam because with your project all finished, you'd finally realize how you felt," Janella sighs. "I guess I was wrong."

"You guys knew?" I ask.

"We had a feeling," Janella admits. "Like Yemi said, you talk about her *a lot* considering she's supposed to be your mortal enemy."

And I guess they're right. And I guess Rani is not my mortal enemy at all.

The only problem is, I've screwed things up so bad, I don't know how I'm supposed to make them right again.

41

RANI

I DON'T KNOW WHY, BUT AFTER THE HORRIBLE FIGHT WITH Meghna, the last thing I want to do is stay in that hotel room right opposite hers. So I grab my things and head out instead, with no idea of where I'm really going.

After a lot of time spent on Google Maps, I figure out how to get the tram into Amsterdam city center, and so that's exactly what I do. The city is beautiful. There are canals and bridges everywhere, and people riding their bikes every which way.

There are even beautiful decorative bikes with flowers around every corner. I take photos of everything. I know that Pari and Neel will be asking me a bajillion questions about my time here, and I'll have to fill them in. I buy an Amsterdam T-shirt for Pari and a packet of stroopwafels for Neel.

Even though it's chilly outside, I decide to walk through town. Past the canals, through the streets. Passing by cheese shops, florists full of beautiful, colorful tulips, and more bikes than I can count. There's something great about the fresh air, the bite of cold in it. It almost—almost—makes me forget about Meghna. But she's still there somewhere, her words niggling in my mind.

I finally pause to enter into a small café that promises to serve Dutch pancakes. Neel looked up all the foods to try while in Amsterdam, and top of her list were frites and Dutch pancakes. I slide into one of their booths and order a plate of the pancakes. The waitress gives me a smile before sauntering off, leaving me to look out the window at the beautiful view of the blue canal against a backdrop of colorful houses.

I wish that Meghna and I weren't fighting. I wish I hadn't said half the things I said to her. Then the two of us could be here together, sharing Dutch pancakes and exploring the city. But I let my anger get the better of me.

Sure, she was wrong for trying to sabotage me. But I knew I was wrong about Zak as soon as the words left my lips. I understood why Meghna wanted to get revenge. Why she wanted to focus our project on him. I could tell he had hurt her in a way that he had never hurt me. Meghna didn't deserve what he did to her.

With the beautiful view of the canal in front of me, with only me and my thoughts here occupying space, what Meghna said about feeling like she didn't measure up to me doesn't even feel so horrible. Because everyone else has always seen me as someone who shouldn't be capable. My parents want me to make myself smaller for Zak—or any guys, really—because they think I shouldn't take up space. Bengali aunties want me to be the same—worthy of being the perfect wife to some man at the expense of myself. Zak wants me to be good at science, but only so long as I'm worse than him.

Meghna, though, actually sees me as competition. She actually sees me as someone who she has to beat. Someone who has achieved things. Someone who's capable of things.

It would be nicer if she was proud of it instead of trying to sabotage me, but it's still a weirdly nice feeling to be seen as competition. Especially by someone like Meghna, who's already so great at everything she does. If anything, I should be the one feeling like I can't measure up to her.

Maybe at the end of the day, it's not about how we see each other, but how we've been made to see each other by other people.

"Everything okay?" the waitress asks as she sets down the plate of pancakes in front of me. It smells sweet, but it does nothing to lessen the dull ache in my heart.

"Everything's fine," I say, with a smile. Though, really, everything isn't fine at all. All I really want to do is talk to Meghna. Find a way past our fight. Except after everything that's been said, I have no idea how we're meant to do that.

42

MEGHNA

I SLEEP SO LITTLE THAT NIGHT THAT, BY THE TIME WE HAVE TO leave the hotel for the museum where the interviews and presentations will take place, my eyes are red-rimmed and there are bags under them. I do the best I can with makeup.

Opening my hotel door, though, I find myself suddenly face-to-face with Rani, who looks just as run-down as I feel. We both look away before we can make eye contact. We haven't spoken since our fight yesterday—I still don't know what to say to her. We definitely haven't practiced our presentation.

Rani takes a right, toward the stairs, so I turn left to take the lift down. We don't need to be near each other until absolutely necessary.

Mrs. Quinn is at the lounge downstairs, looking fresh-faced and ready for the day.

"Good morning!" she says a little too brightly when she sees me. Rani, unfortunately, is right on my heels. "Hope you're both well rested and ready for your big day today."

I give Mrs. Quinn a smile while Rani mumbles something unintelligible under her breath.

"Right." Mrs. Quinn's smile wavers a little, but she doesn't let our demeanor keep her down. "Let's get going, then!"

We make our way out of the hotel and take the tram toward the science museum. Despite the chill in the air, it's a beautiful day out.

The sun is shining and there isn't a cloud in the sky. I watch the city pass by in the tram windows: the beautiful canals stretching over everything, the colorful houses clustered together, the dozens of people zooming by on their bikes. Amsterdam is so different from Dublin, and I wish that I could enjoy it instead of spending my time thinking about how I messed everything up yesterday.

Mrs. Quinn makes the weather the point of conversation during our entire half-hour journey from the hotel all the way to the museum. Somehow, she manages to keep it going for that long with almost no replies from me or Rani.

"I know you girls are nervous," Mrs. Quinn finally says as we get to the lobby of the museum. "But don't worry, you'll be great. Don't psych yourselves out—I think you've got as good a chance at winning this as anyone else. And you've already come so far. You should be proud of yourselves!"

"Thanks, Mrs. Quinn," Rani says. It's the first real sentence she's said all morning.

"Yeah, thank you," I say.

Mrs. Quinn beams at us before she checks us in.

The museum is full of different kinds of displays. If this was any other day, I would be marveling over all of it—especially their half-floor display that's all about water.

"Right, so, Meghna, you're set to speak to the judges first in room 302 on the top floor. It's five past nine, so you'd better hurry up there. And Rani, you've got a slot at nine thirty, in room 303, also top floor. I'll see you both at the conference hall in time for your presentations." She gives us a smile and a thumbs-up for encouragement.

I try to catch Rani's eyes before I turn to leave, but her gaze is glued to her shoes all of a sudden. So I shuffle up the stairs and through weaving corridors until I find room 302. When I knock twice, a deep voice calls me in.

The room's not big, exactly, but it feels overwhelming. There's only one desk in the middle, with two judges sitting on one side, and an empty chair on the other side, for me.

"Meghna Rahman?" one of the judges asks. He's tall, with blond hair.

"Yes, that's me," I say, hoping that the nervousness can't be heard in my voice.

"Take a seat," the second judge says. He has dark brown hair and seems a little more serious out of the two.

I make my way toward the chair and sit down.

"So, Meghna. Your app . . . C.A.T., catch a two-timer." The blond judge chuckles as he looks over our information sheet. "Clever title. I see that you worked on it with a partner. Tell us about it."

"About the app?" I ask.

"And about your process working on it," the second judge says with a small smile.

"Well, my partner, Rani, and I had a shared experience. We were both cheated on by the same guy," I say. "And that's kind of what led to us wanting to create this app. We thought it would have been nice if there was some way we could have known before. And I guess we also thought it would have been nice if there was a way for us to work through how much it sucks to be cheated on."

When both the judges nod encouragingly, I continue.

"I was actually pretty unfamiliar with the process of making an app. My specialty is more in the social sciences, so I guess a lot of my contribution came in the digital therapist aspect, where your digital therapist can talk you through some of your feelings and share some statistics about cheating and relationships that make you feel a little less alone. But . . ." I pause, taking a deep breath. "An app obviously can't function without the coding behind it, and I have to be honest, that was all Rani. She worked on this app day and night trying to make sure that it worked. I just had a simple idea, but she's the person who made it into reality. And she made it better than anything I could have ever imagined. She's probably the best coder *I've* ever met. Granted, I haven't met a lot of coders, but I still think she's one of the best."

The judges continue to smile, a little awkwardly now, like they hadn't quite expected me to ramble on for so long. It probably would have been helpful if I had written any of this down, but when I tried to last night, nothing seemed quite right. After spending so long trying to think of ways to undermine Rani, and even longer trying to figure out all the ways I could outshine her, it was strange to sit down and try and think of the opposite. But sitting here now, I realize that everything out of my mouth is sincere—and it's all true about Rani. I've just been too consumed by my own prejudice to see her clearly.

"So, one of *your* major contributions was the digital therapist aspect?" the brown-haired judge asks with a raised eyebrow. "Tell us more about your work on that."

"Um, I came up with the idea for the digital therapist. I wasn't really sure how to execute it, but Rani had some great ideas about that. Other than the coding, obviously, she also thought about going out and getting our own data. So we did surveys in both of our schools to gather that data. We also researched more widely and compared *our* data sets with the wider data, and that's where a lot of what the digital therapist does comes from. If we had more time to work on it, and more funds, we would probably get a real therapist to make contributions to shape it, but right now, everything really comes from the data we gathered and . . . I guess, a little from our own experiences," I say.

"And if you could improve any part of the app, what would you change?" the brown-haired judge asks.

My fight with Rani and my subsequent conversation with my friends pop up in my mind. What *would* I change?

"I wouldn't make our app centered on spying on your partner. We focused on that, but it didn't help us move on from what happened to us. And the coding of it all is great—which is thanks to Rani—but it's also an invasion of privacy. I think people will always find ways to spy on their partners, regardless of our app, but that doesn't mean we should be helping them do it. If I could improve our app, I would focus on helping people heal from cheating—with the digital therapist, with support groups, and such."

"It certainly seems like a unique app, Meghna," the blond judge says. "We look forward to hearing more about C.A.T. app this afternoon."

I smile, hoping that I've done enough to convince the judges that if anyone deserves the prize out of the two of us, it's Rani, and decidedly not me.

After Rani and I finish our interviews, Mrs. Quinn takes us to lunch in the restaurant at the science museum. She peppers us with questions about the interviews and our presentation later, but

I guess neither of us are feeling particularly chatty. Rani mentions being questioned on the ethics of our app, and I talk about the questions about the digital therapist. After a few too many unenthusiastic answers, she stops trying, probably chalking our lack of enthusiasm up to nervousness.

After lunch, Mrs. Quinn marches Rani and I to the massive conference hall at the other end of the museum. There's a huge stage on one end, where a panel of judges sit. I recognize the two judges I had my interview with, but there are a few more judges sitting alongside them. Facing the stage are rows of seats. Most of them are already filled with students and chaperones from the other countries, along with leading people in different scientific fields who've been invited.

I catch sight of Zak in one corner, speaking to a man who must be the chaperone from his school. He glances up, catches my eye, and does a double take. I try not to smile as I look away. I guess the last thing he expected was to see me here.

"All right, there are three empty seats right here," Mrs. Quinn says. "You two are all set for your presentation, right? I sent in everything you emailed me yesterday, Meghna."

Rani turns to me with a questioning look, but I ignore it.

"Thanks, Mrs. Quinn. Yes, we should be all set," I say.

"What did you send in yesterday?" Rani asks.

"I just looked over everything and refined it," I say. "Don't worry."

Rani frowns but sits down and looks at the stage instead of at me. It doesn't take long for the presentations to begin. Whatever Rani looked up during her research was completely right: Most of the people presenting here are groups of boys. There are no individual girls, and definitely no other all-girl groups, though there are mixed-gender groups.

The projects range from technology to medicine, physics to chemistry and behavioral sciences. There's a group from Portugal who present an investigation into men's mental health in the modern world, another from Malta who present a comparative study into cat owners versus dog owners.

Finally, it's time for me and Rani.

We go backstage a few minutes before while Mrs. Quinn gives us another one of her big thumbs-ups from her seat.

I can see the nerves on Rani's face and from the way her fingers seem to be trembling as she looks out onto the stage. There are almost two hundred people in the audience, consisting of both our peers and leading scientists. It's a little scary to think about.

"We're going to be okay," I whisper to Rani. She glances down at me but doesn't quite seem comforted by my words. I guess after everything I said to her yesterday, I don't see why she would be. She must think that I'm the worst person in the world.

"Meghna, I—"

I don't get to hear the end of her sentence, because the crowd breaks out into applause for the group currently onstage—it's the Croatian guys we met in the hotel lounge yesterday. They give us cocky grins as they pass by. One of them sarcastically mouths, *break a leg*.

I roll my eyes.

Finally, the host announces me and Rani. The two of us step onto the stage. The updated presentation I had sent to Mrs. Quinn last night is on the screen behind us.

"Our project is called C.A.T.—or the catch a two-timer app," Rani begins to explain. "We've, um, created this app which—"

"Makes it easier to figure out if your partner is cheating on you and, if they *are,* it talks you through your feelings and how to deal with being cheated on," I add, interrupting Rani before she can mention anything about Zak.

Rani gives me a questioning look but follows my lead. We slowly go through everything that the two of us prepared. We speak about our app, the coding and design behind it, how it can be used to gather data from your partner but can also just be used to look through what they've already posted online. We go through the digital therapist aspect and the statistics we gathered both from our interviews and surveys and through our research. We even share the texts that show Zak was cheating on us, gathered through our app, but leave out names.

Our original presentation was meant to end with what we discovered about Zak: how we found Julie and how he lied to us about everything. It had the recording of Zak admitting to the cheating, exposing him once and for all for everyone here to see. But when it's time to present all of that, I step in.

"When we originally wanted to create this app, it had a simple purpose: to make it easier to find out if you're being cheated on. But as we developed it, I think it turned into something else. We learned a lot through this app and through our research. We learned that cheating can cause undue harm to both partners in a relationship and have long-lasting effects. Studies show that both those who have cheated and those who have been cheated on report poorer-quality relationships in the future. Ultimately, I think that our app aims to do more than just catch someone who is cheating. It tries to help the ones who have been cheated on, to help them feel less alone, help them work through their emotions: their anger, sadness, whatever they're feeling. And maybe in some ways it can even help the ones who have cheated learn about themselves; why they do it, and how much it can hurt—both themselves and others. Because that's the conclusion that we drew here: Nobody is happy at the end of it. Not even the ones who have cheated."

As the presentation ends, the crowd breaks out into applause. I glance across the stage at Rani, who is looking at me with that frown still on her lips. I did what she wanted—left Zak out of the presentation. She was right in the end: It made the presentation better. Our project never needed to center Zak or our pain, anyway. It's not up to us to expose that to a group of strangers in the hope that they understand us.

But I just hope Rani sees this as supporting her instead of betraying her.

43

RANI

THERE ARE A MILLION THINGS I WANT TO SAY TO MEGHNA, BUT we're ushered back to our seats as soon as our presentation is over so that the next group can present. We sit on either side of Mrs. Quinn for another hour, watching the presentations even though none of it quite registers for me anymore.

Because Meghna gave up her revenge, and she did it for me.

Finally, the presentations are over, and the judges call a short coffee break before the winners are announced. People begin shuffling out of the conference room and toward the coffee area in the next room, but both Meghna and I shake our heads at Mrs. Quinn's offer for coffee.

"So, you changed a lot," I say to Meghna once Mrs. Quinn is out of sight and it's just the two of us. It's the most we've said to each other since our fight yesterday.

"Yeah, I mean, just the stuff about Zak. I wanted to tell you about it earlier, but I didn't really know how to, and I was afraid of getting into another fight, or not being able to explain myself properly. And honestly there wasn't that much time, so I thought I'd just do it and explain everything to you later and hopefully—"

"It's okay, Meghna," I cut her off. This is the most nervous I've ever seen her. "Thanks for changing it, but you didn't have to. I kind of owe you an apology."

Meghna just stares at me for a moment. "You owe *me* an apology?"

"Yeah, I mean . . . Maybe we owe each other apologies? But I don't know, I shouldn't have said the stuff that I did. About Zak and all that, which I don't want to repeat. I get it. He hurt you, and it's okay that you're angry. It's okay that you wanted to get revenge. Just because I didn't feel the same as you doesn't mean that you don't get to feel the way you do," I say. "And I'm sorry if anything I ever said or did made you feel like you had to be different, or someone you're not. Because I don't want you to be different, Meghna. I like you just the way you are."

Meghna takes me in slowly, like she's trying to process my words. "You're not the person who made me feel like I have to be someone I'm not. That's been everyone else, and maybe it's been me to an extent. Comparing myself to you," she says finally. She pauses and glances down at her feet before continuing. "I'm sorry for everything I said to you yesterday. I knew I was being ridiculous for wanting to win against you so badly. I've just had this idea of you in my head for so long because it feels like the two of us are always pitted against each other, and I was just tired of losing. But I could have jeopardized everything we both worked for if I had used those note cards you saw."

"So you didn't use them during your interview this morning?" I ask. She had been so angry at me yesterday that I was sure she would do everything in her power to make sure she got her win. That's the Meghna I knew.

"Of course I didn't," Meghna says, looking at me now like it's the most obvious thing in the world. "I should have never even written them. I told the judges about just how much you put into our app.

That, without you, the app wouldn't be what it was." She smiles at me, and my heart skips a beat. I guess this is the Meghna of now, the one who knows how to say sorry and shed her anger when necessary. And I think I'm somehow even more in love with this version of her.

"You didn't have to do that," I say softly.

"I kind of did. I mean, I was wrong. And the things I said." She pauses like she also doesn't want to repeat any of it. "You're the best thing that came out of Zak cheating on me. Because if he hadn't, I don't know if we would be friends right now."

Meghna is looking at me in a way that she hasn't really looked at me before. Or maybe she has, once, in my bedroom when I was falling apart a little. She's not looking at me like how a friend looks at another friend. But I don't know if it's just me projecting my own feelings onto her, or if this is actually real.

"We're friends?" I ask.

"Well, if you'll forgive me," Meghna says. It sounds like she's joking, but there's genuine worry hidden in there, like I could really stay angry at her.

"I'll forgive you if you'll forgive me," I offer.

Meghna smiles, but there's still something sad behind it. Like she isn't done saying all she wanted to say. "Actually, Rani. There's—"

But she cuts herself off when a figure stops right by our seats. When we look up, we see Zak standing there with a sheepish smile. "Hey, Rani, Meghna," he says.

"What are you doing here?" Meghna asks with a glare.

"I was hoping we could talk," he says. He at least has the decency to look embarrassed after everything he's put us through.

I glance at Meghna, but she's too busy glaring at Zak to notice.

He doesn't wait for us to respond before launching into what he has to say. "I know that the project was about me, even if you didn't mention me. And I just wanted to say that even though it was kind of shitty of you guys to use your app to spy on me, I guess I could have been . . . a better boyfriend."

"No shit, you tried to manipulate me into thinking *I* was the problem," Meghna says. "And Rani was always way too good for you. I don't even know why her parents thought that—"

I reach out and grab Meghna's hand before she can say anything more. She stops in her tracks, looking at me instead of at him.

"He's not worth it," I say. "Let him think whatever he wants. Let him take away from this whatever he wants. It has nothing to do with us."

"Hey, I'm standing right here," Zak says, though he sounds more deflated than angry. I wonder if he *has* actually learned something from all this, but I'm definitely not holding out hope.

I roll my eyes before standing and pulling Meghna up with me. I lead her past him and toward the exit of the conference hall. Zak calls out after us, but we just ignore it. We walk upstairs, to the balcony on the other side of the café. I know we probably don't have a lot of time before they announce the winners, but there's something I need to do first. My conversation with Meghna is not over.

"Meghna, I know you said that we're friends. That all is forgiven, but I feel like there's something I should tell you," I say, pulling her into a secluded corner of the balcony.

"There's something I need to tell you as well," Meghna says. She takes a deep breath, her eyes finding mine. But she doesn't speak. Instead, she steps forward, linking her fingers with mine. There's a flutter in my stomach at the touch.

"Rani, I've been a coward," she says.

"You could never be a coward," I say. "You're, like, the bravest person ever. You always say exactly what's on your mind."

"Not always," Meghna says softly. "Like a few years back, when my dad's company went bankrupt, people started rumors about him being responsible, doing illegal things, and everyone believed the rumors and turned against us. I should have told you that I was hurt, felt betrayed. I shouldn't have taken it out on you. I should have told you that you were my best friend, and the most important person in the world to me. I should have held on to that."

"We were kids," I say, even though this is the explanation I feel like I've been waiting my whole life for. But now it feels like it doesn't even matter. Whatever happened back then happened. And now Meghna and I are here together, friends again.

"Yeah, but we aren't kids anymore. And, Rani, I think I like you a lot more than as a friend. I think I've liked you as more than a friend for a long time," Meghna says. She looks away as she does, like she's afraid of what answer I'll give. Like she really doubts how I feel about her.

"Meghna," I say, even though it feels like my breath is stuck in my throat. Like there's no more air in my lungs. "I think I've been in love with you for pretty much my whole life."

Meghna glances at me, her brown eyes warm and bright as they peer into mine. Then she leans up and presses her lips to mine, and it feels like everything else in the world melts away.

44

MEGHNA

WHEN THE TWO OF US GET BACK INSIDE TO THE CONFERENCE room, the host is mid-speech. Mrs. Quinn frowns at us from the back row as she waves us over. Rani and I hurry down, sitting next to each other this time, instead of on either side of Mrs. Quinn.

"Where were you two?" Mrs. Quinn asks.

"Nowhere," I say quickly, feeling my face flush.

"We got lost coming back from the bathroom," Rani offers as an explanation.

Satisfied with that, Mrs. Quinn turns back to the stage.

"—and each year we see young scientists like you become more and more innovative. It's inspiring for all of us in the field of science to have you all here, dedicated to making the world better with your work. We hope that whether you win or lose today, your work in the field of science continues." The host finishes, flashing a smile at all of us. "And, without further ado, we're excited to announce the winners of the twelfth annual European Young Scientist Exhibition." Someone shuffles up to him with two envelopes.

I take a deep breath, and—almost as if she can sense my nervousness—Rani leans closer and threads her fingers through mine. It feels like the most natural thing in the world all of a sudden. I wonder why we haven't been holding hands and kissing all these years, as I glance at her.

“Do you think we have a shot?” I whisper.

“As much a shot as anyone else,” Rani says.

“The award for the group project goes to . . . Carbon Less, the app to lower carbon footprints, from Croatia!” the host announces. I expect to feel some kind of a gut punch at the loss, but I don’t feel much at all. When the applause begins, I clap my hands together, too, watching the two guys from Croatia make their way up to the stage with huge grins on their faces as they accept their trophies and shake hands with the judges. I wouldn’t go so far as to say I’m *happy* for the winners, but there’s none of my usual resentment that seems to overtake everything else. The only thing left now is the individual prize, which makes my stomach clench. I hope I’ve done enough to convince the judges who really deserves it out of everyone here.

Rani gives me a sympathetic look as the host begins to announce the next winner. “Are you okay?”

I shrug. “Yeah, are you?”

“Yeah, I think I—”

“—Rani Choudhury, for her contribution to the C.A.T. app, made in collaboration with Meghna Rahman!” The host’s booming voice cuts over Rani, whose eyes widen at her name. She sits there for a moment, unmoving. Beside me, Mrs. Quinn is beaming so bright that I’m surprised she hasn’t blinded someone. I can’t help that my face breaks out into a grin, too, as I turn to Rani.

“Rani, you won!” I say.

“I won,” Rani says slowly.

“Rani Choudhury?” the host calls again.

I pull Rani to a stand and push her toward the aisle. She walks up to the stage, her eyes still glazed with confusion. I watch as she accepts her trophy and shakes hands with the judges.

Strangely, Mrs. Quinn turns to face me. "Meghna, I know it must be difficult to see Rani win when you both worked on your project together. But you should look at this as your win, too. The app exists because of both of you."

"I know," I say. And I do. Because I don't feel that usual anger that niggles at me whenever Rani's name comes up. I'm not thinking about when I go back to Dublin and my parents inevitably sing praises of Rani and her win. I'm thinking about the way Rani's walking offstage, carrying the trophy in her arms like it's something precious. How she's smiling so brightly that it could light up the whole room. I'm thinking that losing to Rani Choudhury again isn't that bad after all, especially when she's your friend.

Especially when she's something more.

45

RANI

After a lot of congratulations and what seems like hundreds of photos, I feel like my smile muscles are about to collapse.

"We will let you go back to your hotel room and enjoy your win," one of the judges finally says. "Congratulations again, to all of you."

I wave goodbye to the judges and the boys from the Croatian team before exiting the now-empty conference room. Most people left a long time ago, after the winners were announced and before the photos began. I look around, hoping to see Mrs. Quinn and Meghna waiting for me outside, but they're nowhere to be found.

Something deflates in me, even though I know I'm being silly. They wouldn't wait around for me for so long. I'm more than capable of making my way back to my hotel room. And Meghna probably needed some time away from me, anyway.

"Done with all your photo ops?" I nearly drop my trophy at the sound of Meghna's voice. I whip around to find her approaching from the other side of the room—where they had set up the coffee and snacks.

"Yeah," I say. "Where's Mrs. Quinn?"

"I convinced her to go back to the hotel. I said that we'd be okay making our way back together and if we needed anything, we would call," Meghna says. Her voice is even—normal. I try to study her expression for any sign of anger. I couldn't exactly blame her if she *was* annoyed at me.

"You didn't have to wait around for me. I could have found my way back on my own," I say.

"Seriously?" Meghna asks. She steps forward and takes the trophy out of my hands before looping her free arm through mine. "You win one award and you're already ready to get rid of me?"

"I'm not—"

"I'm joking, Rani," Meghna says, rolling her eyes as she tugs the two of us toward the exit of the museum. "I'm really proud of you. You deserved to win more than anyone else I know."

"You should have won, too," I say. "I mean, we worked on the app together, and I know how much you wanted it."

We step outside the museum, into the chilly November air. Instead of responding to me, Meghna stops us both in our tracks. She places the trophy on the steps behind us before turning around and observing me wordlessly for a moment.

"What?" I ask.

She doesn't reply. Instead, she leans forward and envelops me in a hug. It's unexpected and warm. I wrap my arms around her, too, breathing in the fresh, minty smell of her.

"What was that for?" I ask when she pulls away.

"I don't know. I guess I just know what it feels like to have a boyfriend who doesn't completely support you, and I don't want that to be us," Meghna says. "I just want you to believe what I said. That I'm proud of you. That you deserve this."

Somehow that assuages that gnawing of guilt I've been feeling ever since my name was called. The one clouding my mind when I looked at Meghna over the crowds from up onstage. But I remember, Meghna hadn't seemed angry then, either.

"So now you're my boyfriend?" I ask with a smile.

"Something like that." Meghna smiles before looping our arms together once more. She picks up the trophy and the two of us make our way toward the tram, hand in hand under the twinkling lights of Amsterdam.

When I wake up the next morning in my hotel room, I blink at the bright sunlight flooding in through the paper-white curtains, feeling a strange sense of peace wash over me. Then I remember that it's our last day in Amsterdam.

Thankfully, there's nothing on the itinerary today and no projects to worry about anymore.

"Any plans for your last day in the city, girls?" Mrs. Quinn asks us over breakfast at the hotel restaurant.

Meghna and I exchange a quick glance. We hadn't decided anything, but I remember the list she had shown me when we were at the Dublin airport. Meghna hadn't gotten to do anything on her list, thanks to our fight on the very first day.

"I think we're going to go to the Van Gogh Museum," I say. "Meghna is a fan."

"Good plan." Mrs. Quinn nods appreciatively.

Meghna and I end up doing a lot more than touring the Van Gogh Museum. We explore the city hand in hand; take photos by the canal, share stroopwafels, and catch each other up on so many of the things we missed in each other's lives over the past few years.

"You know, we should do a project for the Irish Young Scientist Exhibition together next year," I suggest tentatively while we're having lunch in a cozy café with an amazing view of the canal.

Meghna looks at me with a confused frown. "Really? Because you kind of have a streak of doing really well, and I have a streak of losing."

I shrug. "We worked pretty well together on this."

"And we *lost*," Meghna says.

"But we made it all the way here. And the only reason our project lost is because we kind of kept getting in our own way. I mean, you made last-minute changes to our presentation. *I* asked you to cut out a huge component that we'd worked really hard on. And . . . we were trying to use our project to get revenge. Plus, I don't think the fact that our app was pretty unethical really helped our case," I say. I can't help but wonder if we had figured out what our project needed earlier whether we could have won the whole thing.

"I don't know. I don't want to, like . . . drag you down," Meghna says. I don't know how she can ever think that she would drag me down when she's the reason why there's a trophy tucked neatly into my suitcase, ready to carry home. I reach out my hand across the table, linking our fingers together. It still feels a little strange to hold her hand, after I've imagined what us being together could look like for God knows how long. But it feels strange in a good way. In the butterflies in the stomach, sparks on our fingertips kind of way.

"If anything, you've made me better," I say. "I mean, our app would look very different if I was the only person working on it. I wouldn't have even thought of something so . . . innovative."

Meghna tilts her head to one side, narrowing her eyes like she really wants to make sure I'm telling the truth. "Your language app was already pretty amazing, though. And I mean, it helped you win."

"Yeah, but you were right about it when you criticized my UI. If you had been my partner for it, it would have been better."

"I only criticized your UI because I was trying to be antagonistic," Meghna says sheepishly. "Your UI was clean and usable."

"But you could have made it better," I say. "I just think we make a pretty good team. I mean, you make me think about things differently. Think about things I maybe wouldn't otherwise."

"Yeah, I guess we do make a pretty good team," Meghna says, squeezing my hand. I savor the warmth of her skin on mine.

"So, a project together next year?" I ask.

"Yes," Meghna agrees.

46

RANI

Meghna's dad is at the gates of the airport, waiting, when we get there. I spot him waving at her frantically before she does. He hurries over, kissing Meghna on the cheek and wrapping her up in a hug like they've been apart for months instead of just three days.

"Abbu, okay, that's enough," Meghna mumbles, pulling away from him and wiping her cheek where he had kissed her. She glances over at me, almost like she's embarrassed that I've seen her dad's display of affection.

"You must be Mr. Rahman," Mrs. Quinn says, holding out her hand. He nods and shakes her hand. "I'm Mrs. Quinn."

"Nice to meet you. And thank you for looking after them," Rahman Uncle says. "Rani, congratulations on winning."

"Oh, um. Thanks, Uncle," I say, feeling myself flush.

"Your abbu isn't here yet?" he asks.

"He's probably going to be at the pickup spot," I say. "Parking fees, you know."

Rahman Uncle nods and takes Meghna's carry-on suitcase from her hands. "We should get going, come on."

Meghna sighs, glances back at me with a smile, and says, "I'll text you later?"

"Okay, bye," I say, already missing our time together in Amsterdam yesterday, when everything seemed less complicated.

She waves at both me and Mrs. Quinn before following after her dad.

Mrs. Quinn waits with me at the pickup area until I spot Abbu's car pull up.

"Congratulations again, Rani," she says, waving me away.

"Thanks for everything, Mrs. Quinn," I call back, hurrying over to Abbu's car. He opens the boot and I stuff my suitcase in there before getting into the passenger side.

"Assalamu alaikum," Abbu says as a greeting. He's already restarting the ignition and pulling into the road. He's barely glanced at me. I try not to let that sense of deflation hit me. I try not to think about how Rahman Uncle's eyes had been alight with excitement when he spotted Meghna.

"Walaikum salam," I say.

"So? Where's the trophy?" Abbu asks. He glances over at me with an overjoyed smile, and I feel a warm tingle of pride spread through me.

"Packed in my suitcase. I'll show you when we get home," I say.

"Your ammu is making biryani so we can all celebrate tomorrow," Abbu says.

"Really?" I ask. "Is she . . . inviting the Sardars?"

Abbu sighs. "She wanted to, but I told her maybe it wasn't such a good idea."

"Really?" I ask again.

Abbu looks over at me again, something unreadable in his expression. "Rani, I know you're unhappy with how we handled things with Zakkariyah. Your ammu and I have been talking about it since you left for Amsterdam, and maybe we pushed you into something too early with Zakkariyah."

"*Really*?" I ask.

"Well, yes. He's still running around with that girl, Julie. While you've won this prestigious competition. Clearly, you two are mismatched," Abbu says.

"Clearly." I mumble. Of course, even Abbu and Ammu's realization of this has more to do with Zak than me.

"So, we've decided we're going to step away from the Sardars for a little while. Even our relationship with them was getting intense. We saw them a lot," Abbu says. "And you know, Uncle talks too much about cricket."

I let out a giggle at that. Uncle does have a lot of cricket anecdotes, and a lot of them come from the time when he was a teenager and used to play in a makeshift cricket team back in Bangladesh.

Abbu lets out a chuckle, too.

"So, can I invite someone else to the celebration tomorrow, then?" I ask after a few moments of silence have passed.

"We've already invited Aarti and her parents," Abbu says. "Your ammu thought you'd want them there."

I smile. I know just how much Aarti annoys Ammu sometimes. "And what about Meghna?"

At that, Abbu's expression dims. It's not like they can forget about all the unpleasantness between them and Meghna's parents so easily.

"It can be just Meghna, her parents don't need to come as well," I say. "It's just, we're friends now, and she was part of the reason why I won at the exhibition. It's only fair that she's there, because it just wouldn't feel right celebrating with—"

"Yes, you can invite Meghna," Abbu concedes, though I can tell it's the last thing he wants to do. "Let me tell your ammu."

"Thanks, Abbu," I say. Some of the weight of everything that's happened in the past few months lifts off my shoulders. Things may not ever be easy with my parents, especially with Ammu, but I can see them slowly coming around, even if it's not always for the right reasons. I'm always going to be their eldest daughter, always going to carry some of this weight around with me, but maybe with time and a little bit of struggle, things can look different.

47

MEGHNA

"Ammu, I'm going out, okay?" I ask, pulling on my winter jacket over my dress.

"Again?" Ammu asks from where she and Abbu are watching a Hindi soap together. "Where to this time?"

"It's the opening night of Yemi's play, Ammu. I told you, Rani, Janella, and I are going together." Usually, I'd be afraid that after the third night of going out in a row, Ammu would be out of patience with me. That she'd demand I go back up to my room and start studying for my upcoming Christmas exams. But I've realized that there are some perks to how much my parents love Rani: If I'm hanging out with Rani, they have very few qualms about my whereabouts.

"Okay, but not out too late," Ammu says, already turning back to the TV screen.

"Okay, khodahafez!" I say, slipping out the door.

It's gotten colder over the two weeks since we got back from Amsterdam. I'm sure it won't be long until we get our first coat of snow this winter. The news has been saying we're supposed to get a *lot* of snow this year, and I can't wait.

Rani is standing in front of the theater when I get off the bus. She's wearing a big, checkered, blue-and-green coat, but still shivering a little in the cold.

"You didn't have to wait out here for me," I say when I reach her.

"Well, I was kind of starting to feel like the third wheel between Janella and her girlfriend," Rani admits. She leans down and kisses me on the corner of my lips. It's quick and not enough, but it'll have to do for now. I intertwine my fingers with Rani's and pull her indoors. We find Janella and Saya near the front and take our seats beside them. There's barely a chance to exchange *hellos* before the curtains open to the very first scene. Yemi comes onstage during the second scene, looking amazing and decked out in costume. We're all captivated as they go into Hamlet's very first soliloquy; the audience is hanging on to every word. By the time the show ends, I can hardly believe that Yemi learned how to play that role in the matter of just a few months for an amateur theater production. They definitely blew every other actor in the production out of the water.

"That was amazing!" we exclaim when we ambush them backstage. Janella gives them the bouquet of flowers we all went in on, and Yemi grins at us like this is the best night of their life. Their dressing table is already overflowing with bouquets of flowers—probably from their cousins in the UK, even though Yemi had told me their cousins were flying down to see the play on closing night and spend Christmas in Dublin with them.

"Really? You don't think I was, like, too much as Hamlet?" Yemi asks.

"You were the best actor on that stage!" Janella says.

Yemi leans in and whispers, "Say it a little quieter, you might make everyone else feel bad."

I roll my eyes at Yemi's cockiness, though it's par for the course.

"We're going to go get some food. Can you come, or do you have to do, like, post-play bonding or something?"

"I can come, just let me get changed out of my costume. Meet you outside in five?"

Twenty minutes later, the five of us are squashed into a booth in Eddie Rocket's, sharing baskets of chips between us and basically showering Yemi with unending praises.

"And that 'To be or not to be' soliloquy, that's the one I was the most afraid of. It's epic, you know? So I really wanted to nail those emotions," Yemi says.

"I think you nailed it," I say. "Honestly, your production was way better than that *Romeo and Juliet* performance we saw for our Junior Cert. Right?"

Janella and Yemi both nod in agreement, though Saya and Rani, not being from our school, obviously didn't watch the same play.

"We actually studied *Merchant of Venice* in our school," Saya admits. "And we didn't even get to watch a theater production of it."

All of us turn to Rani. She hesitates for a moment before saying, "We did *Romeo and Juliet,* and our school actually took us on a trip to London because they were doing a production of it there, and it was pretty good."

Yemi sighs dreamily. "Why couldn't we have gone to a school that took us to a performance at the Globe?"

"It was just our year because they were performing it. Usually, we just go to whatever production we can find here," Rani says. I can tell from how wide her eyes have gotten that all the sudden attention from everyone is getting to her.

"I think *Romeo and Juliet* is Shakespeare's worst play!" I declare, probably loud enough for half the restaurant to hear. "Seriously? He couldn't have picked a better concept than teenagers in love? How boring and clichéd."

"I mean, Shakespeare was writing in the sixteenth century; it probably wasn't boring or clichéd then," Saya says.

"Ignore Meghna, she just likes to be contrarian sometimes," Yemi says, waving my declaration away. I shoot them a small glare, but as the conversation moves on to other topics, I turn to Rani, who has lost some of that deer-in-the-headlights look she gets.

"You okay?" I ask in a hushed voice.

"Yeah," she says. "Your friends are just . . . I mean, I like them. I guess I'm just not used to big groups."

This is definitely not what I would consider a *big* group, but, considering the only friend I ever hear Rani mention is Aarti, I guess I understand why she would think it is.

"We can go, if you want," I offer. We've already been here for over an hour, and I'm pretty sure I've broken my agreement to Ammu to not "be late."

"No, it's okay," Rani says.

"We should go," I say, turning back to my friends. "It's getting late, and we should all probably be studying for our Christmas exams."

"Ugh, don't remind me," Yemi groans, dramatically laying their head down on the table.

"You can take the actor out of the play, but you can't take the play out of the actor," Janella says.

"That doesn't even make any sense." Yemi's voice is muffled against where they've buried their head on the table.

"I'll see you both at school next week. See you later, Saya," I mumble as Rani and I bid our goodbyes. We step out of Eddie Rocket's and head to the bus stop hand in hand. Our buses are on the opposite sides of the road from each other, so we don't have to part yet, but I'm already feeling the dread of saying *goodbye* to Rani. It's strange how just a few weeks can change so much.

"I think you should come back home with me," I say once we're near the bus stops. "I mean, you could sleep over. Ammu would be over the moon. We could study together." I feel like I need to list off all the reasons she could stay, knowing that she has enough reason to say no.

"I really *do* have to study for the Christmas exams," Rani says, just as I anticipated she would.

"I know, but you're going to get all As. We both already know that," I say. "And, like I said, we can wake up early tomorrow morning and study together. I promise."

"I don't know how my parents would feel about it," Rani admits. The last time I saw her parents was the celebration dinner Rani had invited me to at her house. Nothing about it had been unpleasant exactly, but whenever I'm in their presence, it feels like there's unspoken tension hanging over us. After all, no matter what else happened, I can't ignore how easy it was for the two of them to toss Ammu and Abbu away like they meant nothing to them.

"You could ask," I coax. "If you don't ask, they never even get to say no."

Rani sighs. She says that things have been better with her parents ever since they realized they were in the wrong about Zak—even if they realized it for the wrong reasons. But I can tell it's not easy for

Rani to ask things of them. That fear of disappointing them is burrowed in deep, and I can always sense it in Rani's interactions with them, even though I don't quite understand it.

The two of us pause by the side of the road and Rani pulls her phone out of her pocket. She's biting her lips as the phone rings.

"Hi, Ammu . . . um, yeah, it was good," she says. "I was wondering if I could . . . maybe stay over at Meghna's tonight? I know I have the Christmas exams coming up, but Meghna and I were planning to study together anyway, and I think—" She pauses, nodding her head slowly. Her expression doesn't give anything away. "Okay, sure. Khodahafez."

She puts the phone away and turns back to me. "She said . . . okay."

"Really?" Even I'm surprised that it was so easy.

"But only if one of your parents gives me a lift home tomorrow," Rani says.

"They can do that!" I say, trying and failing to hide my grin.

The bus ride home feels quicker than usual, and it's not long before I'm pushing open the front door and waving Rani inside.

"Ammu, I'm home!" I call. "And I brought Rani, she's staying over tonight, okay?"

Rani looks at me with wide eyes like she can hardly believe I'm divulging all this information to my mom before I've even taken off my shoes. Ammu shows up by the door leading to our kitchen, her eyebrows pinched together like I'm already giving her a headache.

"Meghna, when a guest comes home, you invite them inside. Sit them down, offer them a drink. You don't scream into the house," Ammu says, reprimanding me.

Sighing, I turn to Rani. "Would you like something to drink?"

Ammu rolls her eyes and turns to Rani, her expression immediately brightening. "Rani, are your ammu and abbu okay with you staying over?"

"They said it was okay, if you don't mind dropping me off tomorrow morning," Rani says in the prim and proper voice she usually uses to speak to adults.

"Okay, why don't you take off your shoes and come into the kitchen? I'll heat up some dinner for you."

"We already ate at Eddie Rocket's," I say.

Ammu waves her hand like that doesn't register as food, or something. To her, it probably doesn't. Rani follows her to the kitchen happily, though, and, a moment later, so do I. I guess this is the *bad* thing about dating Rani; every time she comes over, I feel like I have to share her with my parents, who are a little too obsessed with feeding her and peppering her with a million questions.

Finally, after Ammu is satisfied that Rani and I have eaten our fill, we manage to excuse ourselves to go upstairs. It's already 10:00 p.m., and after a full day of studying, Yemi's play, and hanging out with everyone, I'm exhausted. I toss myself onto the bed fully clothed, and after a moment Rani lies down beside me. I burrow my head in the crook of her shoulders, closing my eyes and breathing in the familiar scent of her. It feels like this is the first moment we've had to ourselves in a long time.

"I was thinking about our project for next year," I say after the silence has washed over us for a little too long.

"Already?" Rani asks.

"There's no such thing as too soon," I say. "I just thought I'd get the ideas flowing, you know. We could do another app, since you're a coding genius, and I was thinking I could maybe go to a coding course this summer. I've looked it up, and there are some that run just in town. There are some intensive ones and some that run the whole summer. And then I could help you with the coding. I wouldn't be as good as you, obviously—"

"Or I could just teach you," Rani says. "I mean, I probably won't be as good as an intensive course, but I think I could try. If you really want to learn."

We turn toward each other until we're face-to-face on the bed, only inches between us.

"I want to learn. It's a good skill to have," I say. "And then we'd have an even better shot at winning the Young Scientist Exhibition."

"Okay," Rani says with a smile.

"Okay," I say, too, though now I'm thinking a lot less about next September and our potential project and more about all the days leading up to it. All the days Rani and I will get to spend together, talking about coding and science, holding hands and being together, and making up for all our lost time.

Finally, Rani leans in, closing the gap between us and pressing her lips to mine. I close my eyes, thread my hand through her hair, and kiss her back. And, for once, there aren't a million thoughts rushing through my head.

I'm just happy to be in this moment with Rani.

ACKNOWLEDGMENTS

A BOOK IS ONLY AS GOOD AS ALL THE WONDERFUL PEOPLE WHO help make it happen. I was lucky to have some amazing people on my side while working on this one:

Thank you to my amazing agent, Uwe Stender, who has been and continues to be my biggest advocate, for whom I am eternally grateful.

Thank you to my editors, Foyinsi Adegbonmire and Nazima Abdillahi, for helping to make this book into something very special.

Thank you to my publicist, Samantha Sacks, for all of your hard work. Thank you also to the rest of the team at Macmillan: Jean Feiwel, Dawn Ryan, Kim Waymer, John Nora, and Jacob Sammon.

Thank you to Jani Balakumar for the stunning cover art and Samira Iravani for the design!

Thank you to all my friends and family—especially to Faridah, Tammi, Priyanka, Gayatri, Alyssa, and Gavin.

Thank you always to my readers for continuing to pick up my books and give them a chance. Thank you for every book review, every tweet, every Instagram post, TikTok video, and blog post; I am incredibly grateful for all the support.

Also available:

Photo by Lia Car[illegible]otti

Adiba Jaigirdar is the award-winning, critically-acclaimed and bestselling author of *The Henna Wars*, *Hani and Ishu's Guide to Fake Dating*, and *A Million to One*. A Bangladeshi/Irish writer and former teacher, she has an MA in Postcolonial Studies from the University of Kent, England, and a BA in English and History from UCD, Ireland.

She is the winner of the YA Book Prize 2022, the KPMG Children's Books Ireland Awards 2021, and was a finalist for the 2022 Lambda Literary Awards. All of her writing is aided by tea, and a healthy dose of Janelle Monáe and Hayley Kiyoko.

When not writing, she is probably ranting about the ills of colonialism, playing video games, or expanding her overflowing lipstick collection.

She can be found at adibajaigirdar.com or @adiba_j on X and @dibs_j on Instagram.